UNPREDICTABLE
WINDS

a novel

Thomas T. Chin

Relax. Read. Repeat.

Unpredictable Winds
By Thomas T. Chin
Published by TouchPoint Press
Brookland, AR 72417
www.touchpointpress.com

Copyright © 2022 Thomas T. Chin
All rights reserved.

PAPERBACK ISBN: 978-1-956851-33-5

Senior Editor: Kimberly Coghlan
Associate Editor: Becky Marietta
Cover Design: David Ter-Avanesyan @ter33design
Cover Images: Shutterstock

First Edition

Printed in the United States of America.

To my parents for their unconditional love.

Author's Note

The characters and plots in this book are fictional, except for the Second Sino-Japanese War reference. All cultural sites included in this book are actual places, and I have visited them myself. They are open to the general public. The Shanghai French Concession was where my mother and her family used to live. During the Sino-Japanese War, her father, my grandfather, was the chief weapon supplier to the Nationalist Army. Bayer's presence in China dates back to 1882, when the company began selling dyes in China. In 1936, the company began aspirin production in Shanghai. The company's name mentioned in this book is verbatim. (Source: Bayer.com.cn)

1

At five minutes before eight o'clock, the familiar echo of high heels on the marble tiles sounded in the hallway and then in the outer space of his office. Within seconds, there was a gentle knock on the frosted glass door.

"Come in." Lee quickly adjusted his yellow silk bowtie. He felt the subtle crease between his eyebrows relax.

A slender, middle-aged woman in a dark-gray suit walked in with her customary writing pad and some papers in her left hand. She stood tall in her high heels, her back straight. Her dark, pin-curled hair was neatly combed behind her ears. On her smooth, lightly tanned skin, subtle wrinkles around the corners of her eyes suggested she looked younger than her age.

"Good morning, Mr. Lee. I hope you got my note from last night." She fought to hide her haggard voice.

"Good morning to you as well, Mrs. Shen. Yes, I did. Thank you." He looked down at a small piece of beige-colored paper next to his Siemens & Halske handset. "I am delighted that Herr Meyer can come to this year's Chinese New Year's party."

"Well, the Year of the Dragon is special, isn't it? Not to mention it coincides with your birthday, sir."

"Well put, Mrs. Shen. You know how auspicious the dragon is. Nonetheless, I can't predict what the year will bring." He kept his eyes on the note. "And should I assume we are all set for tomorrow night?"

"Yes, sir. The Chang Brothers Jazz Band will return to do their annual Chinese New Year repertoire." Mrs. Shen looked at Lee expectantly from behind her tortoiseshell glasses, and he nodded his approval.

The whistle of a teakettle sounded in the back kitchen inside the office. Mrs. Shen stood. Lee gestured with his right hand for Mrs. Shen to remain seated and quickly walked into the kitchen. The small space was enough for a two-burner electric stove, above which a redwood cabinet hung at his eye level. He took out a tin can and put a pinch of loose White Peony tea leaves into his newly purchased dragon mug and then poured boiling water into it.

After putting the lid back, he looked out the window briefly as was his custom. The morning mist was starting to dissipate, and Pudong was beginning to submerge from the eastside of the Huangpu River. Two tugboats were moving slowly downstream to the south. The gentle wind pushed the crimson swastika flag outside the window to the left to allow him to catch a glimpse of two Japanese soldiers standing next to a bus station. One of them was smoking a cigarette.

"My apologies for the wait, but I can't start my day without my tea." Back to his seat. "Please do continue, Mrs. Shen."

"I have a list of what I have ordered from the new catering service, which I hope is going to be better than last year's."

"Let's hear it!"

"Let's see. . . . . six cases of Schmitt Sohne Riesling and eight cases of Oasis. For hors d'oeuvres, we are going to have stuffed mushrooms, edamame dumplings, cream of crab and cucumber, shrimp cocktail, pearl meatballs, Leeks Royale—everyone is going to love that—and then we have cauliflower cream with smoked salmon caviar. For sweets, we will have Apple Tarte Tatin and Gourmet Fraisiere, and of course, the big cake. I believe that's all." She flipped through her notes to make sure and looked up with a smile. "Do you think we have enough?"

"Everything sounds wonderful. The pearl meatballs will be the only birthday present I need. And thank you for getting this business taken care of, Mrs. Shen."

"That's my job, sir." She grinned again and pushed a stray hair behind her ear. "By the way, here is something that I need you to sign."

After Mrs. Shen left the office, Lee opened his notebook to see the list of phone calls that he needed to make. As he was about to pick up the handset, he heard another pair of high heels briskly walking down the hallway.

"Oh, hello, Miss Wong," he heard Mrs. Shen proclaim from the outer room.

The brass door handle turned, and Lily entered, promptly plunking herself down on the edge of Lee's desk. She was wearing her favorite red trench coat. Under her glowing cheeks, a small pale-green silk choker arranged in the shape of a butterfly wrapped around her long neck. She raised her hand to check her hairpin, while her bare thin legs dangled next to his arm. "I need to talk to you about tomorrow night."

"It's nice to see you too, Lily." He sighed and tried in vain to remove a small stack of papers she was sitting on, and then settled deeper into his chair. He knew exactly what was coming, and he had only himself to blame.

"I can't decide if I should go with Marcel waves or pin curls for tomorrow night. What do you think?" Her legs kept swinging back and forth.

Lee must provide this crucial opinion, or the engagement could be in danger. He took a chance. "I think pin curls would be better."

"You think so?" Lily looked into one of the glass-framed photographs on the wall to see if she could glimpse her hair.

"Yes, Lily. I think the Marcel waves would be too. . . . what's the word I am looking for? Too busy." He was relieved and proud of himself for his answer.

2

Lee's classmate, Johnny, had introduced Lily to him nearly two years ago at the Peace Café.

"You know what? My father is a friend of Charlie Wong's." Johnny pushed his dark pompadour hair back with his stubby fingers.

"Do you mean Charlie Wong from C & W Shipyards in Hong Kong?" Lee squinted his eyes.

"Yes, my friend, and he has a daughter named Lily. She's single as far as I know."

"How do you know she would be interested in me?" he asked, trying to contain his excitement.

"Well. . . ." Johnny took a sip of his hot coffee, "didn't you tell me that when your father gave you that *Men Dang Hu Dui* business, he said the doors from both sides must match? I can tell you this; she is loaded and never has to work."

"Hmm, I see. I did read in the newspaper about that shipyard doing some great work. No wonder—"

"Hey De-Chang, don't change the subject," Johnny said. "I think you two would look very nice together."

"We'd *look* very nice together?" Lee pronounced each word distinctively, staring into his friend's eyes. His mind had already begun to imagine what Lily might look like. He pictured her with the perfect symmetry of a slim body and a sunflower-seed-shaped face. Just like the heroines he'd once admired from his novels, Lily would be the ideal combination of keen intelligence and femininity. She might be shy, but that would suit him fine.

"You know, she is great looking and you are. . . . well, not so bad looking either."

Lee liked the name, as it rhymed with the Chinese word for beauty. *Lily must be the total embodiment of beauty,* he thought.

"Appearance matters, don't you think? I know I like good-looking women myself, but that's me! You both dress well. Besides, you both have money, so—" Johnny's hooded eyes lifted above his thin cheekbones.

"Alright, Johnny. I get your point. So how am I going to meet her?" Lee raised his voice a notch, and he began to rub his fingers against each other.

"Calm down, my friend. She's in Hong Kong now, but she's coming back next week to finish her last semester at McTyeire. When she returns, I can ask her if she would be interested in meeting you." Johnny patted his friend on the shoulder.

"Thank you, Johnny." Lee mechanically pushed his shirtsleeve up to check his watch.

"No need to thank me, De-Chang," Johnny said with a wink. "I am also doing this for your father. The old man was good to me."

Yes. If Lee Senior were alive today, he would be pleased. He would thank Johnny for helping his son to find a wife—well, a potential wife. And what about Elke? She would probably say, "*Mach dir keine Sorgen, mein Schatz.*" She always seemed to have everything figured out.

"I will have Lily call you next week." Johnny tilted his head all the way back with his coffee cup and wiped his mouth with the back of his right hand.

"But—"

"There is no but; it's done."

• • •

Johnny kept his word. On the following Wednesday evening, right after midnight, when Lee was about to finish his weekly note to his manager Mr. Wang, the telephone rang.

"Mr. Lee?" a somewhat forceful female voice sounded from the other end.

"Excuse me . . . you are. . . .?"

"It's Lily. Lily Wong."

"Oh yes! I am sorry. I didn't recognize your voice." His stomach gave a leap. He put the letter down on his desk.

"You wouldn't. We have never met. Johnny told me a lot about you, and I wondered if you would like to meet at some point."

He did? And what did Johnny say? Lee blinked quickly. "Oh. . . . that would be great. I . . . would like that very much." His heart was palpitating.

"Is this a bad time to call?" She obviously sensed Lee's hesitation from the other side of the line.

"No . . . not at all. . . ."

"Good. Are you available tomorrow, say around four in the afternoon?"

"That would be . . . lovely." His right index finger moved about quickly on the calendar on his desk.

"Great! Can you think of a place where you would like us to meet?"

"Would *Café de Flore* work for you?" Elke's favorite place, of course. Where else could he think of? "It's on—"

"I know where that place is. See you then. *Guten Abend!*"

Before he could say anything more, Lily had already hung up the telephone. He stared at the handset for a moment before putting it back in its cradle. A gentle breeze pushed one of the windows open. He walked over and closed it slowly. Suddenly, he felt the excitement of meeting Lily. He tried to match the voice he had just heard with a face, a face of youth, beauty, and perfect proportion. He put his hands in his pockets and paced back and forth, feeling his heart pounding.

3

He was dressed three hours before he needed to leave the house. After changing his clothes five times, he settled on his usual white Oxford pinpoint shirt and a charcoal pinstripe suit, the old-school look. The hallway mirror above the antique marquetry crescent table slowed him down. He squinted into it for a brief second and gave himself a forced grin. Extending his left arm to check the time, he nodded before dashing out.

It was a beautiful spring afternoon. The air was moist but not too humid. The street was full of people going about their business. Some were walking briskly toward their destinations while others were strolling slowly, looking into store windows. At the entrance to a flower shop, he paused and then went inside. Two minutes later, he came out with one red rose in his left hand. He walked quickly toward the French café.

"Good afternoon, Mr. Lee." An older man in a tuxedo at the door gave him a slight bow. "Table for two as usual?"

"Yes, please." He looked at his watch. It was only three-thirty.

He was seated next to a small table near the window in front of a large green leafless plant. The familiar smell of brewing coffee and milk permeated the air. In the back corner of the room, a middle-aged man dressed in a dark tuxedo sat next to a small upright piano, playing *Parlez-moi d'amour.* Between pauses, Lee could hear the clatter of china dishes in the back. Large sepia-toned photographs of France hung elegantly on the cream-colored walls. After placing the red rose carefully on the table, he began to feel overwhelmingly hot, and he pushed the heavy velvet curtain to the side.

As he gazed out the window to remain calm, he suddenly realized that this was his first date . . . ever. He tried to distract himself by focusing on the pedestrians on the street. His mind started to wander. He thought about all the girls from McTyeire who had an interest in him while he was a student at St. John's. But he had never gone out with any of them. His father had always told him that his studies were the priority. Only when Lee Senior became ill did he tell his son to look for a wife, as if it were a social obligation rather than finding love.

"Sorry I'm late." A female voice woke him from his trance. "I know it's almost four-thirty."

Lee instinctively rose from his chair. Only after he stood did he notice the tall, slender, beautiful young woman in a flowery, light-green dress looking straight into his eyes. He noticed her large, dark-brown eyes surrounded by her smooth, pale skin. Her short, dark hair was shiny and held back by a small pink flower nested above her left ear. Her delicate, glossy, crimson-red lips smiled to reveal her even, white teeth. Absolute perfection.

The elderly man in the tuxedo stood not far away, a subtly surprised look on his face.

"Lily." She extended her right hand confidently, her back straight.

"De-Chang," Lee replied rigidly, giving his hand. The warmth of her soft skin gave him a shudder as if it were something he had never touched before.

"Oh, is that for me?" She picked up the red rose from the table.

"Ah . . . yes." Whatever he had prepared to say just went out the window.

"Should I assume this is your first date?" She smiled mischievously.

He suddenly felt the blood rushing into his face.

"I'm sorry for being so blunt, but it's actually a compliment, if you know what I mean."

"I . . . I work a lot and don't have the opportunity and time to. . . ." He started fidgeting, his eyes fixed upon her small red lips.

"I know. You don't have to explain. I was only teasing." She seemed to notice his gaze but was pretending she didn't. "So, what's it like working for Bayer? I mean, *Bayer Pharma Co*? Phew, what a name! Are they all Nazis?" She giggled and then stopped. "I'm sorry. It's not funny."

Lee froze but then managed to squeeze out a few words. "Well, it's just work, and I don't mind it."

"What do you mean you don't mind it? I mean, do you like it?" She placed her chin in her hand and stared across at him.

"I did what my father wanted me to do. He was the. . . ." Lee prepared a safe answer.

"I know. He was the former general manager of Bayer, and you are the new one."

"Yes. My father passed away not long ago, and. . . ."

"I'm sorry."

"Thank you." Lee cleared his throat, trying to stay calm. "Anyway, the work is not hard; it gives me a reason to get up in the morning."

"And everyone needs that, I suppose." Lily smiled. "By the way, didn't your family have some kind of *hardware business*?"

"You are very well-informed," he said, surprised.

"So I've heard." She winked and then turned to signal to the waiter that they were ready to order. Lee couldn't decide what he wanted, so Lily made the decision for both of them. Soon, the waiter came back with a tray, on top of which were two cups of coffee, one glass of warm milk, two croissants, a small cup of butter, and a small jar of strawberry jam.

"I take milk. Do you enjoy sugar with your coffee?" Lily asked.

"I prefer black. Well, I usually drink tea."

"I can see the Germans don't force their Chinese employees to drink coffee." She giggled again.

The two proceeded to eat the buttery croissants with the delectable homemade jam, and Lily took a sip of the coffee.

"Mmm. . . . this isn't bad. Do you come here often?"

"I usually come here with Elke, my stepmother. She doesn't have a lot of friends and needs company."

"That's very nice of you. You must be a good son, I imagine." She looked around the room quickly. "You know what? Now I know why that waiter was staring at me as I came in. Never mind." She steered herself back. "So, Johnny told me where your stepmother came from. Let me try to say this word: *München*." She held her small, protruding lips after speaking the word. "I think French seems easier for me," she said quietly. She added, "Do you two get along?"

"She raised me." He took a sip of his coffee. "She was strict, as one might expect from a German woman, but not in a bad way. I mean, the structure helped me get a lot of things done."

"So, you like to get things done?" She smirked before adding more jam to her croissant.

He paused for a moment. "She's not the greatest cook in the world, but she was always there when I needed her. She washed all my clothes and—"

"How is your German?"

"Decent, I guess, but I prefer not to speak it, as both Elke and Herr Meyer speak decent English. But when they get upset about something, they immediately switch to German."

"What a surprise! Who is Herr Meyer?"

"Oh, I am sorry. He is the German representative from Bayer and—"

"I actually have to go soon." Lily popped another bite into her mouth. "I'm supposed to meet with some friends later and need to change my clothes."

Lee's heart sank. "Will I see you again?"

"Yes. Let's try to meet tomorrow, if you have time."

"I need to check with Mrs. Shen first."

"Who?" Lily lifted her eyebrow.

"Sorry. She's my assistant."

The two finished their coffee quietly without saying much to each other. Whenever their eyes met, Lee would give an awkward smile as if he were finishing a task assigned by Elke. He felt uneasy.

"Well, my friends are expecting me soon. So I'd better get going. Give me a call tomorrow morning."

Reluctantly, he stood. He wanted to say something to keep her but didn't know what to say. He felt his lips moving nervously, but no sound came out. He could've kicked himself. What a buffoon. As Lily turned around, he stood behind the table and watched her leave, still holding his white linen napkin in his left hand. He mechanically lifted his right hand halfway and then felt awkward. She dashed out and left the front glass door open. He continued watching her until she disappeared into the crowded street. Not until the same older man in the tuxedo came to the front to close the door did he sit down again to ponder his first date.

Did she like me? He stared at his empty coffee cup. *If she did, why would she have to leave? Was that an excuse? I have to see her again, and soon!*

4

Lee never had an easy time articulating his feelings, not that he'd ever wanted to or felt that anyone was interested. Elke and his father certainly hadn't been. As a student at St. John's, he'd discovered a passion for romance novels. He hoped to find answers from these books, on perhaps how to feel or love. He cried when he read Flaubert's *Madame Bovary* and Stendhal's *Le Rouge et Le Noir*. He had imagined that he was the protagonist from each of these novels and couldn't put the stories behind him for weeks after reading them. After *Anna Karenina*, he couldn't sleep for several days and pictured himself as Vronsky trying to save Anna. His fantasies brought him both joy and sadness—the protagonists he admired wouldn't have been the kind of people that would meet the approval of his father. He also felt abandoned by the books' characters, who brought him pain without justifying it. He made detailed notes after reading each book and then destroyed them the next day. In the end, he couldn't find his answers, and his confusion deepened.

When he met Lily in the French cafe, he had treated the entire event as if it were a task to be checked off on one of Elke's many lists. Even though he felt an immediate attraction to Lily, he couldn't use the romantic language from his beloved novels or formulate something good on his own. He was very disappointed with himself. He thought his preparation from St. John's would help him get through any challenge in life. He was wrong.

He couldn't make it to the second date the following day because Herr Meyer asked him to attend two meetings, which were expected to last until six in the evening. But he got in touch with Lily and said he would be free on Sunday afternoon. Lily liked the idea, and the two decided to meet at the fountain in Fuxing Park.

• • •

On Sunday afternoon, he showed up early again. A dark-blue cashmere top and a pair of beige linen trousers fit comfortably over his wide shoulders and skinny legs. A lightweight trench coat rested on his left arm. Gazing into the short distance, he watched two young girls feeding the little ducks while their mother chatted with a friend. When the clock on a distant building struck four, Lily appeared from behind a cluster of trees. She wore a pale-yellow polka dot dress with a wide-spread collar under her long neck. A matching small yellow flower nested on her left ear. He also noticed that she was wearing a pair of red gloves that matched the color of her lips.

"See, I'm on time today!" Lily said.

"Thank you for coming." His voice sounded mechanical.

"Shall we go for a little walk?" Lily suggested and pointed down a gravel path, which meandered through the park. Lee began to follow.

"There is something I wanted to ask you, Lily."

"Oh, really?"

"There is a concert at St. John's tonight, and I have two tickets. Would you like to come?" He was surprised at his courage.

"Sure! What's the program?"

"It's Beethoven's violin sonatas, all six of them."

"That sounds very lovely." Lily's face lit up in a smile, and she practically bounced on her feet.

"Great!" He was overjoyed "It starts at six. Perhaps we could get a bite to eat afterward?"

"Wow, you have this all planned out quite nicely! I'm impressed." Lily lifted her eyebrows. "I had a feeling that you were the master of planning!"

"Not really, but I am glad you are in the mood for it." Lee breathed a small sigh of relief at her enthusiasm.

That evening, the two arrived at the music hall half an hour early so Lee could give Lily a little tour before the concert. They strolled inside the grand building as Lee pointed out photographs on the walls and the bronze sculptures in the hallway.

"This bust is the former music director who passed away five years ago," he said with a solemn nod, feeling the sweat on his palms. "And that beautiful piece of tapestry next to the staircase? That is an Aubusson tapestry from Central France, given by a former professor who taught French here for more than twenty years."

Lily listened attentively and gave a small smile. "You seem to know a lot about your alma mater."

"Well, a bit. My father went here too."

"How did you become interested in classical music?" Lily continued.

"My parents," Lee began. "When I was young, they played classical music often. Since Elke came from Munich, I heard a lot of German music. In the evening, after dinner, either Elke or my father would put on a record to play while I did my homework. The music helped me focus, although I didn't realize this until years later." Lee paused and looked at Lily, thankful to see that she held his gaze.

He forged ahead. "Whenever the music played, Elke would put the record cover right next to me so that I couldn't help but notice the composer. Before I even knew it, I had memorized all the names of the composers, and their pieces piled up in my head: Beethoven's *Moonlight Sonata*, Mozart's *Sinfonia Concertante*, and Bach's *Brandenburg Concertos*. One early morning when Elke walked by the washroom, she heard me inside humming the overture of Mozart's *Le Nozze de Figaro*. She smiled and told me that I had become *cultured*." He laughed.

"I'll be the judge of that," Lily said with a grin. "Well, my parents don't play music at home, and I certainly don't know much about Western classical music. Interestingly, my father enjoys singing, which essentially means that he hums around the house when he's not working. And my mother is a housewife. So I have to cultivate myself." Lily checked her watch. "I think it's time for us to go in."

The auditorium was a decent size by university standards, with two levels, though the balcony was rather small. Elongated wall lamps dispersed soft light onto the dark-red velvet wall covering. Over the stage, the heavy gray curtains were pushed to the sides, exposing a baby grand piano in the middle of the stage.

"Wow, tenth row from the stage? Perfect seats!" Lily looked around before she sat down. Lee sat down as soon as Lily removed her gloves. Within a few minutes, the musicians walked on stage and Lily clapped her hands enthusiastically.

The music began, but Lee couldn't concentrate, even though he was looking forward to hearing his favorite piece, *Spring*. He stole a glance at Lily, who looked as calm as the ocean. Her large, brown eyes were fixed on the stage, and her entrancing lips were tightly closed. Her bosom rose and fell with each subtle breath, and her hands firmly clutched her red lambskin gloves. Every time he breathed in, Lily's flowery perfume became part of the air he inhaled. Slowly, the scent penetrated every nerve of his body. He felt the warm blood rush through his body into his head. He debated grabbing one of her hands with one of his own sweaty hands, but he resisted the impulse.

Would she gasp and pull away? I must not make a scene.

When the first piece was over, Lily clapped courteously, and one of her gloves fell to the floor. He bent over, picked it up, and placed it back in her lap. His heart skipped a beat. Lily's eyes remained fixed on the stage, unaware of what had just happened. When the violinist and the pianist took their final bows, he felt his tense muscles begin to relax a bit. As Lily clapped again, he watched her delicate fingers touch, making a shallow sound that only he could hear.

"That was such a lovely concert!" Lily gushed as they left their seats.

"I'm so glad you enjoyed it," he said, still recovering from the sensation he had felt a moment ago. "Some people are a bit bored by classical music." He moved back a bit to let her out first. "I was afraid that perhaps—"

"Oh no, it was simply wonderful." Lily looked up at him, beaming. "Did you like it? You've probably heard it a hundred times."

"I never tire of Beethoven," he said. "Now, where would you like to go for dinner?"

"This is your town. So I'll just follow you. It doesn't have to be fancy."

"Well, there's a noodle shop not far from here. I don't have northern cooking that often. What do you think?"

"Beethoven and noodles. I never thought the two would go together, but why not?" They both laughed.

The noodle shop was small but clean. The smell of fried scallions and garlic permeated the air. Two white paper lanterns, which had the characters for "longevity" and "good fortune" written on them, were suspended from the ceiling. On the small wooden counter in the back of the room stood a woodcarving of a "longevity man." The owners were an older couple, who originally came from Beijing. Since there weren't many restaurants that served northern-style cuisine in this part of town, the couple had almost no competition.

There was an empty table near the window, but it had only one chair next to it. As Lee and Lily approached the table, the older woman quickly brought another chair. Soon, she came back with two cups of hot tea for the couple. Her long white hair was pulled into a knot on the top of her head to form a bun. Above her blue apron, her kind face showed fatigue. "It's getting a bit cool outside," she said with a smile before returning to the kitchen.

While Lily was taking off her gloves, Lee pointed at the menu on the wall. There weren't many dishes, and each was written on a four-inch-wide bamboo stick.

"What's good?" Lily wanted to know.

"Everything is delicious here," he said.

When the old woman returned, he ordered the pork rib noodle soup with Shanghai cabbage. Lily scrunched up her nose and stared at the menu for several long moments. Lee chuckled at her intensity.

Finally, she turned to the woman. "I'll have the noodle soup—I trust the gentleman's taste—but I'll try it with seafood."

When the food arrived, the warmth and the flavor of the noodle soup made Lee sigh with contentment and settle into his chair. The noodles were nested in the white cloudy soup among leaves of Shanghai cabbage, slightly blanched. Three large, tenderly-cooked pork ribs were arranged nicely on top. The smell of soy and anise rushed into his nose.

Before he could say anything about the soup, Lily said, "You know, this is definitely the perfect place, and the food is divine. We should always combine sonatas with noodle soup!"

"It's a deal!"

"Have you always been a . . . how should I say this . . . 'a good boy'?" Lily smiled, wiping her lips.

Unprepared, he said, "I beg your pardon?"

"Well, everything about you seems . . . very orderly." She seemed to be searching for the right words. "I mean, you don't smoke and don't drink, you went to prep school, were the best in class. You know all about books and classical music, and of course, you're head of Bayer. Everything about you seems a bit too logical. No?"

"I did what I was told," he said finally after a long pause, not too proud of his answer.

"That's exactly what I mean!" Lily was looking into his eyes. "Right now, we're being occupied by the Japanese, and here we are enjoying Beethoven as if we don't have a care in the world. Don't you realize there's something wrong with this picture?"

"I . . . see what you mean. I do, but I'm not sure what—"

"Listen, it's getting late, and I need to get back soon." Lily glanced around the room.

"Get back to where?" He was utterly confused by her change in tone.

"Oh, I have an apartment in town. It was my father's, but I live there while I'm in school."

"Right. Johnny said you have one more semester left at McTyeire." He tried to steer the conversation back.

"Yes, I skipped a year," she said abruptly and pushed her chair back to stand. "Are you done?"

Lee nodded and reluctantly followed her. The air was getting cooler outside, and Lily started to shiver. He cautiously moved closer, his cashmere sweater touching Lily's arm. He put his trench coat over her shoulders. The gentle breeze pushed a strand of her hair to his face and it tickled his nose. As he was about to scratch his nose, the smell of her flowery perfume forced him to stop.

"Can you get me a taxi?" Lily put her arms through the sleeves and tightened the trench coat.

"Of course." He was startled from his trance.

When the taxi came, he opened the door, and Lily began climbing into the car. She suddenly stopped and looked back at him, her beautiful eyes sparkling under the blue street lamp. "What about your coat?"

"Don't worry about it. I'll get it later." He closed the passenger door very gently as if any stronger force would shatter the beauty inside. Before he realized what was supposed to happen next, the dark evening pulled the taxi into the evening traffic, along with his heart.

5

5

At exactly seven o'clock, the car of the first guest arrived. Immediately following that, five more drove through the *fleur-de-lis* wrought-iron gate. After the sixth car went through the gate, Lee gazed through the front window as Mr. Ma, the gardener whom Lee had graciously kept on after his father's death, asked one of the hired men if he should tell all other cars to park on the street, for there was no room left in the drive. Guests on foot showed up in pairs, and each carried a little gift bag with them. By seven-thirty, the floor of the ballroom downstairs was full of people. Mrs. Shen had taken care of every detail, and Lee was very pleased.

In the entrance to the front hall, eight large red balloons were suspended from the vaulted ceiling. Gold-colored paper ribbons were across the ceiling, passing through the large crystal Schonbek chandelier in the middle. Mr. Ma had the two antique high-back Hessen chairs removed from the front hall and put into the drawing-room. Not only would this give the guests more places to sit in the drawing-room, but it would also prevent someone from accidentally bumping into the chairs when the area got crowded in the early evening.

The jazz band took the east corner of the room, and the food table was on the opposite side. Elke had put on her red satin Chinese *qi-pao*, which she wore only once a year. The cut of the dress and her slim figure made her look younger than her age. Between her shoulder-length, wavy, sand-colored hair, her large blue eyes revealed a mixture of discipline and straightforwardness. Under her high cheekbones, her thin lips moved subtly as if she were processing her thoughts.

Lee walked around to greet his guests, occasionally bumping into Elke. Each time, she would give his arm a little squeeze and then check his bowtie to make sure it was straight. Lily diligently stood by Lee's side as he greeted the guests. He plastered a smile on his face and gave his hand to a man with a pair of gold-rimmed glasses. "Hey, Meng-Jin and Wei-Wei, it's great to see you two! How is everything at HSBC?" The man's wife deigned to glance at him and took a sip of her Riesling.

"The numbers are up, phew! Considering this kind of climate, I mean—"

"I don't know how you do it. Talent, I guess." Lee smiled. "Oh, do you remember Lily?"

"I do, but *enchanté.*" Meng-Jin gave Lily a polite nod.

The wife pointed at Lily. "That's a lovely *qi-pao.*" Above the man's wife's light-blue-and-pink squaw dress, her small, pale, oval face looked poised, and a pair of blue diamond earrings added a touch of elegance.

"Thank you!" Lily seemed genuinely pleased and enjoyed the attention.

There was a gentle pat on Lee's shoulder. He turned around and confronted a large man with a shock of white hair above his pale-pink face. The man's blue eyes showed warmth and complexity. A bright red bowtie struggled under his excessive chin, below which a small Nazi party pin was fixed onto the collar of his blue pinstriped suit. Next to him, a petite woman with elegant curly white hair was smiling. Although her face did not look young, her large green eyes glowed under the chandelier.

"Herr Meyer *und* Frau Meyer! Thank you for coming!" Lee said to his boss and then turned his face to the older woman. "Frau Meyer, that has to be the most beautiful dress I have seen in recent years. And lavender is one of my favorite colors!"

"*Danke*, Herr Lee! You are always very kind." She put her arm through her husband's.

"I thought you would appreciate my tie. It's good luck to wear red on Chinese New Year, isn't it?" Herr Meyer joined in.

"True, Herr Meyer, true. And it looks great on you!"

"You are very kind, young man." Herr Meyer turned, and his face lit up. Lee followed his gaze and saw the red *qi-pao* emerge from the crowd. "Ah, Frau Elke!" Herr Meyer exclaimed. "*Lange nicht gesehen und wie geht's Ihnen?*"

"*Nicht allzu schlecht und danke, Herr Meyer. Es ist immer gut, Sie an dieser Party zu sehen.*"

"*Vielleicht erinnern Sie sich, meine Frau und ich gehen nicht oft aus wegen meiner Arthrose.*" Herr Meyer sighed and shook his head.

"*Aber wir können nicht diesen Party verpassen!*" Both he and Elke laughed.

"*Haben Sie die chinesische Akupunktur versucht?*" Elke put her right hand on her former boss's left arm.

While the two Germans chatted, Lee and Lily moved away quietly to greet other guests. Lily suddenly noticed someone she knew and ran over to say hello. Lee saw this as an opportunity to refill his glass. He went to the drink table and asked for more Oasis. Before he turned around, he looked up and noticed that the clock on the wall read one minute before eight o'clock. He signaled Lily, who was still talking to her friend, and the two walked toward the jazz band. Lee leaned over to whisper to the trumpet player, and then the band stopped playing. After adjusting his bowtie, Lee took his place beside Lily in front of the musicians.

Under the spotlight, Lee felt happy with his look for the special occasion. His beige tuxedo was beautifully tailored, and the matching bowtie fit nicely over a light-blue shirt. A small red handkerchief peeking from his upper pocket added a nice accent.

And Lily glowed in the attention as well. Dressed in a light-blue satin *qi-pao*, at five feet, eight inches in her heels, she looked almost as tall as Lee. Around her long neck, a natural pearl necklace hung with elegance. A pair of matching earrings dangled from her dainty lobes. Her short, black hair was pushed back, exposing her smooth forehead. She looked up under the bright spotlight, her face glowing and her lips slightly parted, as if she were ready to sing one of her father's favorite songs.

Lee picked up a small fork and struck his crystal glass twice. The crowd quieted down.

"Good evening, ladies, gentlemen, and friends. Thank you very much for coming! Tomorrow is the first day of the Year of the Dragon, and I hope it's going to be a good year for all of us. Also, I will be one year older." The crowd started to cheer. He held up his left hand and continued. "I know we are in the midst of a war, but I am not going to talk about politics."

The guests clapped loudly, and Lee gave a hearty chuckle.

"But I will ask each of you to be very careful out there and don't get yourself hurt. On another note, Lily and I have an important announcement to make tonight." He turned around to give Lily a quick look. "As most of you know, Lily and I have been together for quite a while."

"Yes, quite a while!" Lily chimed in as laughter surged around the room.

"Well, we have some good news," Lee continued. "We're going to be married!"

The crowd started cheering again.

"I can tell you are as excited as we are. We haven't set the date yet, but everyone is invited!"

While the crowd applauded, Lily smiled and gave a little bow.

"Now, back to the important business. Herr Meyer has just confirmed with me that the food tonight is exceptional, and I hope you are going to help me empty those plates!"

A man shouted from the back, "You don't have to worry about that. We've already eaten yours!" Everyone laughed.

"I also want to warn you that Schmitt Shone Riesling is like champagne, right, Herr Meyer?" Lee said, searching for his boss in the crowd and giving him a wink. "It doesn't taste strong, and then suddenly you're being carried home! So, take it easy."

The crowd laughed again.

"Enjoy your evening! By the way, we're going to cut the cake at midnight." Lee gave a wave and the jazz band resumed. As he accompanied Lily toward the bar, he saw Johnny across the ballroom leaning against one of the marble pillars. Johnny raised his Riesling glass and gave Lee a nod. "You are the man of the night, my friend!"

About a dozen couples were dancing on the floor while others continued with their drinks and food. Those who chose not to watch the dancing couples moved into the drawing-room, where Lee Senior's art collections lined the walls. In addition to his Song calligraphy and Ming landscape scrolls, he had been able to acquire two German oil landscapes, one by Renaissance painter A. Altdorfer, and the other by another unknown artist from the Danube School. Lee's father had once told his son that he liked landscapes because they made him feel connected with nature.

Lee wanted to make sure that everyone was having a good time, and he moved around from room to room. From time to time, someone would come up to compliment him on the party. Lee wanted Lily to stay with him, but she insisted on talking to her friends.

Whenever he said to her, "Lily, can I ask you to—" she would reply, "Hold that thought, De-Chang. . . ." and then disappear. When she returned, she'd already forgotten about her fiancé's request. Lee fought hard to put on a smiling face.

By ten o'clock, Lee noticed that Elke's eyelids were struggling to stay open. He led her to a corner chair near the jazz band, her right hand still holding the wine glass. Lily joined them and said, "Frau Elke, the night is still young; why are you not dancing?"

"I would love to, young lady, but my body is not what it used to be. I think I need to get home soon." She gave Lily a sad grin.

"Don't you want to have some birthday cake before you go?"

"That would be too late for me, but thank you. Perhaps you can eat it for me, Fräulein Lily?" She put the glass down and stood up. "I need to get my coat."

"Allow me, Mom," said Lee. He went off to find her coat and asked one of his staff members to get her a taxi. When it arrived, he walked her to the iron gate and held her hand for a moment.

"Congratulations, *mein Schatz*." Elke's voice did not sound enthusiastic.

"*Danke*, Mom."

"So, you and Lily have been together for how long? Two years?"

"Something like that, Mom."

"Are you happy?" Elke moved closer to her stepson.

He hesitated. "I think I am. But—"

"I certainly hope you are." She paused for a moment and then added, "Fräulein Lily certainly looks pretty. . . ." She suddenly went silent and smiled. "Well, goodnight, my son."

When Elke left, he turned around and headed back toward the house. After taking a couple of steps, he stopped at the front garden, staring at the bright lights coming out of the windows and listening to the soft sound of music. The velvet-like melody sounded both joyful and melancholy. Shadows of the dancers moved about on the windows and the walls. Occasionally, he heard cheering. He felt a sudden emptiness, but he held back his tears—he needed to get inside in case Lily wondered where he'd gone.

Upon turning back, he took a moment to stare at the old house, a large, Gothic Revival structure of which Lee Senior had been so proud. For most of the year, ivy covered its light-yellow walls. He missed his father and their laughter together. He missed Lee Senior's voice and his smile when Lee got good grades from school. Even though his father never said much, his quiet approval was an indication that Lee must have done well. This pleased him because he wanted to make his father happy. That is why Lee had never been audacious enough to ask why his father had decided to marry a German woman. He'd often wondered about his biological mother as well, but his questions were buried throughout the years of silence. Lee assumed that his father had kept that part of his life private because he did not want to make Elke feel uncomfortable.

But one day, Lee happened upon a photo of his mother in his father's drawer. He held the sepia photo in his hand for a moment and stared into the face of the young woman. She was petite and had short hair. Her round face made her look younger than she probably was. She wore a dark *qi-pao*; because the photo was not in color, he couldn't tell the shade of the garment. He stared at her, hoping to find himself in her face. He thought his eyes resembled hers, soft and intuitive. He imagined what she was like and wondered if she was an affectionate person, different from Elke. When he heard his father's steps coming up from downstairs, he put the photo back into the drawer quietly, making sure it was in the same place and position as he'd found it.

He had also often been curious as to whether his father had loved

Elke. The word *love* was never mentioned between the two of them, nor to him. As he grew older, Lee wondered what motivated Elke to work so hard and tirelessly around the house. Whenever he brought home an award from school for his academic achievement, Elke would get tears in her eyes as if the award were part of her own achievement, but she wouldn't hold him in her arms to congratulate him.

One day in 1935, a year before his father passed away, Lee Senior asked his son to come to his home office. He had already been diagnosed with lung cancer by then. His face looked thin and tired. He put his hands together and placed them under his chin. After a few moments of silence, he spoke to his son across his desk: "There are a few things that I need to discuss with you."

Lee listened quietly and intently.

"Herr Meyer has confirmed to me that he would be happy to have you take over my work after I am gone. He was very impressed by your academic records and your discipline, which should suit the position very nicely. With your ability and intelligence, you will find that working for Bayer is not going to be difficult, given the fact that you and I have been working together for a while." He paused to have a sip of tea. "As you know, our own company has been doing very well. As much as I hate the war and seeing people killed, it has brought us prosperity. Our annual orders have been increasing steadily for the past five years. You have all the skills you need, and I trust you will do a fine job. Lee Hardware will be in good hands." He looked at his son with confidence.

Lee Junior nodded, feeling the weight of responsibility on his shoulders.

"Also, as you know," his father continued, "because of the nature of our business, we can never discuss what we do openly, especially during wartime. Even if you feel uncomfortable about this secrecy, there is no debate. We need to be extra cautious." Lee Senior stood and paced to the window, his back to his son. After a moment, he returned to his leather chair. "Not all secrets are evil or immoral. Some are kept to save lives."

Lee Junior kept his head down, contemplating the weight of his father's words. This was the first time he had heard his father talk like this.

"It doesn't matter how well you are prepared," his father added. "You will always face challenges you aren't prepared for, and that's how life works. Unfortunately, when I am gone, you will have to find your own answers." Lee Senior got up from his chair and walked to his son. "I think Elke has dinner ready for us. Shall we go downstairs?"

Now, with his father's words still resonating in his memory, Lee headed back to the house. He walked inside to find Herr Meyer and his wife putting on their Loden coats.

"Here you are! We have been looking for you." Herr Meyer patted Lee's shoulder. "I heard the Year of the Dragon brings good luck. So, *Alles Gute zum neuen Jahr!*"

"*Danke*, Herr Meyer. *Danke!*"

"In Germany, we usually say, *Aller guten Dinge sind drei.*"

Lee raised his eyebrows. "Wow, good things come in threes? That's even better than the Chinese double happiness. I certainly hope you are right, Herr Meyer!"

Herr Meyer looked at his wife and then turned back to Lee. "Well, it's getting late, and we old folks need to get in bed early. Sorry we can't stay for the cake, but happy birthday! And thanks very much for having us! *Auf Wiedersehen!*"

The couple shook hands with Lee and then walked to their Mercedes. Lee watched from the doorway. The crimson-red Nazi flag on the left-front of the automobile stood out in the moonlight. The chauffer put on his white gloves, got into the vehicle, and drove away, his charges ensconced safely in the back seat.

Lee turned back inside to look for Lily and found her busily chatting with another young woman. As he turned around and headed toward the kitchen, Johnny grabbed his left arm. "Hey, De-Chang, congratulations! I guess soon we will have to call Lily Mrs. Lee, right? You can thank me with an expensive gift."

Lee laughed and patted Johnny on his shoulder. "Thanks again, my friend."

"So how do you feel?" Johnny asked.

"Feel about what?"

"Being engaged?"

"Well, I don't know. . . ." He was not comfortable with the question.

"What you mean, you don't know? Don't you see each other often?"

"No. I mean, not really. She lives on the other side of town in her apartment. Since she doesn't have to work, she spends a lot of time with her friends. Me? I never have a moment to relax. I spend pretty much every morning at Bayer and then come home early on most days to do more work. So we only see each other on the weekends, and only if she doesn't have a previous engagement with her girlfriends."

"I suppose that's all right." Johnny looked puzzled. "Don't mind me. I'm just a little confused."

"Hey, I've been looking for you!" Lily suddenly appeared in front of them. "Shall we cut the cake? It's five after twelve."

Half an hour later, Mr. Ma, looking very debonair in his well-worn tuxedo and younger than his sixty years, stood by the gate and kept bowing until the last guests left. He then pushed the gate closed and locked it from the inside.

When they were finally alone, Lee met Lily in the hallway upstairs.

"So, did I look all right tonight?" Lily wanted to know.

"Fabulous as always." That was easy. He meant it too.

"I knew you would say that. Thank you!" She paused for a moment and then said, "I am sorry I kept leaving you tonight. It's just that there were many of my friends whom I haven't seen for a while."

"There is no need to apologize," he said dryly.

"Well, it seemed everyone enjoyed themselves tonight. Well done, De-Chang!" She patted him on the shoulder. "See you in the morning."

Before he could say anything more, Lily turned around and went inside her room.

Alone, he stood in the hallway. Staring at the bottom of her door with his hands in his pockets, he heard the gentle sound of the light switch from Lily's nightstand and then saw the shadow of her moving about from the bottom of her door. He shook his head and sighed before he walked toward his own bedroom.

6

Monday afternoon was chilly and overcast, with the sun occasionally popping in and out of the clouds. The less ideal weather kept most people indoors, except the steamed dumpling vendors, who became especially excited as they felt the chilly weather would help them increase sales. All vendors had their "songs" based on the fillings of the dumplings: tender chives with minced pork, lamb with fennel, and baby shrimp with mushrooms. Their "singing" (or cantillation, rather) was rhythmic and soothing. The famous Tian Ren Tea Shop had their own sales pitch: pretty fourteen-year-old Suzhou girls with long ponytails, dressed in red *qi-pao,* holding out small sample cups of tea to pedestrians. Their tender, soft voices made some potential male patrons sample more than one cup of tea and linger afterward.

When Lee arrived at the café, he saw that as always Elke had arrived first. Below her perfectly combed hair she had a gold-colored silk scarf on her shoulders, which looked elegant over her sky-blue Trachten cardigan. She never liked wearing make-up, which she referred to as *der Schild*, or "the shield." *I have nothing to hide* was her favorite phrase. Her smile didn't quite hide the concern on her face.

"Good afternoon, Frau Elke. The same as usual, I presume?" a waiter asked with a smile.

"Yes, please, my dear."

"And you, Mr. Lee?"

"I'm going to have the same thing without the hot milk. Also, could I have one of your Linzer tarts? I haven't had those for a while." Lee felt moisture on the corner of his mouth.

"Yes, Mr. Lee." The waiter left.

"*Mein Schatz*, how are you feeling?" Elke reached across the table to touch her stepson's arm.

"Mom, I'm always feeling tired after a huge party like that. But it's only once a year, so I can't complain. And how about you?"

"I feel more myself today. You know, it took me a while to get home because of traffic. I always forget what a big deal Chinese New Year is here."

Lee smiled at his stepmother. "One would think that you'd just left Germany last year."

Elke wagged a finger at him. "Humor an old woman. My mind forgets."

The waiter came back with the drinks and food. Elke had her regular coffee with warm milk, and Lee had coffee with the Linzer tart. He looked at everything and offered the Linzer tart to Elke.

"*Nein, danke, mein Schatz.* I try not to have too many sweets these days. When you get older, you have to watch what you eat. *Schade!*" She took a sip of her hot coffee and continued, "How is Lily?"

"Oh, she is fine." He took a bite of his tart and gathered his thoughts. It felt awkward to share with Elke the confusion he had about Lily in terms of her lack of interest in intimacy, but at the same time, he needed to let Elke know certain facts about Lily. "Actually," he continued with a sigh, "she is always out and I can never find her, and then she suddenly shows up at my office without telling me first. Mrs. Shen is always very nice about the drop-ins as long as I'm not in a meeting."

"*Ja,* she does seem unpredictable, but again, an unpredictable woman can be more interesting or even exciting, don't you find?" Elke asked with a glint in her eye. "When do you two plan to get married?" She looked at him seriously.

"We haven't really talked about it yet." He glanced sideways briefly. "Perhaps next year." He tried to make his voice sound relaxed.

"You don't sound very enthusiastic."

"It's hard to explain. I don't feel I know her well."

"Then why marry her?"

"Because Father would want it."

"Of course, the *Men Dang Hu Dui* theory. Well, I can certainly see why your father would be happy. She comes from significant wealth." Elke paused for a moment and then continued, "Do you think she wants to marry you for the same reason?"

"Perhaps. I am not sure." He looked down at his hands.

"In Germany, parents want the same thing, of course. I was lucky to have your father as my husband, even though my parents wanted me to marry a German. Your father was a wonderful man. He was generous—much more generous than any German man I've ever known—and he was also very responsible. Now I can see these qualities in you, and I am very proud you have taken his place at Bayer. *Alles geschieht aus einem Grund.* That's what we say in Germany." Elke started on her warm milk, which was cooler now. "You see," she said, pausing for a second, "it appears to me that love relationships in China are very different than in Germany, where everything is obvious."

"How do you mean, Mom?"

Elke put her cup down. "Well, I can't tell if Fräulein Lily is your fiancée or just a friend. It seems something is missing."

Lee kept his eyes on the table instead of looking at Elke.

"What I can tell is that you really like her, but from her end, it seems as though she does everything just for the show. I hope I am wrong."

"I haven't thought about that yet." He was becoming rather uncomfortable, and then he felt Elke's hand on his.

"I just want you to be happy, my son. I am sure your father would have wanted that too."

"Do you need anything, Mom?" He was happy to change the topic.

"Oh no. I am fine. I love my apartment. It's near all the shops and quite convenient. You should come by some day. I can't believe you haven't come for a visit yet." She smiled a bit sadly.

"I know, Mom. I am embarrassed. Dad wouldn't have been pleased about this, as he wanted me to look after you."

7

By nine o'clock in the evening, the narrow street in the western part of the town had become quiet. The poorly kept buildings crowded together, looking like skeletons leaning against each other for support. With few working streetlights, darkness pervaded. Most people had long days of hard work, and one could see the dim lamps extinguishing behind the windows, one after the other.

On the third floor of an old building with rusty-colored bricks, a small lamp near the window was still illuminated. Its faint beam flickered behind cracked windowpanes, barely visible from the street. Behind the lamp, two people sat around a small wooden table, on which two bowls of turnip soup still steamed. Next to the soup bowls, chopsticks sat by two small bowls of rice.

"Let's eat," said the woman.

The couple looked at each other quietly for a moment and then started eating. The man was hungry and ate very fast, while the woman took her time.

"I've been meaning to ask you something, Da-Ming." Her chopsticks were still next to her small lips.

"What is it, Mei?" He did not look up and kept chewing.

"Well, you have been working for the company for three months, and if you can stay there, I thought—" She hesitated and kept her eyes down.

"You thought what?" The man put his chopsticks on the table.

She smiled. "Da-Ming . . . do you like children?"

"I see what you are getting at." He looked serious at first and then smiled at her. "I do like children, but I'm not sure if this is a good time." He scratched his head. "If we could have children, I would want the Japanese out of our motherland first."

"I know. But who knows how long the war is going to last, and I don't want to wait for too long," she said.

"Mei, I know how you feel, but we don't have to decide this right now, all right?" He came around the table and put his arms around his wife. "Don't worry; we will have children one day—and we will have many." He turned to face her. "Here, let me look at you." He pushed her a couple of feet away from him.

"Don't look at me like that. I am embarrassed."

"Stay still, Mei." He kept staring at her.

She lowered her chin to hide her long neck. Mei smoothed out the sleeves of her white blouse and straightened it around her small waist to hide her nervousness.

"Now it's my turn." Mei grabbed her husband's arm, and he stood. He was of medium height with broad shoulders. From time to time, he touched his short black hair. Mei's heart quickened whenever she stared into his deep black eyes. His muscles next to his thin lips twitched a little. He had an awkward look on his face.

"Now you know what it feels like to be stared at," Mei giggled.

He suddenly opened his strong arms and held Mei to his chest.

"Wait, not so tight. I can't breathe. . . ." She continued giggling, running her fingers through his hair. "I love your hair; it's so thick. . . . I like it when it's messy."

He loosened his grip and kissed her.

"Wait, I need to turn the light off." Mei tried to free herself and reach for the light switch. He kept kissing her. By the time she managed to switch the lamp off, she could feel the cool air on her bare shoulders.

8

The weather in June was usually not hot. However, due to poor ventilation, the workshop to which Da-Ming had been assigned was hot and stuffy. It had been three months since Lee Hardware had hired him, and he was glad he was able to find work during wartime. He got along well with his co-workers, and everyone thought he was a hard worker. The lunch bell sounded from the back wall. He put down his last piece of *Mauser* cartridge and walked toward the washroom. After he cleaned his hands, he came out and saw two other men smiling at him.

"Hey, Da-Ming, do you want another chess match today?" The thin, tall man with a mustache smiled at him.

"I would love to, but I can't. I'm feeling a bit tired today."

"No problem. We can try it tomorrow." He patted Da-Ming on the shoulder.

"Are you going to sit with us?" asked a short, stocky man with a worn-out blue hat.

"Of course!"

He followed his friends and walked into the lunchroom, which was starting to get crowded. Most men had brought their lunches, and a few went to the serving window, where cooked vegetables and rice were being sold. Da-Ming put his lunch box on the table and proceeded to open the lid. The two friends who sat next to him leaned over to see into his lunchbox.

"Umm. . . . what's in there? It smells so good! You're a very lucky man," the short, stocky man said.

"Yep, my wife is the best cook in the world!" Da-Ming replied proudly.

"Can you bring some for us tomorrow?" Giggling followed the question.

"Not a chance!" Da-Ming purposely chewed very loudly with his chin up.

"Oh, c'mon!"

"Hey Shorty, leave him alone," the tall man with the mustache said calmly.

"I don't know about you guys, but I miss Suzhou a lot," the man with the blue hat continued.

"Yeah, but there is no work there for us."

"I know, I know. I just miss the pretty girls there, to tell you the truth. The girls here in the big city won't even look at me!"

"Take it easy, Shorty. When we kick the Japanese out, you can have as many Suzhou girls as you want!"

"That's totally unfair because that day will never come!" He shook his head. "You're right; I'm lucky to find work here, but I have to send money home every month."

The tall man patted his friend's shoulder. "Don't feel bad. We all do. Finish your lunch."

One day after work, Da-Ming complained to his wife that he had been having pain in his back, and Mei thought it was probably due to working too hard. She told him that he should take it easy at work. Initially, the pain would come and go. A few weeks later, the pain had become persistent to the point that he had difficulty functioning.

"Did you go to the nurse?" Mei rubbed her husband's back with her hand.

"Yes, I did."

"And?"

"The nurse couldn't tell what was wrong with me, and Manager Wang sent me to a hospital for some testing."

"Why didn't you tell me this sooner?" she asked, agitated.

"I didn't want you to worry."

"That's silly. I'm your wife." She helped him lie down. "When do you expect to see the results?"

● ● ● ●

The hallway was crowded as Mei and Da-Ming entered the hospital. Sick people were sitting and lying on the benches, waiting for their fate. While the floor was clean, the hallway was narrow and dark. Since there weren't enough beds and seating, some patients were lying on the cold concrete floor with their heads resting on their loved ones' legs. Dressed in white, doctors and nurses were busy handling patients and maneuvering through the hallway as if it were a maze.

Mei and Da-Ming were told to wait in the hallway until he was called. She put her arm through her husband's and held tight. Da-Ming looked into the distance and did not show any emotion.

"Mr. and Mrs. Zhou?" asked a soft voice.

They looked up and saw a tall, older man in a white coat with combed-back gray hair standing next to them. He had a square, gaunt face with high cheekbones, and his dark-black eyes looked serious.

"I am Dr. Liu. Would you come with me, please?"

They followed the doctor to a simply furnished, small room, which appeared to be an office. Behind the old pinewood desk, Mei looked up on the slightly cracked gray wall, where two important pieces of papers were carefully framed. On the right side of the desk stood a medium-sized cabinet. Since it had frosted glass doors, Mei couldn't tell what was inside. In the back corner of the office, there stood a dark wooden coat rack with one jacket hanging on it.

"Please sit down," Dr. Liu said politely and then walked behind the old desk. He put on his reading glasses and then organized his papers before he looked at the couple. "I'm afraid I don't have good news for you."

Feeling her stomach drop, Mei grabbed Da-Ming's hand.

The doctor continued. "Mrs. Zhou, your husband has bad kidneys, and they cannot filter his blood well."

Is Da-Ming's life in danger?

"The good news is," Dr. Liu continued, "we should be able to find you a new pair of kidneys. The war made this possible, sad to say, but you should know that it's going to be expensive. You need to pay for the kidneys as well as the surgery." The doctor removed his eyeglasses and put his hands together.

"How much will it cost?" Mei looked at her husband while addressing her question to the doctor.

"I don't have the exact number at the moment, but I would be glad to let your employer know. Perhaps they could help you with the cost, assuming you are in good standing with them. Where do you work?"

"Lee Hardware," Da-Ming said quietly.

"Oh, that's good! I know the manager there, a nice man. I can give him a call. Mrs. Zhou, if I were you, I would go see Manager Wang right away." Dr. Liu smiled and stood.

• • •

When she arrived at Lee Hardware, she apologized to the assistant for not having made an appointment first.

"Don't worry, Mrs. Zhou. Manager Wang is expecting you. Please have a seat inside, and he will be with you momentarily," the assistant said warmly. The assistant stood and opened the door, and Mei followed her inside.

The room was large and bright in the morning sun. A medium-sized oak wooden desk faced the door. Behind the desk was an empty mission-style office chair. On the wall, framed photographs displayed various types of guns, some of which went back to World

War I. A few wooden chairs were in front of the desk, and the assistant gestured for Mei to sit in the one near the desk before she left the room.

Mei sat down with her hands together on her lap, her nervousness preventing her from leaning back. Quick footsteps in leather soles echoed from the entrance of the office.

"Good morning. You must be Mrs. Zhou," a robust voice said warmly. "I thought you might come. I'm Manager Wang."

Mei rose from her chair and saw a wide-shouldered, stocky man with a reddish complexion. He was dressed in a charcoal business suit.

"Please sit down." The man sat behind his desk, gesturing with his hand. "I received a call from Dr. Liu of Tong Ren Hospital, and he said that your husband is not well."

"Thank you, sir, for seeing me, and I'm sorry for this intrusion." She pulled the front corners of her blue blouse. "Yes. It's true. The doctor said my husband needs new kidneys, but the surgery is going to be . . . very expensive."

"I'm very sorry to hear that." Manager Wang pushed some of the papers on the desk carefully to the side and then continued. "Mrs. Zhou, your husband is one of our best workers. If you have any difficulties, we certainly would like to help."

Upon hearing this, Mei felt hopeful.

The man continued. "We normally can handle small illnesses here, but this is an unusual case, which I believe involves surgery that needs to be done in a hospital. We don't want to lose your husband." He leaned back against his chair and put his hands together. "To be honest with you, Mrs. Zhou, covering the cost of surgery is a decision I can't make, but I *am* going to tell Dr. Liu that we will take care of the costs for the tests he's already done."

"That's very kind, Manager Wang, and thank you!" Mei gave Manager Wang a deep bow from her chair.

"Mrs. Zhou, it's quite all right. I suggest that you go see Mr. Lee tomorrow. He is the company boss and should be able to come up with something. He is a nice man. Besides, this illness is quite urgent, and we should not delay the treatment." Manager Wang took a piece of paper from his desk and wrote slowly and carefully on it. "Please take this. He has an office on The Bund. He is usually there in the mornings." He stood and then said, "Please keep me posted. I hope all goes well and we will have Da-Ming back here soon."

"Thank you again, Manager Wang. I am very grateful." Mei stood and gave another bow and then walked out of the office quietly.

• • •

By the time she came home, her husband was in excruciating pain. He tossed back and forth, sweating. Mei gave him one of the pills that Dr. Liu had given them. Within an hour, he had calmed down and gone back to sleep.

She sat by the window and pulled out the piece of paper she had received from Manager Wang. It said:

> *Mr. Lee De-Chang Jr.*
> *Bayer Pharma Co.*
> *100 Shandong Plaza*

9

The Bund was surprisingly hard to find, and it took her much longer than she had expected to arrive at Shandong Plaza because she took the wrong bus.

The big city is so confusing!

"Ah, Mrs. Zhou. I am glad to see you. Please have a seat." Mr. Lee gestured for her to sit. "Mrs. Shen, could you bring Mrs. Zhou some tea, please? Thank you."

"Thank you, Mr. Lee, for seeing me, and I'm very sorry for. . . ." She kept her gaze on the floor.

"It's quite all right. Sometimes things don't always turn out the way we expect, right?"

"I . . . guess." It was probably not a good idea to make eye contact.

"Now, Manager Wang told me that your husband is not well.

How is he feeling at the moment?" He looked at her attentively.

"He's in a lot of pain." She looked up at the kind man and then quickly down, feeling tears forming in her eyes.

"I see." Mr. Lee cleared his throat and shuffled some papers on his desk.

Mrs. Shen came in and put the tea next to Mei on a small table and left without any sound.

"I understand he needs surgery. Is that right?" Mr. Lee asked.

"That's what Dr. Liu said, but we don't know how we're going to afford that." Her hands moved nervously again around the corners of her blouse.

"I see." He nodded slowly, picking up what seemed to be his appointment book from the desk. He looked at it and then checked his watch. "Would it be all right if I asked you to come back later, say sometime after lunch? I have a meeting in a few minutes, but it should be over by the time you come back."

"I'm so sorry for causing so much trouble, Mr. Lee."

"It's no trouble at all. I will see you in a couple of hours. Are we agreed?" He smiled at her again and then stood.

By the time she arrived at Bayer for the second time on the same day, it was one o'clock in the afternoon. While waiting for Mr. Lee, she dared to look around the room. Directly facing her was a large mahogany desk, laden with neatly stacked piles of paper. Near the front of the table, a pair of lion bookstands encompassed hardcover leather-bound books written in different languages. Next to the telephone, a gilded frame held a photograph of a beautiful young woman with large eyes and short, dark hair. On the wall, behind the oak office chair, photographs were framed in dark wood. In the middle, she saw a large sepia photograph of men. All of them were European except the one in the middle, who was a tall, older Chinese man with short, silver hair. Under the photo, the printed words were *Firma Friedrich & Bayer Co, Shanghai 1913.* A smaller photograph to the left showed Mr. Lee with the older man, both in dark tuxedos. Neither of them was smiling. Another photograph was Mr. Lee with an older European woman, who stood stiffly as if a bamboo stick was inserted in her back.

She heard footsteps in the hallway, and within seconds, both Mrs. Shen and Mr. Lee walked into the office. Mei nervously stood. Mr. Lee extended his right hand to signal for her to sit. He took out his pen and wrote something on a piece of paper and gave it to Mrs. Shen, who then left the room quickly. Mr. Lee turned his head toward Mei. "I was worried that you may not come back, Mrs. Zhou, but I'm glad you did."

"Thank you for your time, Mr. Lee." Mei felt his gaze.

"Right before you came back, I made a call to Dr. Liu, and he told me all the details about your husband's illness. It sounds quite serious. This is what I thought could work. . . ." He paused, putting both hands together as he leaned back.

Mei felt the stiffness of her spine; her hands stopped fidgeting, and she waited for her husband's fate.

"If it's all right with you," he began, his eyes searching for approval, "I would be happy to take care of the cost of the surgery."

Mei remained in the same position, processing what he'd just said. *Did I hear what I thought I just heard? Can this be true?*

"But even if your husband gets better and starts paying me back the money he borrowed, it would take a very long time for him to pay off his debt, considering how much he is currently earning."

Mr. Lee stood and came to the front of his desk and sat directly across from Mei. She followed him with the low angle of her eyes as he sat down. She dared to notice his charcoal linen trousers and his brown wingtip shoes.

"I had an idea and wondered if this would be all right with you. I think it's going to be good for all of us."

"How do you mean, Mr. Lee?"

"Well, both my fiancée and I need some help around the house. We do have Mr. Ma, our gardener, but we need someone to work inside. If you don't mind, you could come over and give us some help. Then I can certainly take care of the hospital bill, and your husband never has to pay me a penny back." He sounded enthusiastic.

There was silence. Mei felt her eyelids blinking fast, while her fingers also picked up their speed at the corner of her blouse.

Mr. Lee lowered his head, trying to see her face. "Is . . . that all right? You certainly don't have to—"

"What . . . would you like me to do, Mr. Lee?" She looked up, making eye contact for the first time, noticing a special warm affection in his eyes.

"Well," he said, seemingly relieved to see her eyes finally, "basic house chores, such as cleaning, washing clothes, and cooking. Speaking of which, I certainly hope you like to cook. Since my stepmother moved out, I've been eating out a lot, and I can't wait to have some home cooking." Mei sensed his enthusiasm in his voice. "I hope it's not too much of an imposition. What do you think?"

"I . . . am very grateful, Mr. Lee, but I need to ask my husband first. Could I come back tomorrow and let you know? And yes. I like to cook. I learned that from my father. He taught me many great Suzhou dishes, such as Steamed Lu Fish, Ma-Po Tofu, Northern Style Braised Pork with Mustard Greens, and Drunken Chicken. Would you like to hear more? Oh, I . . . am so sorry; I got carried away. . . ." She felt herself blushing.

"Not at all. I am enjoying learning about your culinary prowess. How about we continue this conversation tomorrow, *if* you come back? If you are not available, I will need to ask Mrs. Shen to find us another person, but I sure hope that person is you." He stood and walked behind his desk, putting his hands together. "See you tomorrow, perhaps?"

10

It was a beautiful summer afternoon. The air was light and moist. A few clouds moved slowly toward the east. Beneath the sky, bustling streets were filled with people and traffic. As she walked by the Lin Grocery Shop, she heard the loud shouting from Mrs. Lin that turnips and Shanghai cabbage were on sale. She saw the bicycles meandering between the rickshaw runners and the buses. Occasionally, she heard the bells from the bicycles and the chants from the rickshaw runners. She checked her pocket to make sure she had enough change for the bus and walked quickly toward the bus station.

When Mei arrived at the French Concession, she noticed the clean, wide street with very few people on it. They were all well-dressed, and none of them seemed to be in any rush. She saw almost all houses here were in Western styles, none of which she had ever seen in Suzhou. She felt her heart start pounding again, and her legs became heavy. In less than three minutes, she arrived at the tall *fleur-de-lis* wrought-iron gate. Behind the gate, she saw the paisley-shaped front garden with many beautiful flowers. A large, Gothic Revival-style house, painted in light yellow with white trim, stood proudly behind the garden. She timidly walked up to the stone wall and checked the number, which said sixty-six.

"*Do not use the main gate; instead, always use the side wooden door*," Mrs. Shen's voice resonated in her head. With her small suitcase in her right hand, she walked to the side door and pressed the doorbell, her heart pounding faster.

The door opened, and an elderly man appeared. "Ah, you must be Mrs. Zhou. We were expecting you!" Medium built and slim, he looked like he should be in his sixties. He had light-gray, receding hair, combed back neatly. His reddish complexion indicated he had been working outdoors. He had narrow but warm eyes above his round cheekbones.

"Greetings, and you must be Mr. Ma."

"Yes, I am. And please let me have your suitcase," the man offered.

She felt embarrassed to have an older man carrying her suitcase but didn't want to contradict him. Mr. Ma took the suitcase from Mei and signaled for her to follow him. She stole a quick glance at the front garden, where she saw pink and white peonies and yellow roses.

"Here you are. Please come in." Mr. Ma pushed the front door open as they reached the top of the stairs. As soon as she walked in, she was immediately embraced by a stream of cool air. "Let me take you to your room, where you can rest for a bit," Mr. Ma added.

I have a room? Mei paused to adjust to the change of light from the bright sun to the darker front hall. She closed her eyes for a moment and then slowly opened her eyes, which were getting wider by seconds. She felt gravity pulling down her jaw, and her canvas shoes planted heavily into the marble floor. With her eyes wide open, she saw a large, gilded crystal chandelier suspended from the vaulted ceiling. Slowly, her eyes traveled downwards to a large gold-leaf framed mirror above the crescent table, a pair of elegant, high-back antique chairs, and a marble statue. At last, she looked at her shoes, which did not belong on the rounded medallion design on the shiny marble floor.

"Are you with me, Mrs. Zhou?" The sound of Mr. Ma woke Mei from her trance. It took some effort for her to move her planted feet. "Here we are. This is a nice room. It's not so big, but it's comfortable." He put the suitcase on the floor next to a cushioned wooden chair. "You must be thirsty, Mrs. Zhou. There is a pitcher of water on the kitchen counter. Do help yourself."

"Thank you, Mr. Ma."

After a quick pause, Mr. Ma added, "Mr. Lee is in his office upstairs and will be here momentarily." He gave Mei a nice smile and then left the room.

She stood there, frozen for a moment. The initial shock of seeing Mr. Lee's house felt overwhelming. Even though Mr. Ma said her room was not big, it looked bigger than the space she and her husband had.

The room was simply furnished. Next to the open window, a small bed was covered with white linen. She gently touched the pillow to feel the softness of the fabric. It was something she had never had. She then turned and stood next to the bed. She began to lower herself, then stopped halfway. She needed to prepare herself for the expensive bed with expensive sheets on it. She closed her eyes and lowered herself all the way onto the plushy bed, *so soft and comfortable.* On the opposite side of the bed stood a redwood wardrobe, which had two small drawers on top and three long drawers on the bottom. Above the wardrobe hung a small mirror framed in a red-lacquered wooden frame. Directly below the window, there was a small wooden desk, on top of which was a banker's lamp with its dark green glass shade. An old double-bell Chinese alarm clock stood next to the lamp.

She stood back up, turned around, and saw a closet door behind the room door. As she was about to open it, she heard footsteps from the hallway approaching her room. She immediately let go of the doorknob and turned around.

Mr. Lee was already standing at the doorway. "Ah, Mrs. Zhou. It's good to see you here!" His voice showed controlled excitement. In his left hand, she saw a teacup. "I'm glad your husband liked my idea. I trust you didn't have too much trouble finding this place today?" He looked animated.

"No trouble at all, Mr. Lee, and it was . . . fine," she murmured, straightening her blouse with her hands.

"Good. First, let me start with the kitchen, and then Mr. Ma can show you the rest of the house." Mr. Lee ushered her to the kitchen, told her to familiarize herself with it, and excused himself with a friendly smile.

In the kitchen, she first saw the large center island with a white and gray marble top. There was not much on it other than a pitcher of cold water next to a small stainless faucet and sink. There were two straw grocery bags hung on a small hook on the side of the center island. Behind the center island were dark redwood kitchen cabinets with a large kitchen sink in the middle, above which was a large open window. A stainless gas stove was situated on the right side of the kitchen counter. On the opposite side of the cabinets and below a smaller window stood a small rosewood antique table with two matching chairs. A Siemens clock hung directly above the window.

Upon opening the first cabinet door carefully, she saw three shelves of tin cans of tea. The yellow can had the words for jasmine tea, red had Wo-Long, white had White Peony, and then Xiang-Pian, chrysanthemum, Long-Jing, Song-Luo, Tian-Chi, Tian-Mu. . . .

That's a lot of teas!

She closed that door and moved to the next one. She saw Ming blue and white dining sets inside: large bowls, small bowls, serving plates, and then soup bowls, all decorated with hand-painted landscapes. The next cabinet consisted of Dresden dining ware, and they were mostly plates. She counted each set with her index finger, eight of everything. The next cabinet was all cooking spices.

After exploring the kitchen, she felt tired, so she thought she should just go take a short nap. She went to her room with a dry throat.

Back in her room, Mei opened her small suitcase and proceeded to take out the contents. She first took out the photograph of her parents and placed it on top of the wardrobe and then took out the smaller items and put them in the two small drawers on top. Since she didn't have many clothes, almost everything fit into one of the large drawers. She unwrapped the newspaper and put her canvas shoes under the bed, neatly together. In the closet, she discovered that there were some towels that she could use. She took one of them and went to the washroom to wash her face.

• • •

"It must've been some kind of a shock to come to the French Concession, wasn't it?" Mr. Ma said warmly.

"It was, and I didn't know what to expect. I feel like I came to a foreign country, with all the strange-looking buildings and beautiful gardens. Even the trees here look bigger. I like the big round leaves. . . ." She looked around as if to confirm her impressions. "This is the first time in my life that I actually heard birds sing. And I don't see any street beggars around here."

Mr. Ma gave a hearty chuckle. "Well, all that is true. I felt the same way when I first came here. But not all Shanghai looks like this. There are still areas that were damaged by the Japanese bombing, which remain unchanged." He raised his palm to point to the surroundings. "This is probably the most elegant part of the city, as you can see yourself. What I like about this area is that it's always quiet, and I hate noise. Even during the Chinese New Year, you won't hear much. The French never allowed the Dragon Dance to be performed in these streets. So each year, I have to go to the city center to see it. It seems that time stands still around here."

"Do the Japanese ever come here?"

"Not usually. Many local residents here are foreigners, mostly Europeans. Only when the Japanese chase someone, say a communist, do they roam around like ants, but soon enough, they return to their bases."

Mei nodded.

"Anyway, we are very pleased to have you, Mrs. Zhou, especially Mr. Lee. In recent days, he has come home with a joyous face and sometimes even humming a tune. That's very unusual for him!"

"You mean he usually is not like that?"

"Oh, no. The young master is usually quiet when he comes home from work. I think he likes to keep everything to himself—that is, until he met you!"

She wasn't quite sure how to respond. "Thank you, Mr. Ma. Actually, I came here by chance."

"What do you mean, Mrs. Zhou?" Mr. Ma looked puzzled. "You weren't applying to work for Mr. Lee?"

"Not exactly." Mei debated how to explain what brought her to Mr. Lee's house.

While she was hesitating, Mr. Ma continued, "It doesn't matter. What matters is that you are here, and we are all happy to have you. I feel like I finally have someone to talk to!" Mr. Ma sounded content. "Mr. Lee hasn't had any decent meals since his stepmother left. He eats out frequently and often brings food back for me as well. He hired a cook not long ago, but the man only lasted for one week because Lily Wong, Mr. Lee's fiancée, did not like his cooking." Mr. Ma shook his head. "I can tell that he likes you, Mrs. Zhou. He also said that he bets you are a very good cook!"

"I hope he likes my cooking."

"I think you will be fine. Miss Wong is the one who is hard to please."

"How do you mean?"

"Well, I don't like bad-mouthing someone, especially someone close to our young master. She actually seems like a decent lady, but there is something unusual about her, and I can't find the right words to describe it."

"I . . . don't quite follow." Mei tightened her forehead.

"She likes to slam things around when she gets upset. Whenever she comes, it seems the entire town knows. And she always walks way ahead of the young master, as if she were late for something." Mr. Ma moved closer to Mei with his hand next to his mouth, almost whispering. "She is nice and everything, but I don't think she is right for our young master."

"What kind of work does she do?" She felt the need to change the topic.

"Work? Oh no, she does not work. She is a rich lady. I believe she is in Hong Kong now with her parents."

"Is she coming back?"

"Oh yes. She comes and goes, like a free bird, and no one can stop her." He shrugged his shoulders. "Well, I guess I have said enough about her. After all, whatever she does is not our business. I just don't want our young master to get hurt, that's all."

"I see what you mean, Mr. Ma. I hope Miss Wong likes me."

"She will, she will. I am sure of that."

• • •

"Mmm . . . everything smells very good!" Mr. Lee walked toward the end of the dining table and then sat down in his chair. "This looks very impressive. You seem like a very experienced cook!"

"I hope you like it." Standing next to Mr. Lee, Mei joined her hands in front of her apron.

"Ah, it looks like you have made my favorite: Steamed Lu Fish." He looked excited. "Let me have a taste." He took a small piece of fish and put it into his mouth. "Mmm . . . it's splendid, so delicious!" His eyes closed for a second. "This has to be the best fish I have ever had!"

Mei felt relieved. She needed to score well with this first dish.

Lee then put his chopstick down. "Wait a minute. This looks like a lot of food for one person. I don't suppose you made anything for yourself?"

"It's all right, Mr. Lee." She was too happy and had forgotten about feeding herself.

"No, it's not all right. Why don't you take out the large fish and half of the cabbage and put them on different plates so that you and Mr. Ma can have something to eat too?"

"But I cooked these for you, Mr. Lee."

"I appreciate this, but you and Mr. Ma have to eat as well." He stood and went to the kitchen and came back with two china plates. He put the bigger fish on the large plate and then took off half of the cabbage and put it on a smaller plate. "Here, now you both have dinner. Why don't you go tell Mr. Ma to come in to eat?"

Mei hesitated for a moment and then went out to find Mr. Ma.

11

It didn't take long for the bus to arrive. Mei asked the driver what would be the best route to get to Tong Ren Hospital and was told that she needed to change buses only once. She was glad to hear that, as navigating around the big city was something she would like to avoid. When she arrived at Dr. Liu's office, he was talking to a patient. She waited outside until the doctor came out with the patient a few moments later.

Dr. Liu shook Mei's hand and asked her to come in. He had a warm and caring expression on his face. "What I wanted to tell you is that it's going to take a bit longer for us to find the new kidneys for your husband; I am guessing perhaps two to three weeks, hopefully not longer than that."

She nodded and tightened her lips, trying to process the information and pondering what it could mean.

Dr. Liu continued, "Given your husband's current health condition, which means he is otherwise strong and healthy, he should be able to handle the waiting period."

That was reassuring.

"I spoke with Mr. Lee about the delay of the surgery, and he has indicated that it would be best if your husband remained here in the hospital while waiting for the new organs to arrive."

"How much will all this cost?"

"Mr. Lee told me not to disclose this information to you because he doesn't want you to worry." Dr. Liu came around the desk and patted Mei on the shoulder and then added, "Don't worry, Mrs. Zhou, we will take good care of your husband. Let me take you to his room." Mei stood and followed the doctor to a room on the second floor.

The space was not big but very bright. Two large windows faced south, and the grassy yard below had benches along the walkways. Patients in hospital pajamas were sitting on the benches, resting and chatting, while nurses in white hats walked by. Even though it was summertime, the air felt cool and comfortable. Da-Ming had his hands resting on a piece of newspaper on his comforter, his eyes closed. Next to Da-Ming on another bed, an older man with a shaved head sat against his pillows. He was very thin, with a dark complexion. His left eye twitched nervously and spasmodically. As soon as he saw Mei and the doctor walk in, he spoke with a sarcastic grin on his face. "Look who is here! It must be my lucky day today!" Dr. Liu gave the man a gentle nod.

The loud voice of the roommate woke up Da-Ming. He opened his eyes. He tried to sit up, and Mei bent over to help him by putting a second pillow behind his back. He gave Mei and Dr. Liu a forced smile. "I thought you might be coming today, Mei." He raised his left hand. "Dr. Liu has been taking very good care of me. We need to thank him. Mei, thank him," he said, his hand still in the air, waiting for Mei to respond.

"I know, Da-Ming. We are very lucky." She wrapped his hand in hers.

"I am going to let you two chat for a while, and Mrs. Zhou, make sure you see me before you leave today." Dr. Liu studied Da-Ming carefully for a second before he left the room.

After the doctor left, Mei turned her face back to her husband. But before the couple could say anything to each other, the man in the next bed started talking again. "This war is very bad, and we're all going to die. So, enjoy each other while you can."

Mei and Da-Ming looked at each other and did not respond.

The man continued, "Do you know why the Japanese are occupying our country? I'll tell you why: their country is too small, and they want ours. *Pei!* Not a chance! They are nothing but a bunch of bastards, very bad people. They probably think we are afraid of them."

"Not I," Da-Ming responded.

Hearing that response, the man seemed to feel encouraged to continue. "Do you know how many Chinese they have killed? And how many women they have raped since they came here?" His breath became agitated, and he paused for a moment. "Well, maybe there are some nice ones among them, but I haven't seen any." He slid down and covered his face with his comforter.

Hearing no more speeches from the other bed, Mei moved closer to her husband. "How are you feeling?" His hand was still in hers.

"Not so bad at this moment."

"Do you need anything?"

"No. I can't think of anything right now." He looked pensive as if processing some deep thoughts. "By the way, what's it like working for Mr. Lee?" he said, changing the topic.

"I've just started and there isn't much to tell, but he seems like a nice person and. . . ."

"And. . . . ?"

"Well, as you know, I have never worked for anyone or had a *job*, not in this kind of capacity, at least."

"You mean as a housekeeper?"

"Yes, as a housekeeper." She looked down for a moment. "I just hope I'll do a good job.

"I am sure you will. I know you. Besides, it doesn't look like we have much choice right now, does it? You know how to clean and all that stuff; on top of that, you're a great cook!"

"While we're on this topic, Mr. Lee seemed to like the Lu Fish I made last night."

Da-Ming didn't seem to hear Mei's sentence. "I owe him. And we can never repay him, and I hate to owe people!" His face suddenly looked sad.

"Don't think about it right now. It's no use." She put her hand on his cheek. "Think that you will be well again—and that we are going to have a family soon!"

"Do you know why I hate to owe people?" Again, he did not seem to hear Mei.

She shook her head. *Why do we have to discuss this right now?*

"I'll tell you why: it gives them the upper hand, if you know what I mean."

"Mr. Lee is not like that. He's very nice."

"I suppose rich people can be nice sometimes." He sighed. "I tend to think too much. But thank you for doing this. I know you're doing this for me, Mei. I know you'd rather go to school. I know that."

"Don't think about it too much, and get some rest."

"You're right, Mei. I *am* actually feeling tired. Perhaps you should go." He pulled his hand out from Mei's.

Mei nodded silently and stood. She tucked Da-Ming's comforter in and walked out quietly.

On her way back to the bus stop, Mei saw a small bookshop on the corner of Shao-Shan Street. She paused and then walked in. When she came out, she had a small dictionary in her hand. Walking back toward Mr. Lee's house, she thought about the chores she needed to do. The anticipation made her anxious.

12

Mei took out some soft cloths, a large and small feather duster, a bottle of wood cleaner, a can of furniture wax, and a broom with a dustpan and headed to the front lobby. She remembered clearly that it was only a couple of days ago when she stood here like a newly planted tree trying to adjust to the new soil.

The front lobby had a marble floor under an old warm-colored Milas Turkish village rug, which she didn't remember seeing before. Beyond the rug, next to the front entrance, a marble statue of a female bust stood on a pedestal. She walked closer to the statue and saw a short phrase carved on the bottom of the statue's chest: *Jehanne d'Arc*. Behind her, against the wall, stood a Georgian Mahogany Demi-Lune crescent hallway table, flanked by two tall, high-back Hessen chairs. The large room to the right was the ballroom, and most furniture pieces in the room were from the Ming Dynasty. On the walls, there were silk scrolls of the Tang and Song Dynasty, Chinese landscape paintings, and calligraphy pieces.

Mei felt her breath getting shorter. She scrutinized every object and walked gingerly as if a faster movement would shatter everything. As she backed out of the formal dining room, her right hip hit the corner of a small walnut table with a porcelain *shou-xing* on it. The movement made a loud sound and she quickly reached out to secure the wobbling statue. *Watch out!* She straightened the furniture carefully and walked quietly to the other side of the ground floor.

It's time to get some work done.

She pondered how much work she had to do and how long it would take her to finish all the chores. It would be unrealistic to think that she could accomplish everything in a couple of hours, so she decided that she should just do the dusting and cleaning the floors and worry about waxing the furniture the next day. She looked at the clock on the wall, and it said three-thirty. If everything went smoothly, she should be able to have the meal ready for Mr. Lee at around six-thirty, a time when Mr. Lee preferred to eat his dinner. She started with the feather dusters for the porcelain and wooden furniture, the large duster for other furniture, and the small duster for porcelain and small objects, some of which required a re-wipe with the soft cloth. As she was cleaning each object, she also paid attention to the motifs of each one—a landscape with little chubby boys playing next to the riverfront on the tall blue and white Ming vase, the wooden legs of the square table with claws on the bottom, and the brass handles on the armoire with a phoenix.

After an hour had passed, the sound of Mr. Lee's car emerged from the front garden. She heard him walk in, go straight to his office, and close the door. Mei finished her cleaning and went to the kitchen to start the dinner. She chopped everything in the necessary shapes and then put the rice on the stove. While she was guarding the rice to make sure it wouldn't overspill when it reached the boiling point, she took out the small dictionary from her straw bag. She first looked through the radical section to see how many words she already knew and then went to look for the characters to see if they had other meanings. She realized that she needed to write the new findings down and made a plan that she should do some studying after work in the evening.

A few minutes after six, Mr. Lee appeared in the kitchen doorway. Still wearing his Oxford pinpoint shirt and linen trousers, he seemed tired but relaxed. "Please don't mind me. I don't want to rush you." He went to the thermal kettle and poured some hot water into his teacup.

Mei turned around and dried her hands on her apron. "It's no rush at all, and dinner is almost ready, Mr. Lee. By the way, here is an envelope for you from Dr. Liu." She took it out from the straw bag and put it in his hand.

"How was your visit to the hospital today? Any good news?"

"It was good. My husband was in a double room, a very nice room, and he seemed to be in good spirits. But. . . ."

"Yes?"

"Well, Dr. Liu said that it might take two to three weeks to get the needed organs. So, we have to wait."

"I see." Mr. Lee nodded. "I trust Dr. Liu. We just need to be patient." Mr. Lee took a sip of his tea and looked casually down on the kitchen counter and saw the small dictionary. "Is this yours?"

"Oh yes. I bought it from a bookshop today," she said, feeling the heat coming to her face.

"I see. Is there anything I can help with?"

She sensed Mr. Lee smiling at her. "Thank you, Mr. Lee. I couldn't trouble you. You've done enough, and I'm sure you are very busy."

"It's no trouble at all. If you'd like to learn to read, from what I am guessing, I'd be glad to help you. Let me take a look at my schedule, and I'll let you know later." Before Mei could say thank you, he walked out of the kitchen, sat in his dining chair, and picked up his newspaper.

The next morning as Mei was preparing the hot water, she remembered to take out the same tea can that she had seen earlier, and she placed it next to the teakettle. She also made two poached eggs for Mr. Lee, and he was very pleased that she remembered this. Before he left the house, he came back to the kitchen and said to Mei, "I should be back by two-thirty this afternoon, and we can read together if you like." His voice sounded sincere.

She gave him a bow.

"Oh please, there is no need to do that." He extended his arm to signal for Mei to stand straight. "I look forward to our reading together this afternoon. It will be fun!" His leather shoes made subtle squeaky noise as he left the room. Within seconds, Mei heard the sound of the engine from Mr. Lee's car.

During lunch break, she sat by the small kitchen table, thinking about the event that would take place in a few hours: reading with Mr. Lee. *One day, I will be as smart as all the women in the city. And I can make my own choices. Then I will have children, a small garden, and little ducks. . . .*

She leaned her head against the window frame with her eyes closed, not realizing how much time elapsed.

• • •

"Mrs. Zhou?" A soft voice sounded next to her.

Still with her eyes closed, she whispered, "What time is it?"

"It's two-thirty."

Mei jumped out of the chair. "I can't believe I dozed off, Mr. Lee. I'm very sorry!" She fixed her hair and straightened her blouse. *How embarrassing.*

"It's quite all right, Mrs. Zhou. I guess it's going to take a while to get used to living here. Is this a good time for us to read?"

"Yes, yes!" She stood, straightening her blouse again.

"Relax, Mrs. Zhou." He was smiling. "I have a copy of today's newspaper and a pencil, and I see you have your dictionary in your hand. I guess we're all set."

She sat back in the same chair, still feeling embarrassed.

"How about a glass of water? It will relax you."

What? Mr. Lee poured ME a glass of water? This cannot be! She smoothed her hair and her blouse.

"I want to get some idea of how much you already know." Mr. Lee sat down across from Mei, putting the newspaper in front of her, while Mei reluctantly took a sip of her water.

"I . . . had some schooling when I was very young and then I was briefly taught by my husband for a while. I don't remember how long but I felt I was making good progress. People like me in Suzhou don't always have the opportunity to go to school, and the war makes it even harder."

"I had an impression that you are from Suzhou." He smiled. "Sorry to change the subject. I get myself distracted here. Shame on me."

She could tell he was staring at her. "You did?" she asked.

"Well, I was guessing from your features. . . ."

Did he pay attention to my features? Why?

"Anyway, that's not related to our reading. Let's see. . . . how about we pick out a paragraph." His voice sounded more natural.

I should get myself ready, she thought, rubbing her eyes.

"Reading the newspaper is not necessarily a good way to learn to read because the language is not always conversational, but this short report could work for us for the moment." His index finger pointed to the lower part of the first page. "Unless you want to read my pharmaceutical books, which I don't think you would like." He laughed, giving her a naughty wink, which seemed out of character.

This side of Mr. Lee she did not expect, but strangely enough, it made her feel more relaxed. "I can give it a try, but I may not do that well."

"Don't worry; just do your best. I also have some novels that I used when I was in college, but I'll have to find them."

Mei sat straight and then started: "*Last night, the Japanese . . . one fishing boat and . . . something five men. They . . . them and later killed three of them. The Nationalist Party said that they . . . something. . . .* I'm sorry, Mr. Lee. This is hard for me." She stopped reading, her eyes still fixed on the paragraph.

"That was very good!"

She was still concentrating on the paragraph.

"You know quite a bit, and well done! See here." He pointed to the words she couldn't read. "All we need to do is find out where these verbs are in your dictionary. After that, everything will make sense." He gave Mei his pencil.

She circled the words that she did not know and proceeded to look them up in her dictionary.

"Why don't we write these characters down on this sheet of paper so that you can review them later?" Mr. Lee handed her a piece of paper.

How organized and thoughtful. She did exactly what he suggested and wrote the words slowly and neatly on the paper.

"So, let's try to read it again." He gave her a confident look.

"Thank you." She cleared her throat to focus herself. "*Last night, the Japanese sunk one fishing boat near . . . Southport and . . . captured five men. They interrogated them and later killed three of them. The Nationalist Party said that those men were their . . . special agents.* Did that sound right?" She looked up to Mr. Lee, waiting for confirmation.

"Bravo! That was excellent, Mrs. Zhou. You see, that wasn't too hard, right?" His eyes were kind and encouraging.

She felt proud.

"How about we try another paragraph?"

13

"Mr. Lee, I have some good news to—" she started as she ran into the house. She stopped her sentence when she saw a beautiful young woman standing in the middle of the kitchen. The woman looked elegant. She was wearing a victory-roll hairstyle with a pair of small, oval-shaped, light-purple sapphire earrings nesting in her delicate ear lobes. Her tightly fitting, light-green polka dot dress revealed her perfectly proportioned body. On her feet, she had a pair of white, bow-trimmed shoes.

"I'm very sorry. . . ." Feeling embarrassed, that was all Mei could come up with.

The young woman put down her drinking glass and extended her right hand. "I'm Lily—Lily Wong—and you must be Mrs. Zhou?"

Mei nodded as if her mouth had been gagged.

"I've heard a lot about you and your great work! But I didn't know you were so . . . pretty." There was a hesitance in her voice.

"Forgive me, Miss . . . Wong." Mei kept her head low. She could tell she must have a terrible blush right now.

"Don't be embarrassed." Miss Wong walked closer and patted Mei on her shoulder. The touch did not make her feel warm or relaxed. "As you may have heard," Miss Wong continued, "I am Mr. Lee's fiancée. I just came back from Hong Kong, where my parents live. As much as I like Shanghai, Hong Kong is where I belong. Do you like Shanghai?" Miss Wong looked at Mei from the corner of her eye. "You must. It's a great city. And you are from . . . Suzhou, I hear? I've never been there, but I hear it's a nice town. And of course, everyone says that Suzhou has many beautiful women. I guess they're right," she said condescendingly, looking at her watch.

While Mei was deciding how to respond, footsteps sounded from the hallway.

"Hey De-Chang, Mrs. Zhou has some good news to share with you," Miss Wong said into the air. "Sorry. I let myself in."

"You are back, Lily!" Mr. Lee came in, looking animated. "What's the news, Mrs. Zhou?" He patted Miss Wong on her back before turning his head to Mei.

Mei gave Mr. Lee a grateful look. "Dr. Liu said that my husband will have his surgery next week."

"That's great! And—" Mr. Lee put his hands together.

"I'm going upstairs for a bit," Miss Wong interjected, and then went to the front lobby to fetch her suitcase.

• • •

The sudden appearance of Lily Wong made Mei feel uneasy, even though Mr. Lee had already said that he and his fiancée needed help around the house. She sensed an aggressiveness about her that she didn't like. She contemplated the length of her stay and wondered how long it would take for her to pay off their debt for the surgery. In addition, she worried that Mr. Lee would spend more time with Miss Wong and wouldn't be able to teach her how to read and learn Chinese characters anymore. She then felt ashamed and selfish to have such thoughts. After all, she was hired under unusual circumstances, and she should not consider any other possibilities until the debt had been paid.

In the morning, Mr. Lee appeared in the kitchen with his usual calmness and equanimity. His morning greeting sounded sincere but rehearsed. "Good morning, Mrs. Zhou. Is everything all right with you?"

Mei had already memorized that phrase by now. He always thanked Mei for the hot water for his tea and for the eggs. But this morning, Mei had Miss Wong on her mind and couldn't look Mr. Lee in the face. She kept herself busy by wiping the countertops more than they needed. Finally, Mr. Lee probably sensed the tension and came closer to Mei. "I like light starch."

He stood very close to her, his mouth almost next to her ear. She could smell his toothpaste breath. "I beg your pardon, Mr. Lee?" she asked, startled.

"I said I like light starch . . . for my shirts." He smiled, the same grin he had used since they first met. "Just one spoon of cornstarch for every two cups of water. And here's a small brush you can use." He boldly grabbed her small hand and put the brush in her palm. She felt the warmth of his large hand.

"Thank you, Mr. Lee. I . . . will do my best."

"No, I should be the one to say thank you!"

14

14

"The surgery was a success!" Dr. Liu proclaimed as Mei walked in from outside. "It took quite a few hours to complete, but all went smoothly."

"Thank you very much for the good news, Dr. Liu. I am so happy!" She gave the doctor a deep bow, feeling relieved. "Do you think I can go see him now?"

"Yes, you can, Mrs. Zhou. He is resting right now. Try not to make him talk. It's better that he just rests." Dr. Liu signaled to Mei that she could go. "By the way, see me before you leave today."

She walked in quietly and saw her husband lying there with his eyes closed. His face looked peaceful, and he was breathing calmly. She put her right hand on his cheek. Feeling the warm touch of her hand, he opened his eyes. He managed to move his lips a little, but Mei put her index finger in front of her lips. She then sat down next to him. He closed his eyes again and remained there peacefully. She remembered that peaceful look very well, a look he had whenever he was content. She also remembered that look when he came home feeling tired from a long day of work.

She walked to the window and observed the quiet hospital yard below. Two men in their hospital robes were sitting on a bench and talking, one of them making gestures with his right hand. A few nurses were walking through the paths with papers in their hands. An elderly woman was sitting alone on a different bench reading a newspaper. From time to time, she would pause and look up as if she were thinking about something.

When Mei looked back at Da-Ming's bed again, her husband had gone to sleep. His breathing was even and quiet. She walked out of the room quietly and again found Dr. Liu in his downstairs office. She asked about the recovery period for her husband and was told that if everything went well, he would be discharged from the hospital in two weeks. The doctor also assured her that his staff would do their best to take good care of him during the recovery.

"Don't worry, Mrs. Zhou. It looks like you'll have your husband home soon. I'll be in touch."

• • •

Da-Ming's pending discharge from the hospital occupied Mei's mind for the rest of the day. She was relieved and grateful that she and her husband would return to their normal life soon.

As such, she was distracted and forgot to lower the heat to simmer the rice until Mr. Lee walked into the kitchen and said, "I hate to bother you, Mrs. Zhou, but do I smell the rice burning?"

Mei dashed to the stove like lightning. "I am so sorry, Mr. Lee!" She hated herself. All of a sudden, she remembered that she had fallen asleep twice already when she was supposed to meet with Mr. Lee, and now, she had just burnt the rice. *I am finished!* She saw one of her hands start to tremble. She stood there in silence, her eyes on her apron, waiting for her sentencing.

"Ah, not to worry, Mrs. Zhou. It's only the bottom of the rice that got burnt; the top is perfectly fine! I don't eat that much anyway, and besides, Lily won't be back for dinner." He sounded unperturbed.

Mei remained on the same spot as if her feet were planted into the ground.

"Mrs. Zhou, it's quite all right." Mr. Lee walked closer. "How about we sit outside for a few minutes after dinner and perhaps you could tell me what's going on in your mind? It's a beautiful evening."

Mei nodded, surprised that Mr. Lee was not upset. She tried to eat her vegetables but couldn't taste the food. She needed to do better, and there would be no more excuses for mistakes.

Thank goodness that Miss Wong was not around. She would have me kicked out of this house in seconds.

After she quickly cleaned everything in the kitchen, Mei arrived in the backyard first. She sat in one of the comfortable white garden chairs but didn't feel comfortable.

Within five minutes (although it felt like an hour), Mr. Lee arrived with his teacup in one hand and a small envelope in another. He sat down next to Mei and took a sip of his tea. "Ah, the evening air feels nice. I think this is the best time of the day in the summer months. Don't you think?" He always sounded relaxed. Mei nodded.

"Are you feeling all right tonight, Mrs. Zhou? It seems you have a lot on your mind."

She nodded again and then asked, "Are you angry at me?"

"Angry about what?" He sounded surprised.

"About the rice that I burned?"

He smiled. "No. I've forgotten about it already. Oh, by the way, if I may change the subject, Dr. Liu called me today and said the surgery for your husband went very well." He frowned slightly. "But you don't seem to be in a celebratory mood."

"I do tend to worry, but I'm very happy about the surgery, Mr. Lee, very happy."

"Let me guess. Are you worried about money and how long you have to work here?"

Mr. Lee must be some kind of mind reader. "You can say that, Mr. Lee." Her fingers started to wrestle with each other over her lap. "I get overwhelmed sometimes by things . . ."

"Well, that's understandable," he said, nodding.

"Could I ask you something, Mr. Lee?"

He moved closer to her.

"Everyone in my family calls me Mei. Could you also call me that?"

"I see. But of course, if that's what you prefer. Which character is your 'Mei'?"

"It's the one for rose, kind of tacky."

"Not at all. Your parents knew you would be beautiful, like a rose."

She had never considered herself beautiful, and hearing the compliment from him made her blush.

He must have noticed her face because there was discomfort in his voice as he said, "I was just . . . making conversation. Take this . . . Mei." He handed her the envelope. "Sorry. It feels strange to call you by your first name. I suppose I'll get used to it at some point. Anyway, I figured you must need some money to pay for things separate from food. In fact, I can give you a small monthly stipend." It didn't seem that there was any room for discussion. He continued, "I suppose you're anxious about what's going to happen to you after your husband is discharged from the hospital. Am I right?"

She sensed his gaze in the warm orange sunlight. She nodded.

"Life can be unpredictable sometimes, especially during war. But some things can make life easier. Allow me to help you, Mei." It sounded almost as if he needed her permission.

"I really don't know what to say, Mr. Lee."

"Say nothing, but do promise that you'll stay and work for me." His voice was pleading.

"I promise."

• • •

Dear Ma and Pa,

> *Da-Ming is coming out of hospital soon, thanks to Mr. Lee. We will once again have our normal life together. My work at Mr. Lee's house is fine. He is a very kind man, unlike what I had imagined. He teaches*

me how to read and write. I don't know if all rich people
are like that, maybe not.

I miss you both very much. Take good care of
yourselves.

Yours,

Mei

July 26th, 1940

15

As usual, Lee was up at six again on Saturday. He had two things on his agenda for the morning: finish his letter to Manager Wang and find out when Lily would come back from her friend's house. The first part was easy, and the second part was not because Lily never told him the address of where she had gone. He had no idea how many friends she was with, not that it ever mattered, but he did know that some of her *ma-jiang* games could last for days. He didn't want to call her if she was in the middle of her games, which usually took place in the afternoons and evenings. After all, her social life had always been her priority, and the engagement to Lee had not changed a thing. "My friends are important to me," she had once told Lee.

Upon finishing his tea and his letter to Manager Wang, he walked to the windows to open the glass panes for some fresh air. He saw Mei walking out, approaching Mr. Ma in the front garden.

"*Zao*, Mr. Ma." Her voice sounded fresh and relaxed.

"*Zao*, Mrs. Zhou. Where are you going so early in the morning?"

"I'm dropping off a letter to my parents at the post office. Can I get you anything, Mr. Ma?"

"Oh, I am fine for now. Thank you." He looked down at the garden. "You know what I hate? The weeds! They are anarchists and keep coming out perniciously."

"Excuse me?"

"Oh, every time I turn around, they creep out. They think I don't see them."

"They must have their own minds, Mr. Ma, ha, ha, but the garden looks amazing, Mr. Ma. Always." She looked around, impressed.

"Thank you, Mrs. Zhou. I do enjoy working in the garden. The work keeps my mind clear."

"So, how about I bring you back a *you-tiao*; isn't that your favorite for breakfast, Mr. Ma?"

"You mustn't spoil me, Mrs. Zhou. Your memory amazes me. I would like to have a *you-tiao* and a bowl of hot soymilk in the morning, but at my age, I should watch out for fried food, and the temptation really kills me!"

"An occasional treat won't hurt, right?"

"You are very persuasive, Mrs. Zhou. All right." He reached into his shirt pocket, took out a paper bill, and handed it to Mei. "I'm going to treat myself today!"

"I'll make sure all will be hot when I come back." She walked through the small wooden side door next to the gate, which opened to the street.

Lee's eyes followed Mei's back until she made the turn at the street corner. He liked her short, quick pace, as if every errand was urgent, exactly like his own.

He waited until after ten, when he felt it might be a good time to find out where Lily was. He called several of her friends' houses but was told that she had left earlier. Finally, he thought he should ring her apartment.

"What is it, De-Chang?" She sounded flustered.

"I'm sorry, Lily. Are you still in bed?"

"No, I am not. I'm having my coffee." Her voice was agitated. "What's up?"

"You don't sound like you're in a good mood, Lily. Did the *ma-jiang* games go well?"

"No. I lost a lot of money this time."

Since when did she care about money? "I'm sorry to hear that." What else could he say? After a short pause, he dared to add, "Perhaps you would like to come back later today . . . and we can spend some time together?"

"I don't know. I can't think that far right now. Just tell Mr. Ma not to lock the front door." She hung up. He sank back into his chair, not knowing what to do. Perhaps he should forget about Lily for a while and give her a call later.

When noon arrived, his body seemed to guide him toward the kitchen—there might be some leftovers from the previous night. He was not that hungry, but it was better not to disrupt his routine. Upon approaching the kitchen doorway, he heard unfamiliar soft singing coming from inside. He tiptoed toward the doorway, where he saw Mei standing next to the ironing board with her back facing him and her front facing the open window. He saw her pale thin arms lift up over her head, and her slim fingers moved quickly to pin down her hair. The back of her long neck revealed itself for the first time above her delicate shoulders, which were covered by her light-pink blouse. Under her pale-blue trousers, he saw her small bare feet standing on the wooden floor, her canvas shoes not far from the ironing board. She mixed the cornstarch efficiently and spread it out on the collar evenly with the small brush that he had given her.

He froze, feeling like a statue standing at the kitchen doorway, not blinking, watching her arms move back and forth. The rising steam embraced her face above the ironing board. He saw a few strands of hair dangling next to her ears, moving about in the cool breeze, and he felt a surge of blood rushing to his head. He couldn't concentrate on the lyrics she was singing, and he only heard random words: little brook, birds chirping, water, blue . . . he felt his breathing shorten, his heart pounding fast. Suddenly, he imagined Mei in his arms, and he was gently caressing her.

She must not notice that I am watching her.

He backed away like a shadow. Back in his office, forgetting lunch, he shut the door before sinking into his chair. He covered his face, admitting to himself that his feelings for Mei had become a reality, a reality that he was afraid of, a reality that could never be revealed. Having feelings for a married woman was never on his agenda, nor was it an action he had expected.

I feel like Vronsky or Julien Sorel, but those would've been the kind of men that my father would spit on.

It was true. His father would have been ashamed. Elke would also be ashamed, and she would have to give him a lecture on how to be an honorable man. It would be a scandal in the French Concession, and Herr Meyer would have no choice but to have his title as the general manager for Bayer stripped. It would be a disgrace for the whole Lee family. His ancestors would have to come back to punish him by having him sit on the bottom of the family well for two weeks without food, and his name would be crossed out in the Lee family book with the darkest pine ink one could find in China.

Lily must never find out about this.

● ● ●

"Look at you." Lily had an affected grin on her face. "What a pretty face and figure you have. If you put on decent clothes, someone could easily mistake you for Mrs. Lee!" The words came out as if from Lily's nose, her eyes slanting toward Mei.

Lee saw Mei's face blushing like a ripe peach.

"Please don't mind me. I was just joking," Lily added.

"Thank you for making my shirts look so good, Mrs. Zhou." Back to formality, Lee tried to ease the tension. "They look like they were done by a professional!"

"Well, I guess you won't need to go back to that old cleaner anymore, De-Chang, for *obvious* reasons," Lily added sarcastically, but Lee ignored her undertone.

"That's true. Mrs. Zhou is very good at what she does." Upon taking his shirts from Mei's hands, he felt her soft skin. "I'm going to put my shirts in my room."

"So, how have you been, Mrs. Zhou?" Lily changed her voice back to normal, not nasal anymore.

"I'm getting used to the work here now, and Mr. Lee is very kind."

"I am sure of that. And I can see he is very fond of you, especially by the way he looks at you. He thinks I can't tell. You know what? I don't care."

"Miss Wong . . . I. . . ."

"Oh, don't mind me; my mouth has no guards. By the way, in case you haven't heard," Lily's face changed, becoming serious, "the Japanese are going crazy lately because the communists are having a lot of activities around the city."

"Are we in immediate danger?"

"Probably not, but you never know for sure. Underground activities are going on right now, and some attacks on the Japanese may be imminent. That's just what I've heard. I hope I am right."

"Do you think we're safe here?"

"Well, I don't think any major battles will take place near where we are. My guess is that most likely they will occur outside the city to avoid civilian casualties. Nice thought from the communists, but that will never happen. Civilians always get caught in the middle."

"Are you a part of any of the 'activities'?"

"You mean am I a communist?" Lily shook her head and added, "Oh no, I am not a communist, my little sister. As much as I care about our motherland, I think I am a coward, and I don't try to hide it. Even if a Japanese soldier was standing in front of me, I don't think I could kill him. I don't know. It's too complicated. I just hope they leave China soon."

16

The sound of two gunshots woke him. It came not far from the house.

He quickly removed his book from his lap and walked to the window. The street looked as calm as usual. He turned around and checked his watch, seeing that it was seven minutes after midnight. He sat back in his reading chair. In less than five minutes, the doorbell on his front gate rang, and he got up again. With the large lamps switched back on, Lee could see Mr. Ma open the side door, and three Japanese soldiers and a translator walked in. There was no time to think. He rushed into Lily's room without knocking. "We have some unexpected guests downstairs," he said, trying to keep his voice calm as usual. "Come with me."

By the time they reached downstairs, Mr. Ma and the unexpected guests were already standing in the front lobby. The two short soldiers stood side by side behind a young, tall commander. The skinny translator wore a black raincoat and a Fedora hat. "Good evening, Mr. Lee," the translator said while he was removing his hat. "Sorry to disturb you at this late hour." His unusually high-pitched voice sounded as if he'd just had his vocal cords recently replaced.

"What can I do for you?" Lee responded, Lily standing on his left. She stood with her back straight, looking defiantly at their unexpected guests.

"Well. . . ." he looked at the Japanese soldiers and then turned his eyes back to Lee. "Someone just fired at us and ran this direction. We wanted to see if he is hiding in one of these houses." He looked at the young commander, who nodded.

Unlike most Japanese Lee had seen, the commander looked about six feet tall. Under his hat and given the length of his sideburns, he must have short, dark hair. Above his prominent cheekbones, his almond-shaped eyes revealed intelligence and a hint of humanity. Between his square jaws, his lips were thin, showing his curiosity and ability in articulation.

"This is Captain Aoki and—"

"We have not seen anyone coming this way, but please let the captain know that the house is open for search," Lee cut the translator off.

The translator quickly translated everything to the captain. Holding their Arisaka rifles, the two soldiers stood behind the captain as if they were sculptures. They kept their heads straight, and no one could tell where or at whom they were looking. Mr. Ma remained where he was near the doorway, silent and expressionless. The captain contemplated for a moment and then said something to the translator. He had a deep, clear voice.

"The captain wants to know if you have anyone else in this house."

All of a sudden, Lee realized that Mei was still in her bedroom, perhaps sleeping. "Yes. We do." He signaled for Mr. Ma to bring Mei to the front lobby. A moment later, Mei walked in with her eyes barely open, obviously trying to adjust to the bright light from the chandelier.

"And who is this?" The translator's eyes lit up.

"She is Mrs. Zhou, our housekeeper," Mr. Ma answered from a distance.

"She is what?"

"Mr. Ma is right. She is our housekeeper," Lee confirmed.

"Well, let me ask her who she is myself." The translator approached Mei and stopped within a few inches from her face.

It took a few seconds for Mei to realize what was going on. Her eyes were fixed on the swords mounted on top of the Arisaka rifles. In his peripheral vision, Lee saw that Mei's legs were trembling.

The translator put his right hand over his mouth and cleared his throat. "And what's your name?" He was squinting his eyes, putting his hand down.

"Mrs. Zhou," she said mechanically.

Her tightened eyebrows might be indicating her reaction to the translator's cheap alcoholic breath, Lee thought.

"And what are you doing here in this house?"

"I am . . . the cook and . . . the housekeeper."

"I see. Have you seen a—"

Before the translator could finish his sentence, Captain Aoki lifted his left hand in his white glove briefly in the air, and the translator stopped. With his eyes blinking fast, the captain paced slowly back and forth in his shiny leather boots, and the squeaky noise sent chills through the spines of everyone in the room. He stopped in front of Mei and look down at her face as if he were studying her features.

Meanwhile, Mei still kept her gaze on those swords. Looking at Mei, the captain revealed a slight grin. Within seconds, Lee noticed that Mei's whole body was trembling. With the captain standing in the way of Mei's gaze, it looked to Lee almost as if Mei were studying the details of his captain's uniform: the new wool, the leather gun strap, so close she must be able to smell it, the military medal on his left chest, and a chain for the pocket watch next to it.

This could be the last few moments with Mei at my house. Since the Japanese didn't find the man they were going after, they could arrest Mei instead. The soldiers could take her away under suspicion of being a communist—and no proof of evidence would be needed, Lee thought. He mentally began preparing himself to defend Mei. He could verify that she was not a communist. But what if the Japanese did not believe him or her? What should he do? The only possible alternative would be to offer himself to be taken away in order to save Mei's life.

While Captain Aoki had his eyes locked onto Mei, the translator whispered something to the captain. Captain Aoki listened carefully, shook his head, and walked away from Mei. Lee felt momentary relief, but the danger was not over yet.

Captain Aoki paused for a moment without saying a word. The few seconds of his pause felt like an hour. With gentle poise, he slowly pulled out his pocket watch, looked at it, and then said something to the translator. He sounded calm and non-threatening.

The translator responded, "*Hai, hai!*" before he faced Lee. "Well, the captain trusts what you told us, Mr. Lee, and we won't search the house this time." He put his hat back on. "The captain wishes you all a good night."

Captain Aoki walked out quickly in big strides first, followed by the two soldiers and the translator. Mr. Ma gave Lee a relieved look before he left to lock the front gate.

Lily's face turned red. She raised both of her hands. "That was it? I can't believe how powerless we are! Unless we get those bastards out of our country, we will never have peace!" If there had been a piece of furniture next to her, Lee knew she would have smashed it into pieces.

"There is nothing we can do, Lily. They are the occupiers right now. We just have to learn to live with it," Lee said, trying to calm her down. "No one is hurt, so let's go to bed."

As Lily climbed the stairs, she kept saying, "bastards." Lee heard the loud slam of her bedroom door, the force of which could shatter the chandelier.

Mei jumped, startled by the sound, and Lee saw her looking at him. "Everyone is okay." Mei's whole body was still trembling. "Let me walk with you to your room."

17

"Wow, everything looks *schön*!" Elke walked in. "Ha, ha. It looks like Mrs. Zhou didn't trust the dexterity of my hands," she said, looking at the only set of silverware on the table.

"Mrs. Zhou always thinks about this kind of thing ahead of me," Lee responded. "I hope you are not offended, Mom."

"Of course not. You want the old German lady to learn how to use chopsticks?" She smiled. "You can't teach an old cow new tricks. Isn't that what we say in English?"

Mei left the dining room quietly.

"I like the—how should I say it?—the presentation of her dishes. *Alles sieht sehr schön aus!*" Elke added. "I suppose that's part of the Chinese cuisine, right?"

"Frau Elke, my fiancé knows how to find the best in town," Lily responded.

"I suppose that includes you as well, Fräulein Lily?"

"Thank you, Frau Elke!" Lily blushed but seemed pleased.

"Would you like to start, Mom?" Lee pointed the dishes out to Elke.

After a quick glance at everything, Elke reached into the pork with her fork and then put the meat into her mouth slowly. She chewed it with special care as if the dish were from a different planet. "Umm, this pork dish is exceptionally delicious and tender! It reminds me of what we ate at home. In Germany, we like to eat a lot of pork, except Mrs. Zhou's dish is not as salty." She sounded pleased. "Where did you find such a good cook, *mein Schatz?*"

"It's a long story, Mom. I think we're just lucky."

"Yup. We all need luck sometimes, don't we? The Japanese could have taken us all away the other night. I say we all are pretty lucky," Lily added, and took a sip of her Riesling.

Lee tightened his eyebrows, disappointed that Lily had brought up the unpleasant subject.

"What happened?" Elke looked puzzled.

"It's nothing, Mom." Lee did not want to bring up the confrontation with Captain Aoki and his soldiers. "It's really nothing."

"No, no. I want to hear this." She put her fork down.

Lily appeared to realize what she had started. "Well, a group of Japanese soldiers came to the house at night, really late."

"Why?"

"They were chasing a man who had fired a couple of shots at them. Apparently, he was running toward this direction."

"So they thought he might be hiding in this house."

"Exactly." Lily took another sip of her drink. "But for some reason, they did nothing and left."

"How strange." Elke shook her head.

"It was. The captain stood in front of Mrs. Zhou for a while, and we thought perhaps he was going to take her away, and I could tell that my fiancé was worried about her safety, but guess what? After he stared at her for a bit, he walked away. He might have said something to her, but none of us understands Japanese. It was really weird."

"Let's put this episode of drama behind us, shall we?" Lee said, feeling the need to interject.

"So, what do you think is going to happen to Shanghai? I mean, are the Japanese going to stay here long?" Elke asked. She continued before anyone could respond, "I certainly hope not. I still remember the bombing three years ago. It was devastating, and we all were lucky to have survived that. They really are crazy people." She shook her head and added some food to her plate.

"Well, I don't know, Frau Elke." Lily gave a cold smirk. "The real issue, I think, is that the nationalists need to take care of their own problems, and the communists aren't strong enough to fight the Japanese alone. In my opinion, the two sides have to work together to fight the Japanese. Will it work? We have to wait and see."

Elke nodded. "You seem to know things, Fräulein Lily." She squinted at her.

"A bit, just a bit. I care about what's going on around here. My fiancé probably cares too, except he won't discuss it with anyone." Lily patted Lee's hand.

Lee wanted to change the subject but didn't know what would be a better dinner conversation.

"I think the Japanese are just like the Nazis, except they are in Asia. They are merciless people. Don't you think, Frau Elke?"

Elke stopped chewing and looked at Lily seriously. She seemed to want to respond, but nothing came out. She stared straight into Lily's face, and Lee slowed his chewing.

"I know nothing about the Japanese other than seeing what they did to this city. And of course, they are occupying China right now," Elke said coldly.

"It just occurred to me, Frau Elke, that the reason we were spared that night was that they knew that my fiancé works for Bayer." Lily sounded very sure.

"Excuse me?" Elke sounded confused.

"Aren't the Germans and the Japanese on the same side? Now I've got it!"

Elke put her fork down. "Are you saying that I am a Nazi because I am a German citizen?" Elke asked in a loud voice. She turned her eyes to Lee, who, feeling uneasy, chose to be silent.

Lily continued, "Allow me to finish, Frau Elke. I know Bayer is a good company, but Herr Meyer is a Nazi party member, isn't he?"

Lee nodded in silence. Nodding was all he needed to do right now.

"And I know he has to be; otherwise, he wouldn't be appointed by the *Führer*. This makes perfect sense. You see? I was right," she said, looking at Lee. "Have you heard that Jews are migrating to this city now? And you must know why." Lily turned her face back to Elke. "Are we on the side of the Nazis?"

"I have not heard about Jews migrating to the city, and yes, we both know the reasons, but let me tell you something, young lady. . . ." Elke wagged her finger at Lily.

"Take it easy, you two." Lee wanted to stop this conversation before it was too late.

"No, no, let me finish," Elke insisted. "Things are not as simple as they seem sometimes. Do you know something, Fräulein Lily?" Her voice was firm. "I am not a Nazi, and none of my family members are, but the Nazis *are* in charge. We need to do what we have to do to survive. Besides, I guess there have to be good Japanese people out there, although I don't know any." Elke sat straight as if preparing for the next battle.

"Well, in that case, let me ask you this: What do you think of the *Führer*?" Lily pressed on.

"What do *I* think of him?" Elke paused for a moment and then continued. "He actually has done a few good things for the Germans; otherwise, he wouldn't have been elected, but he seems to have a troubled soul. But that's just my opinion. What do I know?"

"So do you have any plans to return to Germany?" Lily persisted.

"Not right now. My fate has taken me to China. So, this is where I belong."

"Ever?"

"I don't know, young lady. I really don't know." She was looking at Lee, and their eyes met. "Maybe when the war is over, I can take my son back to Germany. I would like for him to meet his German grandparents."

Lee met Elke's warm eyes.

"That would be nice. Perhaps I can come too!" Lily patted Lee's shoulder and then turned to face Elke. "But Frau Elke, please don't get upset with me. I am no politician. I say whatever comes to my mind. I suppose I should be grateful to the *Führer*, otherwise, my fiancé wouldn't have a job! And the funny thing is, Herr Meyer seems like a nice old man, even though he is a Nazi. I exchanged a few words with him during our New Year's Party. I think he always has an eye for young women." She giggled.

"*Pretty* young women," Elke corrected Lily.

Lee had to laugh, hoping this topic was finally coming to an end.

"I think you are a very smart girl, Fräulein Lily. Just make sure you watch yourself, if you want a word of advice from an old woman." Elke looked less tense.

"Thank you, Frau Elke. I know my mouth has no guard. But hey! I have nothing against the Germans—as a people, I mean. It's the leader we have to watch out for. Right?" Lily took a couple more bites of her food. "Mmm, this is really good!"

18

"Thank you very much again, Dr. Liu!" Both Mei and her husband bowed.

"When you go back to work, just take it easy for a few weeks, and try not to lift heavy objects." Dr. Liu shook his patient's hand. "And I hope I don't have to see you both again, unless you want to invite me for dinner!" He gave a hearty laugh as he walked out of the hospital building with the young couple.

Mei and Da-Ming thanked Dr. Liu again before they headed for the bus station. Once they were on the bus, Mei sat close to her husband and held his hand in hers. She studied his face for a while: he looked thin, and his hair was messy.

"I am a very lucky man," he said quietly, looking at his wife. "Can we go for a walk? I have not seen the city for a while."

The two got off the bus a couple of stops early and started walking toward their small apartment. He opened his eyes wide as if it were his first time seeing the streets, letting the gentle air massage his thin face. He smiled at people as they walked by. When he saw a street vendor selling sticky rice cakes, he asked Mei if he could have some. Mei pointed out to the seller the two kinds they would like to have, and the woman wrapped up two pieces each of the hawthorn-flavored and red-bean-flavored sticky rice cakes.

Once they arrived at home, she told him that she needed to finish some work for Mr. Lee and should be back later in the day. He said he needed to rest anyway and waved at his wife before she left.

After Mei was gone, Da-Ming found a piece of paper and a pen. He paused for a moment and then started to write:

Dear Mr. Lee,

> *I can never thank you enough for what you have done for me. I am just an ordinary worker and feel undeserving of this kind of generosity and kindness, which I know I can never repay. I hope my wife has been some help to you and that you would let her stay to continue working for you even after our debt has been paid, whenever that time might be.*

> *Wishing you the Best of Health,*
> *Your humble worker,*
> *Zhou Da-Ming*
> *August 18, 1940*

* * *

Within two weeks, Da-Ming contacted Manager Wang and told him that he was feeling ready to go back to work and would like to start on Monday. Even though he was not feeling one hundred percent, he thought he should at least try so that Mei would be happy about his effort. The manager was pleased and confirmed that, despite the increase in work at the plant, he would give him the day shift so that he could spend the evening with his wife. Da-Ming was very grateful.

Early on Monday morning, he arrived at the plant before the night shift got off. After changing his clothes, he went to the rest area, where he saw some of his friends. A taller man noticed him first and came toward him with his right hand extended. "Hey, brothers, Da-Ming is back!"

Within seconds, he was surrounded. Some patted his shoulders, and others put their hands through his hair.

"We thought you weren't going to make it."

"What are you talking about? This guy is tough!"

"Hey, Da-Ming. I'm glad you're back because I want a rematch of our chess game, and I hope you still remember that."

"I don't know about you guys, but I miss his wife's cooking!"

Da-Ming thought he should go say "hello" to Manager Wang before he punched in. He left the rest area and went upstairs, where Manager Wang was already busy.

Manager Wang was concentrating on his paperwork until he heard the gentle knock on the glass door. "Hey, look who is here!" He removed his glasses and came around the desk.

Da-Ming gave a bow and met the manager's hand with his. "It's good to be back, sir, and thank you for having me back." He looked his boss in the eye.

"We know you just came out of the hospital. So, take it easy for a few days, and don't push yourself too hard." Manager Wang smiled at him.

"Thank you, sir. I won't disappoint you."

"All right, young man. Be careful out there, and I'll see you around." Manager Wang patted Da-Ming on the shoulder.

• • •

It had been two weeks since Da-Ming returned to work. Each day he felt stronger, and Mei was very pleased. Mr. Lee was also pleased with the news. He asked Mei to prepare his dinners early so that she could leave before dark to get the meals ready for both her husband and herself. The daily travels were not easy for her in the first few days because she did not plan well for the things she needed to do for Mr. Lee and the chores at home. Mr. Lee sensed that but didn't want to say anything. He thought it would be best for Mei to figure out her own system of managing things.

Mei realized it too. Whenever she forgot to do something for Mr. Lee, he never said anything. Knowing how conscientious her employer was, Mei was thankful that he kept silent about her mistakes. She tried her best to keep things going as smoothly as possible, and Da-Ming was very pleased with his wife. Whenever he walked into the door, a meal was always ready. Even though Mei was often tired by the end of the day, she never said anything to her husband because she thought the work at the factory must be ten times harder than her house chores.

She enjoyed watching him eat, always like a "tiger," she often said. Sometimes she forgot to eat because watching him distracted her, and he never paid attention to Mei's gaze. Occasionally, he would eat the whole meal without leaving any for his wife. Only after he was done did he realize that Mei had not eaten yet. Then, he was very apologetic, and Mei would smile at him and say nothing.

Whenever Mei asked him about work, he always gave her the same answer: "It's very good."

One day before Mei asked him about his day, she noticed he had a serious face, and she thought something was wrong.

"I have some news to share with you." His voice sounded ominous.

"What happened?" Mei put down her chopsticks, preparing herself for the possible bad news.

He burst into naughty laughter. "Sorry I scared you. Manager Wang asked me today if I'd be interested in the workshop manager position, and I said yes. Aren't you happy for me?"

Mei punched him gently on the arm. "It's not funny to tease me like that, but congratulations! I'm very happy for you!" She put her fingers through his hair.

When he started eating, Mei did not. She watched him eat as usual and contemplated the news. She imagined what the promotion meant for him and for both of them. She realized this could mean that she wouldn't have to wait long for them to start a family, and the prospect made her elated. A moment later, she was less enthusiastic because she was worried that her husband might not be ready to accept the responsibility of having children. Still, she felt she should bring up the topic, but she needed to find the right time.

A month after he returned to work, he started coming home at irregular hours. Sometimes, he didn't come home until after eight o'clock, and that made Mei worried. When she asked him about it, he said that he had more work to finish, and on certain days, he was playing chess with friends. She believed him, but one night, Mei thought she should have a talk with her husband about coming home late. "Da-Ming, you do know we are at war right now. Don't you?"

"You sound strange, Mei. Is there something wrong?"

"No, there is nothing wrong." She wanted to bring up meeting Captain Aoki in the middle of the night at Mr. Lee's house but decided it wouldn't be wise, as this would make him worry and he might ask her to stay home all day.

"Then why are you acting so strangely?"

"I'm just worried about you, that's all." She paused for a moment and then added, "I would prefer that you come home before dark. From what I know, if you get caught breaking the curfew, you could be taken away."

"Don't worry about me. I'm always careful." Seeing no response from his wife, he added, "Hey, I said not to worry, all right?" Then, he started wolfing down the food.

Mei wanted to bring up the "family" topic but couldn't. The words came up to her lips, and she stopped them. The timing was probably not right.

That night, she laid awake in bed while her husband snored loudly. She was pleased to have their life back, and the news about her husband's recent promotion made her happy. She was happy that Mr. Wang liked his work, and his new role meant that the factory would start taking him seriously, and he could be on his way to becoming permanent staff.

On the other hand, she was not sure if she would be able to handle the amount of work if her husband agreed to have a family, especially during wartime, when things seemed unpredictable. Moreover, Mr. Lee might not like the idea of having an infant in the house while she was doing her chores. She finally told herself that she should give it some time. If her husband continued to do well and moved up to an even higher position, she might not need to work for Mr. Lee anymore. The prospect of a new life pleased her.

· · ·

Da-Ming ignored Mei's advice—and the curfew. His coming home late became a pattern. On certain nights, he would come back very late, and Mei couldn't wait for him, so she had to eat first. She assumed it was probably for the same reasons he had told her earlier and didn't want to give him a hard time about it. Until one night, he came back to the apartment out of breath as if he had been chased.

"What happened? Are you all right?" she asked, concerned.

"I thought I was being followed. There's something I need to tell you," he said quickly while catching his breath. "I've been going to meetings lately," he said in a low voice.

"What do you mean? What kind of *meetings*?" Mei put her kitchen towel down on the chopping board.

"Well, I've been approached by the nationalist army, and they want me to join them."

"*Join* them? Join who?" Mei felt her eyes widen.

"Join the army to fight the Japanese."

Mei couldn't talk. She stood, left the room, and sat on their bed. She felt as if thunder had struck her.

Da-Ming came and sat next to her on the bed. He put his arm around her shoulders and then said, "Do you remember telling me about what Dr. Liu said about me being lucky?"

"Yes?"

"Well, I thought about what he said a lot lately, and I want to make great contributions to our motherland. I think I'm ready for that." His voice sounded determined.

"But what about your work at the factory?" She couldn't look at him.

"Manager Wang would understand, I think. But look, I just want to join them for one year and then come back."

"How can you be so sure about this decision?"

"I'm not sure about it—not really, but I want to give it a try. I want to kick the Japanese out of our motherland."

"What about me?"

"You can still work for Mr. Lee, and I'm sure he will protect you."

"But that's beside the point. And—"

"Look. I'm not the only person doing this. Think of it this way: If no one joins the army, how are we going to kick the Japanese out of our country? Besides, I'm healthy and strong—"

Mei put her hand on Da-Ming's lips. She realized that her husband had already made up his mind. It was better not to try to talk him out of it. "Just for one year, right?"

"I promise, and I'll write to you whenever I can." He put his head on her shoulder.

"When do you plan to leave?"

"I think they want me to join them next week, so I have a few days to get ready. I need to talk to Manager Wang tomorrow."

Mei couldn't sleep that night. She thought about the sleepless night not long ago when she'd heard the good news about her husband's promotion and was looking forward to a new life. Now, all her dreams were shattered. She turned sideways on the bed with her back facing her husband. Soon, her pillow was moist with tears.

After a while, when her husband was in a deep sleep, she got up from her bed and sat in the small wooden chair by the window. She pushed the old curtains open and saw the full moon above the trees in the distance. The street was quiet, except for the sound of crickets singing rhythmically from behind the buildings. She sat there, staring at the moon until she felt tired, and put her head down on the table. By the time she felt cool air coming through the window, it was dawn. She sighed heavily, woke her husband, and went to the washroom to get ready for the day.

• • •

The day of Da-Ming's departure came sooner than she had hoped. Mei got up early and started helping her husband put his things in his suitcase. She gave him a small piece of jade, which was given to her by her grandmother as a lucky charm. It was a carved monkey. She found a piece of red twine and made a string out of it to put through the small hole formed by the monkey's arms so that Da-Ming could wear it on his neck.

After supper, they sat on the bed, and neither had anything to say. They looked at each other for a while until the hand of the clock pointed at eight-thirty. When their feet stood on the dusty floor again, Mei wrapped up the steamed buns she had prepared for him for the road in her scarf. He grabbed his suitcase, and they walked downstairs.

The street was quiet, and only a few windows had lights on. It was a moonless night, and the air was chilly. She put her right arm through her husband's, and the two walked toward the bus stop to catch the last ride. In less than an hour, they reached Song-Gang Wharf. They got off the bus and walked slowly toward the riverbank, where two men in long, dark-blue robes were already waiting by a small boat. Da-Ming introduced his wife to the two men, and they shook hands. One of the men took the suitcase from him as he climbed into the boat.

Mei handed her bag to her husband and then said, "The food inside is still warm. Don't forget to eat it." She felt her eyes become moist, and her husband's face began to look blurry. She wiped her eyes with her thin fingers and pushed a few strands of her hair back.

"Don't cry, Mei. I promise I will write. I promise."

"I will miss you," she said, trying to hold her tears back.

One of the two men started rowing. As the small boat wobbled slowly away from the riverbank, Mei waved at her husband while her other hand wiped tears from her cold cheeks. She was not sure if her husband could see her, but she kept waving until the small boat vanished in the darkness.

19

With her coffee cup in hand, Lily sat in the armchair by the window. She glanced at the clock on the dresser, which indicated that she had a couple of hours before Ah-Fang and Lan-Lan arrived. She should let De-Chang know that she wouldn't be able to join him for afternoon tea. She dialed his number, and when he answered, she said, "De-Chang, it's me. I just wanted to tell you that I won't be able to meet you today."

"Are you all right?" The voice on the other end sounded disappointed.

"Yes. Everything is fine. I am just not in the mood to be in the French Concession area today. I have asked both Ah-Fang and Lan-Lan to come here for lunch instead."

"Perhaps I can join you? I had planned to take the second half of the day off so that you and I could be together." His voice was eager.

"Please don't. I'm sorry to cancel on you since we haven't seen each other for a while."

"How about after lunch?"

"No. We're going shopping together. I'd like to check out the new dresses at *The Lafayette*. Let's try another time, okay? I'll let you know when." She took a sip of her coffee and added, "Besides, we'll be talking about politics, and you aren't that interested."

• • • •

Honestly, she was happy to be engaged to Lee—happy in the sense that her father's honor would be protected and the future of the shipyard would be in good hands. The problem was intimacy. The idea of sleeping with a man in the same bed made her shudder; she found the idea of being touched by a man repulsive. She felt that a woman's body was sacred, and to be touched would feel like a violation. Whenever De-Chang tried to get close to her, she'd get very nervous and lose her composure. To her, this feeling made perfect sense. However, she couldn't let anyone know how she felt about intimacy—including her fiancé.

She finished her coffee. She needed to get ready for her friends. Before she knew it, Ah-Fang and Lan-Lan had walked in with white pastry boxes in their hands. "*Maison Angles*, my favorite!" Lily made a quick waltz spin. "What would you like?" She put the pastry boxes on the kitchen counter. "I have *Laubade* and *Château D'Yquem*."

"*Laubade* for me, *s'il vous plaît!*" Ah-Fang sounded playful. "And by the way, Johnny told me that you have a high tolerance for alcohol. Is that true?"

"Yeah, somewhat." She shrugged. "You won't believe this. . . ."

"Tell us!"

"Some white men tried to get me drunk once, but after six shots, I was still in charge of the conversation. Then they realized they had made a mistake and started worrying about their wallets."

Loud laughter erupted from both young women. "Boy, I can see that the sinister side of their plan failed!" Ah-Fang looked animated. "Why do you always say that you're a social drinker then?"

"Well, I need a secret weapon to protect myself, just in case. Anything for you, Lan-Lan?"

"I'll have whatever Ah-Fang is having. It sounds fancy." Lan-Lan sat down and grabbed the picture of Lily and Lee. "Wow, I like this picture of you two. What a perfect-looking couple! Mr. Lee Jr. certainly has good taste!"

"He's not so shabby himself, Lan-Lan," Ah-Fang said.

"Yeah, that is a good picture." Lily gave Lan-Lan the wine. "That was a fun party."

"Mr. Lee Jr. looks like. . . . how should I say this? A 'good boy,' if you know what I mean," Ah-Fang added mischievously.

"Everyone says that." She realized she sounded a bit flat. "I mean, he *is* good. He is *really* good!" *There. That should correct the preceding tone.*

"But he also seems . . . very sedate."

Lily didn't catch the last word. "Sorry, Lan-Lan, what was that?"

"Oh, it's nothing," she replied, shaking her head.

"Should we go sit down?" Lily suggested. "But first, cheers!"

A short moment later, the phone rang. "That must be the concierge." Lily jumped up from the sofa.

"Miss Wong? Sorry for the disturbance. I have two gentlemen here from *Chez L'Auvergnat*. Should I send them up?"

• • •

"That was the best lunch I have ever had, Lily!" Ah-Fang exclaimed, and then she turned her head to look at Lan-Lan, who was still chewing and nodding. "Bouillabaisse is my favorite," she said, wiping her lips with a perfumed napkin.

"What do you expect? Shanghai never runs out of seafood, and. . . ." Lily felt proud even though she hadn't cooked the lunch. "Well, we are also lucky. When you have a war going on, you never know what's available."

"By the way, did you read today's paper?" Ah-Fang cut in. "Sorry to change the topic."

"Yes. I did." Lily shook her head. "It seems that the nationalists are a bunch of cowards."

"What is it?" Lan-Lan wanted to know.

"Well, to make a long story short, they made a plan with the Red Army to cut off the escape route for the Japanese for the Battle of Jinan, but they left right before the battle started." Lily threw her napkin over her shoulder. "A lot of casualties from the Red Army's side. You can never trust the nationalists!"

"A bunch of cowards indeed! I thought they would do the opposite, considering they are armed by the Americans." Lan-Lan sounded angry. "What if Mao's Red Army never collaborated with the nationalists?"

"Well, that was the best option for the time being because the Japanese are better armed than the Red Army." Lily needed to clarify this. "I think Mao knows what he's doing, although I'm sure he doesn't trust the nationalists."

"What exactly does 'Greater East Asia' mean to Japan?" Ah-Fang asked.

"Natural resources, which they don't have, mainly oil." Lily turned her head to her friend. "That's part of their imperial ambition, I think."

"What's the significance of the Tripartite Pack? I mean to Japan?" Ah-Fang was looking at both Lily and Lan-Lan.

Lily stood. "I think it brings two advantages to Japan. First, it boosts Japan's ambition to take over more countries outside of China, specifically Southeast Asia. That's just what I think. Second, if Americans were to attack Japan, Germany and Italy would come to assist."

"So, what's the significance of occupying China in relation to Southeast Asia?" Ah-Fang wanted to know. Lan-Lan was nodding, obviously curious about the question too.

"Well, you may have heard that Sir Harold Mackinder has a book on the Heartland Theory that whoever controls the 'Heartland' will have control over the world."

"Can you elaborate on what the Heartland consists of, Lily?" Ah-Fang asked.

"Basically, the Heartland is the area of Europe and Asia combined. I'm certain that's what Hitler and Japan have in their minds."

"So if Japan had control over China, the rest of Asia would be a cinch?"

"Exactly, except they need to work out a deal with the British." Lily picked her napkin up from the floor. "Anyone in the mood for some *Mille Feuilles* and *Paris-Brest*?"

20

Two weeks after her husband left, Mei found a letter sitting on the kitchen counter when she returned from her grocery shopping.

Mei,

> *Sorry for taking so long to write you. I am safe. The boat ride was fine, although it took much longer than I had originally thought it would. The wind was cold that night, but your food kept me warm. Thank you.*
> *I am not supposed to give you my exact location, but everything is fine here. We have been training very hard, and I am feeling a bit tired. The commanders are nice, and I think they like me. They told me that I have a great future in the army. How could they tell? I just got here! Isn't that funny?*

The food here is not nearly as good as yours, but at least we have food. They say that once we go into the battles, food could be a problem, and what we can bring with us is limited. But I am not so worried.

I hope everything is going well for you at home and that you still enjoy working for Mr. Lee. He is a good man. I will write again soon. At the moment, you won't be able to write me back, but I was told when we go to Changsha, we will be able to receive letters from home.

Take good care of yourself,
Da-Ming
October 30, 1940

• • •

"Is everything all right with your husband?" Mr. Lee walked into the kitchen as Mei was putting the groceries away.

"Oh, Mr. Lee." She turned to face him. "I have been meaning to say that I am not entirely happy about my husband joining the army."

"Why not?"

"Well, I feel that he has been selfish and ungrateful—instead of repaying your kindness for helping him with the surgery, he decided to leave the factory where he had just received a promotion."

"I see your point here. But you, or should I say *we*, should be grateful to him as he is risking his life to defend our motherland against the invaders."

She nodded. "I guess you're right, Mr. Lee. I just think the timing of it—"

"Let's have this discussion another time, Mei." He looked at his watch. "I need to finish some work upstairs. Why don't you take the afternoon off and go to the bookstore perhaps? I know you have been wanting to get another dictionary for your studies for a while. In fact, Miss Wong just told me that she wanted us to go out to eat tonight. So, there is no need to worry about making dinner for us."

• • •

She remembered when Da-Ming first came out of the hospital and the stroll they had taken and the street food they had eaten together. She also remembered the joy and relief on her husband's face, as if he had once again been given the chance to rejoin humanity. It had also been a beautiful day—one that felt like it was made for him, and she was part of his joy too. But now, she had no idea where her husband was.

To distract herself from thinking about Da-Ming, she turned her attention to passerby. It felt odd that she only saw children or that they were the only people on the street to whom she paid attention. She imagined they were hers. She smiled and waved at them as they walked by. The children kept turning their heads toward her until their mothers dragged them away by force.

As she was making her way toward the bookstore, a man's voice sounded from behind her. "Good afternoon, Mrs. Zhou. Is that you?"

The voice was familiar, but she couldn't recognize it. She knew she had no friends in Shanghai and was convinced that this person was making a mistake. She turned around suspiciously. As she looked up in front of her, there stood a tall, handsome young man. He had kind, black eyes—large and intelligent—and dark, thoughtful eyebrows. His square jaw was prominent, his shoulders wide, and his light-gray suit fitted him perfectly. She looked at the stranger with bewilderment.

"Ah, it *is* you, Mrs. Zhou. I was right," he said warmly. "Do you remember me?"

"No. You are. . . . ?"

"I am Captain Aoki. We met a while ago at your employer's house. Do you remember me now?"

Mei couldn't believe her ears. Suddenly, she recognized him, and everything that had happened on that scary night appeared in her head. I *should run, run as fast as I can.* Or what else should she do? She needed to decide within five—or no, perhaps *two* seconds. She quickened her steps.

"Please wait, Mrs. Zhou. Please!" He went after her.

She had to stop; otherwise, there was a good possibility that she would be shot in the head from behind, and her brain would splatter all over the street, just like in the story she'd read the other night. *He is going to take me away on suspicion of helping the communists. He's going to interrogate me and ask me where my husband is. Then what I am going to do? I'll have to lie.* Her hands were getting sweaty, her heart beating faster and faster.

"I just wanted to say hello, Mrs. Zhou," he said softly, catching up with her from behind. "I promise I won't hurt you."

"You . . . speak Chinese?" She was trying hard to keep her composure.

"Yes, I do. Could we have a couple of minutes so that I can explain myself?" He walked closer to her.

She should not speak unless she was forced to. She stood still and didn't make eye contact with the captain. Anything could happen: he could let her go or arrest her. This could be her last few seconds of free air.

I am very sorry, Da-Ming. I am very sorry, Mr. Lee. I didn't mean to let this happen to me. Please forgive me. . . .

"Let me formally introduce myself. I am Captain Aoki." He extended his hand and waited for Mei's response.

She had no choice. She raised her hand, slowly, reluctantly. *This is very odd. Do all Japanese soldiers shake their prisoners' hands before they arrest them?* She saw her hand shaking violently as it extended itself to meet his, until she felt a firm grip, which she assumed would crush her bones. Instead, she felt warmth.

"I hope you don't mind me walking with you a bit." He sounded grateful. "It's a beautiful day, isn't it?"

Now what? He wants to talk about the weather before he takes me away? She should keep her mouth shut and let the captain decide what her fate would be. That was all she could do. She tried as hard as she could to hide the shaking of her legs as she walked slowly next to him, her feet feeling as if they were tied to heavy rocks.

"Today is Sunday, and I am off duty. As you can tell, I am wearing civilian clothes today." From the corner of her eye, she could see Captain Aoki moving his hands over his nicely cut suit. "Ah, I like weekends, when I can wear my own clothes."

Da-Ming used to say that people who have power are never hurried because they can see everything in their heads and know what will happen. He was right. Captain Aoki seemed poised and not hurried, whereas her life of twenty-one years, as short as it seemed, was about to end. So for the last minutes of her life, she should at least have some dignity so that her husband would be proud of her. If he were here, he would say, "Mei, show the Japanese what we are made of!" She kept her back straight, keeping pace with Captain Aoki, feeling the weight on her feet getting lighter and each stride getting stronger. She must not show fear.

"Yes, I do speak Chinese whenever I am by myself. I use translators only when I am with my fellow soldiers so that they can hear what's going on." He turned his face toward Mei. "I'm sorry if I startled you. I didn't mean to, and I understand your reaction." He stopped walking. "I know we are the occupiers right now, and you have every reason to be afraid of me."

She kept her head up but her eyes low. *So, what's next?*

"Thank you for walking with me."

She sensed he was smiling at her.

"May I ask—are you from Shanghai? The reason I am asking is that when I first saw you, I suspected that you might be from a different place, but I don't know why I had that feeling."

What should he care? But this could be one of Captain Aoki's interrogation techniques, so Mei had to answer the question. "Yes. I am from Suzhou." She sounded calm and she was proud of herself for that.

"I see. I have heard that Suzhou has the most beautiful women in the region, and you have proven that what I heard was accurate." He seemed enthusiastic. "I am from Yokohama. Have you ever heard of that city?"

Surprised by his self-introduction, Mei debated on how to respond. First of all, she had never heard of this "Yoko-something" place, as she barely knew the cities in China. And second of all, why would a Japanese captain tell her where he came from? "My father once told me there is a place called Tokyo or East Capital in Japan."

Captain Aoki clapped his hands. "That's wonderful you know Tokyo! Yokohama is not far from Tokyo. If you take a bus from Tokyo, you will get there in a little over an hour."

"Is that where you learned to speak Chinese?" Mei was shocked that she had asked a question to a Japanese army captain, but it was too late to take her words back.

"That's correct, Mrs. Zhou." Captain Aoki cleared his throat as if he were nervous too. It was kind of strange, in a way. "I have always been interested in Chinese culture, and many people in Japan feel that Japanese culture originally came from China. I learned Chinese at my school, and we had a very good teacher. His name was Mr. Tang."

Perhaps she was too naïve, but so far, this did not sound like an interrogation, not that she had ever seen any. She needed to figure out Captain Aoki's intentions. For the moment, his fluency in Mandarin impressed her. In fact, his Mandarin was better than hers in some ways. She thought she had done well in getting rid of her southern accent. Only until she heard how Captain Aoki spoke did she realize that she needed to work harder.

A foreigner who speaks better Mandarin than I do. How can it be? Her fascination with Captain Aoki's linguistic ability made her feel less defensive, and Captain Aoki seemed to have sensed that. She looked up at him for a quick second unintentionally, and she caught his smile.

"I have only been here for one year and like the city very much. I think Shanghai is a very interesting city. Don't you think so?"

"I haven't the time to think about it." She felt calmer.

He turned his face toward her again. "I can sense that you are still nervous." His voice sounded calm and deep, like the ocean. "You have every reason to be afraid of me, and I don't blame you. Our army has the epithet of brutality, and I can't defend what we have been doing to China. As you know, I am a soldier, and I follow orders. That's my duty, at least for now. Well, let's not talk about politics." He paused for a moment, looking down the street for a while. Then he spoke again. "I'm sorry, Mrs. Zhou. I'm afraid I have taken too much of your time today, but thank you for talking with me. Perhaps I will see you some other time?"

Did he just say "see me some other time"? I would rather not. But his courtesy surprised her. She kept silent.

"Great! I hope I'll bump into you again soon." He raised his right hand, gave her a small wave, and then turned around and walked swiftly in big strides in the opposite direction.

21

Da-Ming

> *I hope you never have to find out the reason I
> wrote this letter because things have happened in
> life beyond my control. If it comes to the point
> where I am no longer around, please remember
> that I did love you and that you were my husband,
> and of course, my little monkey. (It makes me
> laugh every time you make that silly face of yours.
> Only you know how to make that face!)*
> *I would also like it to be remembered that I
> loved our motherland although I never dared to
> be like you, going to battles. I wish we had a son
> together. He would be just like you, I imagine.*

> *Yours always,*

Mei
November 8, 1940

She reread the letter several times before folding it carefully and then sealing the edges around it. She made her mind up that she would never tell anyone about her encounter with Captain Aoki.

Anyone would have done what I have done, she told herself. There weren't any choices.

22

22

Lily wanted to see her parents, and ten days after she left, a letter arrived for Lee from Hong Kong. Lee recognized the familiar handwriting. He opened the letter with his usual carefulness and read:

De-Chang,

Finally, the weather has become cooler, and autumn is probably the best time of the year in this city. It has been great to be back here, where I feel at home. No offense. Only when I start eating dim-sum again do I realize how much I missed them when I was away.

As usual, the British keep the city in good order, and I have made a few acquaintances with them. I don't think they like the Japanese very much, and they don't *envy me when I return to Shanghai. I think one of them is interested in me, but don't worry; he is not my type. Still, it's fun to chat with them.*

Both Ma and Pa are very happy to see me, as always. I only wish they didn't spoil me too much— believe it or not. Pa is busy as usual, and his business is going quite well, hard to fathom in these uncertain times. I guess partly because he keeps his business mainly in Southeast Asia. And he won't do any business with the Japanese. Who can blame him?

How is everything in Shanghai? I suppose Mrs. Zhou is still around, as you seem agitated when she is not. As time goes by, you won't believe how much you rely on her. From what I can see, you seem to like her a lot. But don't get upset; I am not the jealous type.

I should probably take the advice from Frau Elke and put a guard on my mouth! But hey, don't mind me. I am just a straight arrow. How is Frau Elke doing? I hope she doesn't hate me. Women have their intuitions, unlike men, who use reason.

By the way, what's it like profiting from the war? Have you ever thought about it?

Take care,
Lily
November 20, 1940

He put the letter down on his desk and then took out a piece of paper from his desk drawer. After a short pause, he picked up his pen and wrote:

Dear Lily,

I was glad to have received your letter today. It's a relief to know that all is well in Hong Kong. It's reassuring to know that your father has been doing well in this kind of economic and political climate. Luckily, most of his clients are not from the mainland, and that's the reason for his success.

True, while millions of our people suffer and die from this war, I am one of the few who profits from it. I am as equally guilty as anyone who profits from this war. However, I am not an avaricious man, nor am I without conscience, except I don't think about the war as often as you do. Perhaps I should. But one day I will redeem myself, I hope.

As you have predicted, Mrs. Zhou has been doing very well here. She has been attending an adult school now, only one day a week. She enjoys it. I think you are right about me depending on her. She keeps the house very clean and never complains. She has made my life much easier so that I can concentrate on my work.

Elke is trying to keep herself up. Her health is not as good as it used to be. People her age tend to have aches here and there. I suppose that's normal. I try to have my usual meetings with her at the French café whenever I can. She tries to keep herself busy, and I wish she had more friends. I am sure she doesn't hate you, but I think you two seem to share certain personality traits—you both never hesitate to speak what's on your minds! Still, I hope the two of you get along. After all, she is the one who raised me.

Please give my best regards to your parents, and take good care of yourself.

Let me know when your next boat comes.
De-Chang
November 26, 1940

He put his pen down. The telephone rang. It was Manager Wang.

"I'm sorry to bother you, sir, at this hour. I think one of our workshop managers was just taken into custody by the Japanese."

"I see. Tell me more." He took a deep breath and pushed his letter to Lily to the side.

"He works the second shift but never showed up for work today. A friend of his told us that he saw two Japanese soldiers go to his apartment earlier today and take him away."

"Do you know where they took him?"

"I'm not sure, but I can find out by tomorrow."

"Okay. I'm going to give you a call tomorrow around noontime. Please be by your desk and wait for my call." He put the handset down and rubbed his face with his hand. He picked up his notebook and looked through it in hopes of finding the names of the main detention centers in the city where the Japanese kept their communist suspects. He found two names and looked at their addresses, thinking about the quickest ways of getting there by taxi. At exactly noon the next day, he dialed Manager Wang.

"I have the name of the detention center, sir. He is held at Xitangzhen."

● ● ●

When he arrived at the detention center, he saw many people standing outside the entrance, hoping to get in. Two Japanese soldiers were checking papers and deciding who should go in first. He went to the translator and showed him his identification card and then gave him the name of the person he wanted to see. One of the soldiers signaled for him to follow him inside the building. They walked through a long, dark hallway and entered a dimly-lit and simply-furnished office at the end of the hall. Behind the desk sat a middle-aged officer with eyeglasses on his wide face, his hat on the desk in front of him. Next to him stood a skinny, tall translator, who was wearing a dark-beige suit. The soldier pulled up a chair and signaled for Lee to sit down.

The officer looked at him for a moment and then said something to the translator, who cleared his throat and spoke in a high voice. "You must be Mr. Liang's boss. If he were a good citizen like yourself, mister, he wouldn't be in here."

"What did he do?" Lee asked, and the translator relayed the question.

The officer in eyeglasses answered in his coarse voice, and the high voice sounded again: "Well, he is a communist. What a waste of time! Still, he should consider himself very lucky today because he has a chance to see you before he dies tomorrow."

"Can I see him now?"

The officer signaled for the soldier on his left to take Lee to the detainee's cell.

He followed the soldier to the dark basement, where he was embraced by a sudden shot of cold air. After making a few turns in the dark, narrow passage, the soldier pulled out one of his keys and opened the metal door. Lee walked in quietly and saw a man in his mid-thirties lying on the concrete floor. His torn shirt was covered in bloodstains, and dark bruises were visible on his face. One of his eyes was so swollen that he probably couldn't see through it. He sat up slowly as Lee walked in, squinting his only good eye.

"I am Lee De-Chang, and Manager Wang told me you were here," he said with his usual calmness, sitting down on a small stool.

"Nice coat." The corner of the prisoner's mouth dropped. "Are you going to get me out of here?" he asked coldly.

"I wish I could."

"I see. Then why are you here?" He struggled to squeeze his words out, sounding angry.

"I came here to see if you perhaps have some last words for your family." He tried to get closer to the man, who seemed to be in great pain.

"Yes, I have a wife . . . and a son. Tell my son. . . ." He tightened his lips. "When he grows up, I want him to kill those bastards." He looked at the door and turned his head back. "Don't worry; we can say whatever we want. Those bastards don't understand a word of Chinese. I feel bad I won't be able to kill them all. I wish I could finish my mission." He clinched his teeth.

Lee listened quietly and then said, "Could you give me your home address so that I can visit them?" He took out a small notebook and a pen. The man murmured something, and Lee wrote everything down and then put the notebook back in his breast pocket. "I promise I will go see them for you right away. I promise." He put his hand on the man's shoulder and kept it there for a while.

"Thank you, mister. You seem like a nice person."

"No, thank *you*." Lee stood. "I will go see your family now." He banged the rusty metal door twice, and the soldier opened the door. He gave the man one last look before he left.

• • •

He gently knocked on the door, and a young boy opened it.

"Who is there, Fuzi?" A woman's voice sounded from within.

"Hello, Mrs. Liang." He made sure his voice was loud enough for her to hear it.

A woman came to the door and pulled the boy behind her. "Yes, mister?"

He noticed her untidy hair. The lines on her face made her look older than she probably was. Her faded dark-blue blouse was patched. He stared into her large, eager eyes. "Forgive my intrusion, Mrs. Liang. I am your husband's employer. May I come in?"

The woman paused for a moment and then gestured hesitantly for him to enter. "Please excuse us, mister. We don't have a comfortable place for you to sit." She pointed to a small wooden chair, looking embarrassed.

Once Lee sat down, she picked up the red-cheeked, chubby-faced boy, took him to a smaller room, and closed the door behind her. She came back with a pensive look on her face. "Is he all right? Did he get himself hurt? I've always told him to be careful, and he never listens. I knew it. I just knew it! So did he—" She looked agitated.

"It's not like that at all, Mrs. Liang. It's not like that." Lee put his hand up to calm her down. "He's all right and has asked me to tell you that."

"Really! So, is he coming home soon?"

"I am afraid not."

"Why not? You just said he is all right."

"Well, let me start from the beginning." He took a deep breath, preparing himself to share the awful news. "Mrs. Liang, he is in a Japanese prison, and it's unlikely that they will release your husband."

The woman froze, her jaw dropping. "What! Why is he in a Japanese prison, and what do you mean they won't release him?"

"He is a communist."

"But what did he do? How come I didn't know this? I can tell you this much about our marriage: he never tells me anything! Never." Her face turned red.

"Mrs. Liang, your husband is a hero—a hero for our motherland."

"That's good to know. But what about us? What about us? Is he coming out soon?" Her voice became louder and agitated.

"I am afraid not." He realized the weight of his words.

"So the Japanese are going to kill him. Am I right? Am I right?" She started sobbing, using her hands to cover her face. Between her fingers, Lee heard the muffled words as she continued, "I knew something bad was going to happen to him. I just knew it!" The woman suddenly grabbed Lee's trench coat with all her force. "Help him! I know you can help him!"

He could see her tears streaming down her cheeks. Soon, her face turned a deeper red. He wanted to comfort her but didn't know how.

The woman sank onto the concrete floor, sobbing louder, her head leaning against Lee's leg. "I knew it! I just knew he would join the communists." She wiped her face with one of her sleeves. "What are we going to do?"

"Mrs. Liang, your husband is a brave man. He is going to be a martyr for our motherland."

"But what am I going to do? How are we going to survive? My son is too young, and. . . ." Her voice sounded desperate, and she was having trouble breathing. She coughed between her weeping and finally managed to breathe more evenly.

"Mrs. Liang, here. I have something here for you." Lee pulled a brown envelope out from his breast pocket and put it in her hands. "Please take this. It's not much, but it should last both of you for a while." He stood from his chair and walked to the door. "I am very sorry about your husband, Mrs. Liang. He will be remembered by all of us."

He opened the door, stepped outside, and then closed the door quietly behind him.

23

A second letter from Da-Ming arrived. Mei was anxious to find out the latest news from her husband.

Mei,

> *I wanted to write you sooner but couldn't. It has been a lucky week for us. I had my first battle about a week ago, and we were victorious. Only one of us was hurt, but not seriously. We killed a dozen Japanese soldiers and captured two alive. The commanders are very pleased with their strategies, but some say we just got lucky this time, and I believe them.*

> *I hate to say this: the Japanese soldiers are much better trained than we are. Many of our soldiers are uneducated, and they don't know that bravery alone is*

not enough. We need to use our brains. I keep telling them that, but they don't like hearing me saying this because I am new. I know I am new, but I have a feeling that I will be very good at fighting and you will be very proud of me.

How have you been? I wish I could see your face and hear your voice. Is everything in the city all right? Manager Wang must be counting down the days for me to come back. He is a nice man. Please write me whenever you can. You can save your letters until we get to Changsha so that you can send all of them to me. I miss you.

Da-Ming
December 3, 1940

She wrote back immediately:

Da-Ming,

I was very happy to have received both of your letters. I have been very worried about your safety and if you have enough clothes to keep you warm. Then I thought you have uniforms, silly me. I knew you would miss me when you were cold, and I like it when we cuddle.

It must be very dangerous to fight in battles, and it scares me to think about it. Mr. Lee said he admires your courage, and so do I. I have some good news to share with you. I have been attending an adult school in the city. Mr. Lee paid the tuition for me. He knows the head of the school. My classes are in the mornings, and I still have time to do my chores. I can't believe everything worked out so well. My teachers are all very good. They are patient and know how to teach. As you can see, I can write a letter like this, thanks to my teachers. I will write again soon.

Please be careful.
Mei
December 7, 1940

24

January 1941 felt much colder than usual. Whenever Mei went out, she needed to wear extra layers. She started using the silk scarf that her mother had given her. She remembered that her parents never liked cold weather because it made them feel vulnerable. Her mother said she was convinced that the combination of cold and dampness had hollowed out her backbone, which prevented her from standing straight. Even though Southern China was not as cold as the north, most houses in Suzhou did not have heat. Those lucky ones who had means of finding coal managed to have small coal-burning stoves in their homes. The unlucky ones would just have to endure the cold. At this time every year, she worried about her parents. On top of that, war made everything more difficult.

A letter from her father came just in time to ease her worries:

Mei,

It's never the same without you in the house. Winter here in Suzhou is difficult, especially this year, when the weather seems much colder than usual. The house is not warm, and we only have enough coal to keep us warm for a couple of hours a day, but we consider ourselves lucky. If you were here, your presence would bring us warmth.

Ever since you left, your mother tends to get sentimental sometimes. Her back pain persists and she can't do much around the house. We are hoping that you might be able to come home for the Chinese New Year this year, as we did not see you last year. It's on the 27th. There is nothing much to celebrate other than seeing you, as you can imagine, but it would be good to have you around again and learn about your life in the big city. You can stay as long as you want although we know you have work to do. Please let us know if Mr. Lee would let you go. He sounds like a nice man, and we are happy he has been a great help.

Look forward to hearing from you soon.
Pa
January 14, 1941

Mei wrote back:

Pa,

It makes me sad to see your letter even when there is no bad news. I am sorry to learn about Ma's health and feel powerless. I wish I could do my daughterly *duty to be with her and care for her. Even though this has been a tough winter, Mr. Lee has a nice furnace that keeps the house warm. I feel very guilty living in such luxury, something I know I don't deserve. Please forgive me.*

I have been going to an adult school and enjoying it very much. You and Ma would be very proud of me. I am making a lot of progress in my writing and have been receiving very good marks. In case I haven't told you, I also am taking an English course, and it's a very interesting language which I may or may not be able to use. I already feel I am smart now, like a city woman.

I know it is very unfair of me to share my joy with you, knowing how difficult life must be for both you and Ma in Suzhou. I feel guilty that Da-Ming is away fighting the Japanese and I am here in the city enjoying the good life.

Please don't think badly of me. I am still the same daughter you raised. I will ask Mr. Lee if he would let me spend the Chinese New Year with you and Ma. I think he is going to let me go. I am hoping to be able to come home on New Year's Eve.

I miss you all.
Mei
January 21, 1941

Beyond what Mei had expected, Mr. Lee not only granted her wish to spend the Chinese New Year with her parents, but he also let her decide the length of her stay in Suzhou. All she would need to do was send him a note when she was ready to return. She was overjoyed. One afternoon, when she walked into the front garden after doing her daily grocery shopping, she saw the front door of the house wide open. She looked around and did not see Mr. Lee's car. She thought it might be Mr. Ma inside the house. Upon entering the front door, she called out, "Mr. Ma, is that you?"

She heard the sound of high heels, and soon someone in a bright pink satin dress emerged from the drawing-room. "Hello, Mrs. Zhou," the woman said calmly, almost coldly.

Mei was taken by surprise. "Miss Wong! I wasn't—"

"You weren't expecting me? Is that what you were going to say?"

"Well, Mr. Lee did not say that you had returned from Hong Kong, and I didn't get enough food for dinner." She looked into her straw bag quickly. "Let me go back to the store to get more food."

"That won't be necessary, Mrs. Zhou." Miss Wong gave Mei a slight hand gesture to stop her from leaving the house. "I've already spoken with Mr. Lee, and we're going out to eat. So you are off the hook tonight!"

"In that case. . . ."

"In that case, perhaps we could chat a little, if you don't mind."

"Oh, Miss Wong, I am not much of a . . . conversationalist, and besides—"

"My goodness, is that a new word? So I have heard," she walked closer to Mei, "that you have been going to school lately. That must be great for you. Am I right?" Miss Wong crossed her arms in front of her chest.

"I am very embarrassed to talk about this, Miss Wong."

"Don't be, my little sis. So, you must be doing exceedingly well, I gather?"

"I try." She kept her head low.

"I'm sure you are not just trying. Mr. Lee told me that you are super-smart and are a fast learner. I bet one day you could work for him in his company."

"I am—"

"Don't be embarrassed, my sis. There's nothing wrong with being smart. I can tell you this: we women are no less intelligent than men. It's just that they are more tenacious and aggressive than we are."

"Mr. Lee has been very supportive about my studies and I am very grateful to have this opportunity."

"I bet you are. Mr. Lee's generosity knows no boundaries, especially when it comes to helping you!"

"I didn't—"

"I know you didn't ask him to help you with your school and everything because I know what kind of a person he is." Miss Wong paced around Mei slowly and then stopped in front of her. "So, let me ask you this." Miss Wong leaned her head to the side. "And I just want to hear your opinion. . . ."

She wants to hear my opinion? Mei had trouble trusting her ears.

"Do you think that the establishment of Japanese Nationalism was not just for the national pride of the Japanese people but rather aimed for an imperialistic ambition, which results in Fascism?"

"Miss Wong, I—"

"Or do you think that the Japanese would never take the Chinese Communist Party seriously because they think the CCP members are nothing but a bunch of peasants with bird guns trying to scratch the ass of the well-trained imperial army?"

"Miss Wong, my knowledge on politics is very limited at this point and—"

"I know, I know. That was very cruel of me, I admit." Miss Wong turned her back to Mei for a brief second and then turned around again. "My little sis—or Mrs. Zhou—I know you are a very smart young woman; otherwise, Mr. Lee wouldn't be so. . . . how should I say this? Well, let's just say that he is very fond of you. He has never said this, but I can tell. And that pretty face of yours can get you. . . ." Miss Wong squinted her eyes. "Wait a minute. I think I'm off the track right now."

"Miss Wong, I don't quite follow. . . ."

"Precisely. Innocence can be a virtue sometimes." Miss Wong sounded philosophical. "But Mr. Lee is not his usual self these days." She was beaming down at Mei.

"Miss Wong?"

"Well, ever since he learned that you are leaving for Suzhou to visit your parents, he seems agitated and sometimes gets flustered with me, if you know what I mean."

"I will try to come back as soon as I can. My mother is not well, and I worry about her."

"Well, my little sis," Miss Wong said as she patted Mei on the shoulder, "I didn't mean to be unkind. There is something special about you. You just don't know it, and that could be a good thing." Miss Wong once again checked her watch. "Why don't we just stop our chat for now? I'm sure you have a lot to do." She removed her high heels and walked quickly on the soft carpet up the stairs toward her room. When she reached the top, she paused. "Oh, by the way, Mrs.

Zhou, why don't you make something nice for Mr. Ma and yourself tonight? I think the old man would like that."

Within a few seconds, Mei heard Miss Wong close her room door, gently this time. She stood there, still recovering from the odd conversation. She decided she should try to forget that the conversation ever took place. After all, she needed to get her mind ready for her trip to visit her parents, whom she missed very much.

25

"The braised yellow fish with hot pepper sauce was delicious, Mrs. Zhou!" Mr. Ma looked content. "It had just the right amount of spiciness; otherwise, my old stomach wouldn't be able to handle it."

Mei gave a small bow. "I am glad you liked it, Mr. Ma. We rarely get a chance to sit down and chat even though we see each other all the time."

"Now you mention it, time does seem to go by fast."

She paused and then asked, "Do you think life is very hard? I hope this question doesn't sound too random."

"It can be." Mr. Ma turned to look at her. "Are you feeling all right today? I hope you are not ill?"

"I am feeling a bit anxious at the moment, but I don't think I need a doctor."

"I see what you mean." He took a deep breath and looked out at the sky. "There are many things in life beyond our control. We have no choice but to accept our fate."

"Do you believe in fate, Mr. Ma?"

"I think most people my age do."

Mei nodded. "I don't know what to believe. Maybe I should believe in something, don't you think?"

"You sound confused, but don't feel bad. I was once confused too. But I can tell you this: if you don't think about yourself too much, you will feel better."

"Mr. Ma, I hope you don't mind me asking you again—what happened to your family?"

"You have such a wonderful memory, Mrs. Zhou, and I knew you would come back to our last conversation at some point."

"I'm sorry."

"It's all right. I don't mind at all." He dusted his sleeves, looking pensive, and continued, "I was once married a long time ago. It was an arranged marriage between my parents and my wife's parents, who were friends of my parents. Both she and I were the only children in our families."

There was joy on his face. He blinked his eyes quickly and gazed into space as if trying to recapture all the precious moments. "I had just graduated from high school, and so had she. I knew nothing about her and vice versa; therefore, there was no . . . how should I say it? *Love*, the kind of word people your age use. But that was not the reason people got married. They married because they were expected to, and no one wanted to upset their parents. You can say it was more of a social obligation.

"At the beginning of our marriage, we slept in separate rooms: I slept in the kitchen, and she in the family room. It wasn't my idea. It lasted about six months, until one cold winter night, a strong wind broke one of our kitchen windows, which already had a crack in it. She asked me to come into the family room, and I slept on the floor. The next night, she asked me not to go back to the kitchen again. She saw me shivering on the hard stone floor and asked me to squeeze in with her on the small bed so that we could keep each other warm." Mr. Ma's face was animated, and everything seemed to have returned to him with great clarity.

"Was she a nice person?"

"Yes, she was, and I was very lucky." He had a grateful expression on his face.

"So, what was she like?"

"Well, she was not a talkative person and was quite shy. It was hard to get to know someone who didn't say much. But she showed who she was in her actions. Without me asking, she kept our small home very clean and cooked all the meals. I found a job as a construction worker, and we managed to get by on my meager salary. Every night when I came home, she said I needed to clean myself before I went to bed; she would warm water for me and wash me every night. She said since I couldn't reach my back, she would have to do it for me. So every night, she would wash my back with her soft hands. I liked that. Because she didn't talk much, like I said earlier, I was always the one who talked and talked. She just sat there and listened to me, and I never knew whether she liked what I said or not because she wouldn't offer any of her opinions. Still, we had a very happy life together for several years, and she gave us a daughter who was almost as beautiful as you are."

Mei felt heat coming up to her cheeks. "So, what happened to her then?"

After a short pause, Mr. Ma continued, "One day, she took a boat from the city to visit her aunt in Ningbo. It was a rainy day. I took the day off from work so that I could see her off. She had a small suitcase with her, and we waved at each other as she got on the boat. She never made it to Ningbo, and that was the last time I saw her. I later learned that the boat had an accident, and all four people on board drowned. I tried to look for her body for several days but had no luck."

His eyes were moist, and he had to stop for a moment. Mei wiped tears off of her face and remained silent. Mr. Ma gazed into the distance as if trying to bring all his memories back. "My daughter was a lovely girl. She was smart and enjoyed going to school. She was a good student. For many years, she was the only person who kept me company."

"Did something happen to her?"

Mr. Ma sighed deeply, a sad look on his face. "When she got older, we discovered that she had a talent for Beijing opera. She had a nice voice and wanted to go to Beijing to pursue her dream. The problem was that they only accepted boys. As you may have heard, many men performed female roles in the Beijing opera. But she was determined and wouldn't give up her dream. One day, she shaved her head and asked me to take her to Beijing. We went to the famous Beijing Opera Preparatory School together for an audition, and she was accepted on the spot. We both liked the school and were so happy. I said to her that if her mother were alive, she would be very proud of her."

Mei saw some joy come back to Mr. Ma's face. For a brief moment, she imagined herself as Mr. Ma's daughter studying in Beijing.

"She was doing fine for a while but had one problem."

"What kind of problem?"

"Well, after each rehearsal, the boys would take showers together, and my daughter couldn't go with them. She made many excuses in the beginning and got away with it until she finally ran out of excuses. One day, one of the boys touched her pants and the secret came out. The boys started making fun of her, and the taunting lasted for several weeks. She had no place to hide. On New Year's Eve, when all the boys went home, she hung herself with the shirt that her mother had made for her. She did it on the wooden beam in her dorm." Mr. Ma started choking up and couldn't continue.

Mei couldn't believe her ears. She fought hard to hold back her tears, wiping her face with her sleeves.

After a long silence, Mr. Ma managed to calm himself down. He stood and said he needed to go back to his room to rest a bit.

26

When they walked into *Chez L'Auvergnat*, a middle-aged, half-bald man in a tuxedo gave Lee and Lily a slight bow. "*Bonjour*, Monsieur Lee; *Bonjour,* Mademoiselle."

"Even though I like French food, I think I prefer the British way in Hong Kong. Or perhaps I should say I am used to it?" Lily said upon being seated.

"How do you mean?" Lee pulled his chair closer to the table.

"Well, the British like things in a certain order, and I like their sense of humor. They can insult you and still make you laugh at the same time."

"And you like that?"

"I choose my battles, as you know. The ones I tend to spend time with seem to be a combination of intellectuals and drunks."

He had to laugh. "That's not a bad combination at all! Besides, they could be synonymous."

"Ha, ha! And the best thing about them is that they seem to wear their characters on their sleeves. In a way, it's a good thing, I suppose, because it leaves nothing for you to guess about. And I like straightforwardness."

"Interesting observations, Lily. Interesting." He nodded. "But—"

"But what?"

"Well, knowing you as I do, I wonder if you have thought about Colonialism."

"Gee, I never thought you had that in you—I mean political sensitivity. Every time I think of you, I think about you and your novels. But there is nothing wrong with that. You are who you are." Lily shrugged her shoulders. "I just hope you're not trying to get even with me for what I said about benefiting from the war."

"I forgot about that already." He shrugged.

"So, let me see. . . ." She tapped the soft white linen cloth with her short, perfectly French-manicured nails. "Actually, it does bother me, thinking about how they occupy Hong Kong and have for more than forty years." She continued, showing her pensive side, "The funny thing is that although Colonialism bothers me, I don't hate the Brits as individuals. Some of my friends there seem like decent people. Are they all puppets of the Queen? I really don't know. Monarchy is a strange thing, not that feudalism is any better."

"You must have read Thomas Paine's *Common Sense*, haven't you?"

"I flipped through a few pages of it and know he was not a fan of the monarchs. He was a sharp writer, I must say."

"So do you have a new conclusion now?"

"The truth of the matter is," she looked around the room, "when it comes to history, no one is innocent. We had been fighting among ourselves for hundreds of years until the Japanese came. I think this is the time for unification."

She had a point there. "Isn't that what the nationalists and the communists are doing right now?"

"Yes. Our current national crisis is the Japanese, right?" She turned her face toward the tall waiter, who came back and lowered himself.

"*Voulez-vous boire quelque chose, Mademoiselle?*" He looked at Lily attentively, his hand behind his back.

"Obviously, his Chinese is not very good. I don't know, De-Chang. I'll drink whatever you like. This is your territory." She giggled.

"*Deux Ravat Chardonnay, s'il vous plaît.*" Simple enough.

"*Merci.*" He walked away soundlessly.

Lily's eyes followed the waiter for a few seconds, and then she turned back. "Well, I had a little chat with Mrs. Zhou today. I thought you would like to know." Lily put her napkin on her lap.

"You did? And what prompted you to do that?"

"No reason." She spread her lips sideways.

"So. . . . how did it go?"

"I think I was kind of mean to her."

He did not sense regret from her tone of voice. "What did you say to her?"

"Well, I think she must have gone through a lot, even though she is younger than I am. I was thinking more about how I felt rather than from her viewpoint. It was unfair."

Lee couldn't respond to this statement because he didn't want to take a side and jeopardize his relationship with either Mei or Lily. What seemed obvious was that she was not going to disclose what she had said to Mei and how she'd said it.

"So what do you think of her?" Lily asked Lee.

"What do you mean?" He was uncomfortable with the question.

"Well, ever since you learned that she was going to visit her parents, you've seemed, how should I say this. . . . ? Not quite yourself. True?"

"Ah, I see. I hope I didn't make a complete fool of myself." He was surprised by Lily's perception and wondered if he had done anything that might have given her the hint that he was attracted to Mei. As a matter of fact, Lily might have already been feeling that both she and Mei had been sharing Lee's attention. After all, women's intuition was something beyond the reach of his reasoning skills. Would Lily be jealous of Mei? So far, her confident nature had indicated that it would be unlikely that she would allow herself to be jealous of anyone. If she had any competition, it would most likely be herself. Perhaps she was merely teasing Mei? And who knew how many had been victims of her teasing, including him, perhaps.

"No, you didn't. But you seem distracted lately, and that's not the person I know. And I can tell she has a lot to do with this *distraction*. Am I right?"

He was feeling cornered and did not like it one bit. "I wasn't aware of this, Lily. I wasn't," he said, feeling heat coming to his face.

"Of course you weren't. So, you admit you have been distracted by her?" Lily was relentless.

The waiter came back with two large glasses of chardonnay. "I will return with the menu in a moment," he said in his decent English, and then walked away with his tray.

"As you have sensed, Lily, Mrs. Zhou has many challenges in her life. Her husband just had his surgery and. . . ."

"There is no need to run through the list, De-Chang. I know she did not apply for this housekeeper position of yours, but it was no coincidence that she showed up in front of the *fleur-de-lis* gate out of the blue."

"I thought you knew how she got here. Should I repeat Mrs. Zhou's story?"

"That won't be necessary."

"It seems I have been interrogated if not investigated. No?"

"Don't be offended, De-Chang. I just don't want you to get hurt, that's all." She stared at the ceiling. "Life is like a game sometimes, don't you think?"

"That's an interesting perspective, Lily. Is that how you see everything?"

Lily put her hand up. "Easy, De-Chang, easy. I don't want to get into a ping-pong game with you. I appreciate Mrs. Zhou as much as you do."

"Do you?"

"Yes, I do. Even though I'm not at your house much, she washed all my clothes while I was there. She has been great, I must say. I am amazed that I actually like her. As you know, there aren't that many people whom I like." Lily put her index finger under her chin. "But I think she burned one of my blouses."

"She what?"

"Well, one of its sleeves has a brown spot on it, but please don't say anything to her. I know it was an accident. I don't care. I can always buy another one." She gave him an awkward smile. "The most important thing is that all your shirts are perfectly pressed and starched. We wouldn't want you to look bad in front of Herr Meyer, right? In any case, you have trained her well!"

"I didn't—I mean, I never *trained* her. You can ask her."

The waiter came back with the menu.

"Well, let's see what they have." She looked through the pages. "I do love French cuisine, which I think is exquisite. Can I say the same thing about their people?" She was squinting her eyes.

Lee shook his head, sighing. "Phew! I should consider myself lucky."

"Oh, c'mon! Am I that bad? Hey, what do I know about the French? I'm from Hong Kong. Remember?" She took a sip of her wine. "Oh, by the way, when is Mrs. Zhou leaving?"

He had to answer this question. "I think it's the day after tomorrow."

"Are you taking her to the bus station?"

"Yes, I am."

"I shouldn't have asked."

• • •

"The French sure know how to cook." Lily seemed content as they walked outside. "I thought my *Boeuf Bourguignon* was tender and light. How was your *Confit de Canard*?"

"It was lovely. The slow cooking made all the difference. I prefer that method to frying." Lee looked the sky over. "It's still early. Could we go sit by the lake for a bit? It's only a couple of blocks from here."

"I actually need to get back. I'm expecting a phone call from Lan-Lan. But thanks for the delicious meal!"

His heart sank. For several months, he had been trying to find opportunities to spend time with Lily but without much luck. Lily's social schedule seemed to keep her busy. Since she never needed to work, there was no difference between weekdays and weekends to her. If she was not with her friends, she was most likely out shopping. *She can never have too many dresses and shoes.*

"When . . . can I see you again?" He moved closer to her and dared to grab her hand; her smooth, soft skin made his heart pound. A gentle breeze came in, and he felt Lily's hair on his face. He was once again embraced by her familiar scent.

"I'm not sure," she said, trying to free her hand, "but . . . wait, there is a taxi. Taxi!" Lily shouted with her arm up. As she ran toward her ride, she turned her head and said, "Call me tomorrow!"

He stood there, feeling deflated.

27

Before Lee could suggest anything for the Chinese New Year's Day, Lily informed him that she had already made plans for both of them. They would go to Yuyuan Garden to have tea and steamed dumplings and pastries in the afternoon, and then in the evening, they would go to the Peace Café for their Chinese New Year's party. Lily would bring Ah-Fang and Lan-Lan plus Johnny. Lee couldn't think of anything better to do; besides, he hadn't seen Johnny for a while. He told Lily that he liked the plan.

* * *

The Peace Café was famous for its Bauhaus ambiance and its clientele. Celebrities, including movie stars and politicians, frequented it on a daily basis. Unless you paid attention to calendars, every day seemed like a holiday there. Before nine o'clock in the evening, the restaurant served regular meals. Only afterward would the dance floor open, and the jazz band would begin to play.

The evening was mild and calm. Since it was the Chinese New Year, there was not much traffic. Lee and Lily arrived at the Peace Café within less than twenty minutes. When they stepped out of their taxi, they saw that Lily's two classmates were already waiting at the entrance. At Lee's suggestion, Lily had put on her bright pink satin *qipao* with turquoise trim. She'd decided, however, to wear her fox collar, which she claimed she only wore on special occasions; plus, it matched her alligator skin purse. She had also decided that she should wear her bow-pump high heels, and Lee couldn't agree with her more. In his usual holiday white tuxedo, he followed behind Lily as if he were her backdrop.

Without waiting for Lee, she walked in quickly and greeted the three of them. "Happy Year of the Snake!" They kissed each other on the cheeks. "I can't believe we are back here again. Where did the time go?"

Lee stood there, knowing he was being ignored.

"It's good to see you, Mr. Lee." Ah-Fang approached Lee.

"Oh geez. I'm terribly sorry, De-Chang. You remember Ah-Fang and Lan-Lan. Right?" Lily grabbed his arm.

He shook their hands mechanically and then followed them inside the dining room. After the restaurant staff took their coats, they were seated at a table near the jazz band. While Lily continued her chat with her friends, Lee looked at his watch, hoping that Johnny would show up soon. He heard loud laughs from Lily's friends. The waiter came to the table, and Lee told him to come back later as they were expecting one more guest. While the young women chatted away, the jazz band started their tuning.

Unlike Lily, who was like a fish in water, Lee was less at ease in social events, especially in a group of young women who frequented these places regularly. He didn't know what to say to them and was feeling like there were needles in his chair. As he was debating how to join in the conversation with Lily, Johnny walked in.

"I'm so sorry for being late, De-Chang. I had to take a detour because the Japanese blocked the road that I was on." Johnny went over to greet Lily and her friends before he grabbed the empty chair next to his friend.

"I'm glad you made it, Johnny. You saved me," Lee said, relieved. He waved at the waiter.

Before long, everyone had ordered alcoholic drinks except Lee, who ordered lemon-flavored seltzer. The waiter also brought some cold cuts, mixed nuts, and dried fruits. "Do you come here often, Johnny?" Lee put some nuts into his mouth.

"Well, I used to. Do you remember Danny Tang, the guy with the crazy messy hair who always sat in the back of the class?"

"Yes."

"He and I used to come here a lot, but now he's gone, who knows where, and I don't like to come here by myself. You and I could come here more often, but you like to go to bed early. I know—you have to be up early for work." He held his glass up and took a sip of his whiskey.

"What happened to Danny?"

"You haven't heard? He joined the army and is now fighting the Japanese."

"Which one?"

"Oh, the communist army, of course. You may recall, he was always on the left."

"I see. I'm so poorly informed about our classmates."

Johnny looked over at Lily and then leaned forward. "How is everything between you and our Princess?"

"Pretty much the same," he said casually, looking to see what was on other plates.

"That's a vague answer." Johnny moved his eyebrows a bit and put a piece of five-spice beef in his mouth.

"What do you want to know?" he said, shrugging.

Johnny paused for a second to hear what the jazz band was playing and then came back to his friend. "Well, anything *sizzling* you want to share?"

"My goodness, you haven't changed, Johnny. I wish I had something 'sizzling' to share with you." He took a sip of his drink. "The only thing that's sizzling right now is my seltzer."

"Nice try, my friend. You see, I know people like you. You approach everything from an intellectual level, and that'll never work, I'm telling you. Why don't you get yourself a glass of whiskey, then you'll understand what I mean!"

"Hey Johnny, I'm not clueless, all right? We all have our own predicaments. Or maybe you don't."

"Let's put it this way: Lily is a hot chick and very smart. Isn't that what you want?"

"You're right, Johnny, but looks aren't everything."

"I don't know what has gotten into your head, my friend; maybe it's your books. I don't suppose you want a housewife. But if you do, she is not it."

"*That* I know." Lee shrugged his shoulders.

"This is what I heard. . . ." Johnny said. He checked to see if Lily was listening. The women were talking fast to each other, and no one was paying attention to the two men. "I heard her father likes you very much, even though he hasn't met you yet."

"How do you know that?"

"My parents told me. They go to Hong Kong often and—" Before Johnny could finish his sentence, the front door opened, and four Japanese officers walked in. As a man in a bowtie led them to a round table in a corner, everyone stopped chatting and followed the soldiers with their eyes.

One of Lily's friends stood up. "This is outrageous! We can't celebrate the holiday without having those animals interfering with us. I want to leave!"

Lily also stood and put her hands on her friend's shoulders. "Calm down, Lan-Lan. This is *our* place, and we're not leaving. *They* are the ones who should be leaving."

Lan-Lan appeared to think about what her friend said for a moment and sat down in her seat. She pushed her hair back and resumed the conversation. The four officers ordered several bottles of hard liquor and some meat dishes. In a short while, they started making a lot of noise, which caused the people from the neighboring tables to leave. The soldiers were oblivious to this and continued enjoying themselves.

Before Johnny could resume his conversation with Lee, a short older man from the jazz band walked to the microphone. "Ladies and gentlemen, we have a special guest tonight. Please put your hands together and give a warm welcome to Miss Lily Wong!"

Before Lee realized what was happening, Lily stood up. "Hold this for me." Lily put her fox collar into Lee's hands and walked onto the stage.

Johnny had his mouth wide open. "Did you know anything about this, my friend?"

"I knew nothing, Johnny. I didn't know she could sing." He opened his eyes equally wide.

Johnny reacted with a glare.

"It's true! I am just as surprised as you are." He didn't know what to think or how to feel but was certainly pleasantly surprised. He felt his heartbeat move faster, a similar feeling to the one he'd had when he and Lily went to a Beethoven concert. He locked his eyes onto Lily, and even thunder couldn't move him.

Lily's face glowed under the bright red and blue light, the same kind of glow he remembered when they first announced their engagement at the Year of the Dragon party. Her short, dark hair was neatly pushed back and her red lips were shiny. She had the same white pearl earrings on that he was very familiar with. She gently put her hands in front of her and walked closer to the microphone.

"This is my father's favorite song. It's called *If You Love Me*. He used to sing it when I was a little girl. At that time, I was too young to understand what each word meant. But now I think I do. So this is for you, Dad." She turned around and gave a nod to the band.

The soft music led off with the bass, and then the saxophone emerged in a rhythm of longing. After taking a deep breath, Lily's lips gently parted.

If you love me, please meet me by the fountain when the moon rises

If you love me, please read your letters to me

I wonder what makes you pause

I wonder what makes you strong

If you love me, please don't let me fall

If you love me, please hold my hand and take me wherever you go

As the last note faded away, there was a silence in the room, and then all of a sudden, the crowd burst into loud applause. Everyone stood. Lee stood with the crowd; finally, he could breathe, his hands clapping so hard they hurt. His eyes were still locked onto Lily's face. Lily took a simple stage bow and walked back to her seat.

When she came back to the table, both of her friends rushed in to hug her. Lee waited until it was his turn. "I had no idea you could sing," Lee said in Lily's ear, his right hand behind her back. "I wish you'd told me." He felt moisture in his eyes. He wanted to kiss her so badly but couldn't. *Not in public.* "Can I say. . . ." He was debating about whether he should let her know what he was thinking.

"Say what?" Lily looked into his eyes.

"I think your singing is as beautiful as you are." He'd said it. It wasn't as difficult as he thought it would be.

"That's sweet, De-Chang." Lily patted his cheek with her soft hand. It was the first time since they had been together that he'd felt her hand on his face. The last time he'd felt a female hand on his face was when he was five, and it had been Elke's.

"I just had no idea." He kept his right hand in the same place behind Lily's waist. The satin felt soft and smooth, thin enough for him to feel her body through it. He didn't want to let go.

"I wanted to surprise you. I guess I did." She didn't push his hand away this time.

Lily's friends were ecstatic. "Wow, that was so beautiful, Lily! And—"

Another person jumped right in. "That was truly amazing; I love that moist, clear sound of yours. I don't know how to describe it. If I were a guy, I would have fallen for you!"

"Hey, Lily. That was great! Really!" Johnny commented last.

"Thank you all! I enjoyed singing that song." Lily turned around and whispered to Lee, "I guess you can let me go now."

"Oh, I'm sorry." He removed his hand from Lily's waist.

"So, aren't you impressed?' Johnny was smirking at him.

"I don't know what to say right now, Johnny. I am just. . . ." He felt he barely knew Lily.

"Overwhelmed? I bet you are. I told you. She is something, isn't she?"

When the clock struck midnight, couples walked to the open area in front of the band and started dancing. Lily and her friends got up, getting ready to dance.

"Don't you want to have a tango with me, De-Chang?" Lily turned around. "Well, actually, I think waltz is probably more your style, given your background."

He sensed that Lily's words were more courtesy or even social obligation. She said it loudly so that everyone could hear her.

"Except the music right now is not waltz. Why don't you go ahead with your friends, and I can stay here until they play the Strauss." He then turned around to Johnny. "Why don't you go with them too?"

"All right then." Lily looked happy to go with her friends, and Johnny followed.

Soon, Lee saw his friend dancing with Ah-Fang, and Lily paired up with her friend, Lan-Lan. Lee was feeling sleepy but realized he needed to stay awake. With his chopsticks in hand, he picked out little pieces of food from dish to dish. Food could keep him awake a bit longer. Occasionally, he looked up to watch the dancers.

One of the Japanese officers got up and walked to the jazz band. He whispered something to the bandleader and walked away. Within a short moment, the sound of *Sakura* was heard. Suddenly, all the dancers stopped dancing. Two Japanese officers came back, grabbed two young women from the dance floor, and started dancing with them. One of them was Lily's friend, Lan-Lan.

The soldier had trouble standing straight. He seemed very drunk. As he leaned toward Lan-Lan to try and kiss her, Lan-Lan turned her face to the side in disgust and pushed the soldier as hard as she could. The soldier fell back like a sandbag; luckily, one of his comrades was standing right behind him and caught his shoulders.

In a second, the falling soldier took out his handgun and fired one shot at Lan-Lan. He missed. He pulled the trigger one more time, and nothing came out. As he was checking his gun, Johnny leaped from his chair and covered Lan-Lan's body with his, and both of them landed on the floor. The standing Japanese officer quickly reached from behind and grabbed his comrade's gun. Lee heard loud screams followed by pandemonium.

Lily quickly got a solid hold of her friend. "Are you hurt? Are you all right?"

"I am . . . fine. . . ." Lan-Lan replied, shaking violently.

Two of the Japanese officers dragged their drunken comrade toward the front door, and the fourth one followed behind.

The chaos began to recede slowly after the Japanese left. "Is everyone all right?" someone next to the jazz band asked loudly.

"We are okay, I think," Lily responded as she stood from the floor.

"Thank you, Johnny." Lan-Lan turned to face Lee's friend.

"We were lucky. I think his gun was jammed or ran out of bullets." Johnny patted Lan-Lan's shoulder.

"Let's go home." Lee looked at everyone before he walked out to get the taxi.

28

Hello, Mr. Lee,

I hope you had a nice holiday. It has been very good to see my parents. My father is doing alright, but my mother is not. Her back pain makes it hard for her to cope with daily activities. Still, she seems to be in good spirits. They both asked me to stay in Suzhou, but I told them I have work to do in Shanghai.

I plan to take the four o'clock bus on February 12th and wonder if I could trouble you to pick me up at the bus station. I am scared to take the city bus at night by myself.

Thank you and see you soon.

Wishing you good health,
Mei
February 8, 1941

By the time Mei got on the bus, it seemed more crowded than when she had left Shanghai. Luckily, her suitcase did not feel heavier when she fought to put it onto the luggage rack, even though she had two more new blouses in it, thanks to her mother. She was told that she needed to look better. Why? Because her mother said an educated person, such as herself, should always look nicer than an uneducated one.

The roads out of Suzhou were often bumpy, and none of the buses she took ever seemed to have any suspension. Whenever the bus went over a bump or rough surface, it felt like everyone was bouncing off the seat, and it rocked back and forth as if it were making *yuanxiao* or sweet sticky rice dumplings. Looking out the window, she saw farm fields and small irrigation ditches. Modest-looking houses were scattered in the distance as decorations for nature. However, she wasn't enjoying this all-familiar scenery. She had other things to worry about. She didn't know where her husband was or whether he was fighting in a battle. She worried about his safety.

She wondered if she should check with Mr. Lee to find out if she was getting closer to paying off her debt. She recalled asking him one day about the surgery cost, and his response was, "It would be best if I did not disclose that information, as it would make you worry." On a lighter note, she thought about her school and reminded herself that she needed to ask his advice on what classes she should take in the spring. "You are making great progress!" Mr. Lee had told her right before she left.

Soon, the "lighter note" was interrupted by the voice of her mother, and the unwanted conversation they'd had before she'd left resonated in the back of Mei's head.

"When are we going to see our grandson, Mei?"

"Hopefully soon, Ma. Soon."

"How soon?"

"I don't know, Ma. The war makes everything hard."

"Let me tell you the reason, Mei. After giving birth to you, I couldn't have any more children because giving birth to you hurt my *qi*; that's what the doctor said. And that's why I am still not well." She paused and then patted Mei on the shoulder. "Mei, please don't cry; I wasn't blaming you for my illness. I would just like to have a boy in the house. And I thought . . . I thought having a grandson would be nice."

"Ma, there is a war going on right now, and besides, I have to wait until Da-Ming comes back."

"Will you talk to him when he comes back?"

"Yes, I will, Ma. Don't pressure me on this right now, all right?"

She couldn't remember how long she had been on the bus, but the road felt smoother, and the sky was getting dark. She put her head on the handrail on the seat in front of her and dozed off.

Suddenly, loud gun shots woke her. She heard the driver quickly slam on the brake, and the bus came to a screeching halt and turned sideways off the road, perching in a slant over a ditch. She rubbed her eyes and looked around. She saw half of the front windshield was gone, and blood gushed out from the driver's head.

In a muddled voice, the driver shouted, "Get down!"

When she and all the other passengers looked outside, they saw a truck ahead taking most of the gunfire, which brightened the dark sky. She heard a loud male voice yell, "We are under attack!"

Then the pandemonium began. People pushed themselves toward the only small door. Many began to climb out of the windows. Bullets whizzed toward the bus, and many were shot in the process of forcing themselves out of the bus. Mei kept her head as low as she could, covering her ears with her hands. She saw bodies on the passenger seats as well as in the aisle, accompanied by the sound of moaning and screaming. The gunfire intensified, and bullets whistled through the broken bus windows.

When she dared to glance up, she saw that the bus door was open, with one body over the steps. She eased toward the steps and pushed the body with one of her hands, but she saw no movement. She looked down and saw that her hand was wet with blood. Because there was no time to hesitate, she crawled over the dead body. Her hands touched the ground first and she felt the cold air. She lifted her head to see where she was and glimpsed the Shanghai skyline in the near distance. Before she could make up her mind on where she should crawl, she felt something strike her head, and everything went black.

29

When she opened her eyes, she saw Dr. Liu standing next to her hospital bed. "Where am I?" She felt pain on the left side of her head.

"You are in the hospital, Mrs. Zhou." Dr. Liu smiled. "It's good to see you awake. How are you feeling?"

"My head hurts." She touched her head and felt the gauze wrapped around it.

"I know, but you are lucky. The gunshot wound is only superficial, and you will recover soon." A nurse came to the room and said something to Dr. Liu. He turned to Mei. "I'm going to take care of something and will see you shortly."

After the doctor left, Mei tried to sit up from the bed, still feeling confused, not sure how she'd got here. She glanced at the nightstand and saw a newspaper on it.

She picked it up and read:

Ambush
Shanghai, February 13.

Last night, a bus carrying passengers from Suzhou ran into an ambush, which was intended for a truck carrying Japanese soldiers riding in front of it. A group of unknown resistance guerillas claimed they have killed at least twelve Japanese soldiers, and unknown numbers were injured.

During the gunfight, an unknown number of civilian passengers from the bus were also injured or killed. The truck managed to get away. The bus was badly damaged, and the surviving passengers left the bus on foot. The bus driver is reportedly missing.

She put the newspaper down, trying to remember what had happened.

"I see you must have read the front-page article, Mrs. Zhou," Dr. Liu said as he walked in, "and you must wonder how you got here."

Mei looked at the doctor and then at the newspaper. "I can't say I remember what happened to me," she replied, shaking her head.

"Well, you were on that Suzhou to Shanghai bus that took fire from the resistance guerilas. The target was a truck carrying Japanese soldiers riding in front of the bus. Apparently, the darkness made the ambush more difficult, and there were many civilian casualties."

"How did I get here?"

"Mr. Lee brought you here. He said he found you on the ground, your head bleeding, not far from that bus. He wrapped your head with his shirt and then drove you here."

"I see." She still felt puzzled by all the information. "For some reason, I don't remember any of this."

"Don't worry about it, Mrs. Zhou. The important thing is that you are all right. I will have the nurse change your gauze after lunch. So get some rest." Dr. Liu smiled again and then left the room.

30

A few days after Mei was discharged from the hospital, she came down with a bad cold, a high fever, and a sore throat. She couldn't tell if the pain in her head was part of the cold or the lingering effect from the gunshot wound. She felt dizzy, and standing on her feet became a task.

Mr. Lee made himself her sole caretaker. While he preferred giving Mei Bayer aspirin, Dr. Liu suggested that Mei should also add herbal medicine to her daily medication, as it would be gentler to her stomach. Mr. Lee made a schedule for her, which seemed somewhat regimented, but she followed it in order to get better.

At eight o'clock, she was to rise from bed. After freshening up in the bathroom, hot milk and one hardboiled egg followed. *Where did he learn how to make a hardboiled egg?* she wondered. At nine o'clock, she was given the first bowl of herbal medicine made up of twigs, orange peels, and leaves of some sort. It tasted very bitter. At noon, Mr. Lee brought in lunch, purchased outside (probably by Mr. Ma), followed by another bowl of the bitter and murky liquid. A nap followed, and then Mr. Lee read to her, just a bit. At six o'clock, Mr. Lee brought in dinner, purchased outside again, and then Mei drank the last bowl of medicine before bedtime. Every day, the bitter odor of the medicine permeated the whole house, and the smell of it never left; Mei could even smell it from her room.

Mr. Lee brought in more pillows whenever she was feeling less tired so that he could prop her up for a short while. Eating often required significant effort from her. She didn't have much appetite and ate very slowly. When she became tired, Mr. Lee would come over and help feed her. This made eating much easier for her. She was embarrassed but accepted defeat.

"I'm so sorry, Mr. Lee," she said one day after breakfast.

"Sorry for what, Mei?" He had the same smile, warm and calm.

"I thought I was supposed to take care of you, Mr. Lee, but—"

"Don't worry, Mei. Life can be unpredictable sometimes. You see, I have often wondered what it would be like to take care of someone, and now you have given me that opportunity. I hope I'm doing a good job!" He sounded happy.

She felt embarrassed and did not know what to say.

Mr. Lee left the room for a few minutes and then came back with something in his hand. "Here, I have a couple of letters for you. I think they're from your husband. Would you like to read them?" He handed the letters to her.

"I don't think I can concentrate for very long at the moment. Could I trouble you to read one of them to me?"

"I would be happy to." He sat on the edge of her bed and read the letter:

> "*Mei, I have not been able to write you because we constantly move from place to place. I am feeling very cold right now and please excuse my handwriting, as my hand feels very stiff. If you were here with me, you could keep me warm. I wish you could hold me in your arms right now.*
>
> *We have been waiting for the enemy for several days here outside in the cold. Someone must have gotten the information wrong. I don't know how long I can endure this hardship. It's a test of my stamina....*"

Mr. Lee looked at Mei. "Should I continue?"

"Yes, please."

> "*Something bad happened recently. We went to a small village last week, and three of our soldiers raped two women, and I was there when it happened. One of the women was a young mother with whom we'd stayed for a few days. One day, a cousin of hers came for dinner, and she brought us rice wine. There were four of us, plus the two women. They cooked the meal, and everything was delicious. After dinner, two of our guys got a bit drunk, and one of them started flirting with the two women. Before I knew it, they jumped onto the women. I tried to stop them, but one of them was an officer, and he told me that if I told anyone about this, he would shoot me. He asked me to join*

*them, but I refused. I was very angry with them, but
there was nothing I could do.*

*What makes me even more upset is that one of the
two soldiers had
actually saved my life not long ago when we were
attacked. A Japanese
soldier threw a hand grenade at us, but I didn't see it.
One of those two
soldiers used his body to cover mine. Luckily, he only
got a scratch. How could a good soldier be a rapist? I
am so confused. I miss you very much.*

Da-Ming, February 18, 1941."

She sat against her pillows quietly, trying to process what her husband had written. The moral dilemma her husband had experienced reminded her of her own encounter with Captain Aoki, whose politeness had surprised her. *People are not what they appear to be sometimes,* she concluded. "Thank you, Mr. Lee. Perhaps we could read the other letter tomorrow? I am feeling tired right now."

"Of course, Mei. Would you like to sit in the drawing-room? I think we have the sun coming through the window right now."

"I like that idea, Mr. Lee."

"Let me help you up." He pushed her comforter to the side so that she could get up, and he put her slippers on her feet. "I have a blanket on the sofa there, I think."

Mr. Lee was right. When she sat down on the sofa, she felt the warmth of the sun. "It looks nice outside. Mr. Ma is probably working in the garden right now." She leaned back as Mr. Lee covered her with the blanket. "What's in your hand?" She noticed something before Mr. Lee sat down next to her.

"Oh, it's a little lighthearted book. I have a habit of carrying a book around the house sometimes."

"Perhaps you could read it to me, just a bit?" This would be a good distraction from her worries about her husband.

"I would be glad to, Mei." He opened the book where it was bookmarked and read:

> "*The sun started to descend, dodging in and out from behind the clouds as if it were playing hide-and-seek. When all the clouds moved away, the sun's warm radiance reflected on his youthful face. His smooth skin had an orange glow at first, but soon the orange turned into red. He stood on the large boulder, gazing into the pale-blue mist emerging in the distance. Slowly, it enveloped the small village above the horizon. He dusted his ripped shorts, picked up his walking stick, and walked his sheep down from the high cliff.*"

Feeling the warmth of the sun coming through the window, Mei leaned back and tucked her arms under the blanket. Unconsciously, her head slid to one side and onto Mr. Lee's shoulder. Mr. Lee did not move and continued his reading. Before long, her eyelids closed without her permission.

The next day, Mr. Lee punctually came back and read the second letter aloud to her:

> "*Mei, I am in Changsha now, and it's good to be here. I like the city, and I have a feeling that we might get some decent food. There is a rumor that we might*"

be able to stay here for more than a week, finally. The truth of the matter is, we all need rest. Please write me and use the address on the back of the envelope. I never know how long it will take for the mail to travel, but if you could write me soon, the chance of me getting it would be better. I want to tell you something, but I don't want you to worry.

During a battle a couple of days ago, I was injured, but it's not serious. A bullet went over my left shoulder, and it took a small piece of skin with it.

At least it seemed that way. I feel a little sore, but it's no big deal. I was very lucky because the man who was next to me is dead. Whenever I go to sleep, I hear the sound of bullets flying around me in my dreams. They sound like whistles. Sometimes it's hard for me to tell whether I am awake or dreaming. Maybe it's better that way. I am still very troubled by the incident that I mentioned in my last letter. I had always thought that bad things are committed by the enemies and never realized that anything like that could happen during war; even good men can do bad things. After that bad night, one of the women told me that she was raped by the Japanese soldiers not long ago, and she couldn't believe that our own soldiers would do the same. She cried all night that night. I tried to comfort her. Please write soon. Da-Ming, February 22, 1941."

Mr. Lee leaned closer to her after reading the letter. "You seem worried," he said.

"I should write him back right away before he leaves Changsha." She paused for a moment. "Do you think, Mr. Lee, that if I tell you what I wanted to say, perhaps you could put a nice letter together for me? I hope it's not too much trouble."

"No trouble at all! That would be my pleasure, Mei. Besides, this will be a nice change of pace from my day job."

"Mr. Lee, I just realized that you have not been to your office for so many days . . . because of me. It's all my fault."

"It's quite all right, Mei. I already made all the arrangements with Mrs. Shen last week, and she knows this is an unusual circumstance. Just give me one moment." He left the room and then came back with a writing pad and a pencil. "I'm ready. Where should we begin?"

"I want to tell my husband that I am relieved to have received his letters and to learn that he is safe." She paused to gather her thoughts. "And. . . ."

Mr. Lee listened attentively and wrote everything down with great efficiency. When Mei finally stopped talking, he said, "Let me rearrange the letter a bit, and I'll read it back to you, and then you can tell me what you think."

Mei closed her eyes to rest, but she heard the busy sound of the pencil on the writing pad moving about. Within a few minutes, Mr. Lee said softly, "I think this pretty much covers what you have told me." He began:

> "Da-Ming: It's good to know that you are all right.
> I have had a bad cold lately, and Mr. Lee is very kind
> to help me write this letter to you. I hope you don't
> mind. I was very relieved to receive your recent letters,
> which brought me both joy and sadness. What worries
> me most is still your safety. War is ugly, and bullets
> don't have eyes. Knowing how courageous you are, I
> want you to be extra careful because I want you to come
> back unharmed. I spent the Chinese New Year with my

parents in Suzhou, and Mr. Lee was very kind to let me go. It was great to see them.

I also visited your parents, and they cried when they saw me. I told them where I thought you might be, and they are disappointed that you have not written them. Please write them if you have time. They miss you very much. I have spent most of my days in bed for more than a week, I think.

Luckily, Mr. Lee has been taking very good care of me. It shouldn't be this way, but I have no choice right now. I look forward to getting better and returning to both what I was hired to do here and to my classes. I have been learning a lot, and you would be very proud of me. I realize it's very selfish of me to share this with you, but I don't have the courage that you have. Improving myself is all I can do right now. Please forgive me. Please write soon, and let me know if you have fully recovered from your injury.

Mei, February 27, 1941."

"I like it. It sounded very good, Mr. Lee. I wish I could write that well."

"I notice that you did not mention the gunshot wound on your head. Should we add that?"

"I thought about mentioning it, but I don't want my husband to worry about me."

Mr. Lee nodded and then folded the letter.

31

Da-Ming received his wife's letter two days before he was scheduled to leave Changsha. He kept all her letters in his pocket. Whenever he had the chance, he would take them out and read them over and over again. They made him feel as if she were there with him. On the day of his departure from the city, the army served a good lunch, which he had wished for. It was braised pork with potatoes. He hadn't had a decent meal for a while and ate quite a bit of it. After lunch, everyone was told that they were going to leave in an hour. He sat on a bench, wanting to reread one of his wife's letters. As he was about to start, Sergeant Fang came by.

"Hey, Da-Ming, if you keep reading those letters, eventually the thin papers will evaporate!"

"Oh, Sergeant Fang. Thanks again for saving the extra food for me."

"How is your wife doing in Shanghai?" the middle-aged man asked kindly. He was thin and tall, with wide shoulders. Above his bold eyebrows, he had a scar near his left eye. When he walked, his right leg tremored slightly.

"She is fighting a bad cold right now; otherwise, she is doing all right, I guess."

"It sounds like everyone is fighting something these days!" Sergeant Fang giggled at his own wit.

"There is more, Sergeant. She is actually taking some courses in an adult school."

"You better watch out, young man. One day, she will be smarter than you are!" Sergeant Fang laughed warmly.

"She already is. I have always thought she is smarter and better than I am anyway."

"I heard she is a great cook. Am I right?"

"Yes, she is. I had hoped you wouldn't mention it because whenever I am hungry, I think about her cooking."

"Well, when the war is over, you two can resume your good meals. Maybe you can invite me over one day?"

"That's a promise, Sergeant."

"Tell your wife I said 'hello' next time."

"I will. By the way, Sergeant, do you know where we are going next?"

"We are going north, and that's all I can tell you." He stood up and patted Da-Ming on the shoulder. "When the bullets start to fly, watch yourself, young man."

In less than half an hour, everyone climbed into the back of the two trucks. Da-Ming checked his food bag, the knife on his right side, and his rifle. He propped the collar of his overcoat up and put his hands together. The road was bumpy, and he felt as if his lunch were about to come out from his stomach. The soldier who sat across from him kept staring at him, and it made him uncomfortable. He told the man to turn his head away.

In a while, some of the men started to doze off as they traveled on the dusty road. The soldiers who sat in the front used their overcoats to cover their faces, and Da-Ming did the same. He couldn't tell how much time had elapsed, but right before the sky turned dark, the two trucks stopped. He opened his eyes and looked around. They were in the middle of nowhere. The narrow valley was flanked by dark hills, and the rocks ahead prevented them from moving forward. The word came from the front that they needed to spend the night here.

He and two other soldiers found a small shallow cave up on the hill. They removed their blankets from their backs and set them on the ground. Da-Ming took out a steamed bun and started eating. He looked up behind the mountain on the other side of the road and saw the sky turning a dark purple. A chilly wind came, and dust started dancing in front of him. Behind him, the other two soldiers were quarreling about something. He turned around and told them to lower their voices. After eating, he saw the first group of three night guards walking around the two trucks. In a little while, a soldier came and told three of them that sergeant wanted them to do the four o'clock to six o'clock shift. Da-Ming checked his watch and thanked sergeant in his head for giving him the later shift.

Holding his weapon to his chest, he closed his eyes and imagined what his wife might be doing. He saw her on her way to her school, smiling. He heard her voice saying words that he had never heard of. He imagined her coming back from her school and showing him her writings—pages and pages of words he had never learned himself. She was using ancient idioms that only his father would use. He also imagined her finding a good job in the big city, and she changed her small-town-girl look into that of a sophisticated young woman. He imagined himself coming back from the war and watching her come out of an office building with her attaché in her hand. On her high heels, she would walk by him on the street without noticing him standing on the street corner with his crutches under his arms, bandages on his head, and the medals dangling from his uniform.

Although he had never been to Mr. Lee's house, he imagined Mei working in his large kitchen and how happy she must be. He started feeling jealous of his boss because he was having her cooking every day. He also imagined that the debt he owed to Mr. Lee would be paid off soon, and most of all, that the war would be over soon too.

The cold night was finally finished. It took only half an hour for the soldiers to clear the road. Before long, the two trucks continued moving north. Still, he did not know where they were going and how long the trip would be. As the road became smoother, the two trucks started to pick up speed, though the dust never left them. The soldiers once again covered their faces and lowered their helmets. By late afternoon, a small village emerged in the distance ahead. He was relieved.

Soon the trucks stopped, and a group of men in civilian clothes stood near the entrance to the village. He saw Sergeant Fang, Captain

Yin, and a few other officers walk to the group. They spoke for a few minutes, and everyone was told to get off the trucks. In less than ten minutes, they were gathered in a schoolyard.

"There will be a battle tomorrow morning at four a.m., and I want to make sure that everyone gets a good night's sleep," Captain Yin said calmly. Although Da-Ming didn't know Captain Yin very well, he had heard that he was not a talkative man. Coming from Shenyang, he was the only son of his family. A man of medium build with gray hair, he liked to meditate and play chess.

"This group of Japanese may be larger than our group; however, our advantage is the hills. As always, we need to do our best not to let a single soldier get away. The good news is that we have the village fighters assisting us. I feel confident that we will win this battle. The sergeants will give you the details later." He looked at the plain-clothed men. "I think we are going to have some home cooking tonight. So, enjoy!" He smiled at everyone before he left the yard with two other officers.

After dinner, everyone was told to sleep in the school classrooms. Da-Ming was glad to be able to find a corner in the large room. Even though it was not heated, he thought the walls would prevent the cold draft from coming through. As before each battle, he wanted to prepare himself by contemplating for a few minutes. He lay on the cold, uneven brick floor with his blanket wrapped around him, thinking about the upcoming battle in the morning. He checked the wound in his left shoulder, and it felt fine. After the last two comrades finished their card games, the night came without further delay. The familiar loud snoring once again persisted in the darkness, and he covered his ears with the sleeve of his coat.

It felt more like a quick nap rather than a night's sleep. At three o'clock sharp, they rose almost soundlessly. Within minutes, everyone packed and gathered in the schoolyard. Captain Yin gave a short briefing, and the soldiers marched toward the hills. Despite the brief sleep, Da-Ming felt good. He had a feeling that this battle would be short and quick; he could almost taste the victory. He marched with his head up, looking at the dark sky, where stars were still twinkling as if saying "good morning" to the soldiers below. He was glad to have the battle in good weather and remembered how much he hated fighting in the rain. He had once complained to Sergeant Fang that rain prevented him from seeing well.

"Maybe you should get yourself an umbrella and draw the enemies toward you," the sergeant had responded sarcastically.

By the time they arrived at their battle location, Da-Ming saw a group of lightly armed villagers waiting on a small hill, where the Japanese troops were expected to pass by below. The officers spoke with the leader from the village fighters. Soon, the group was divided into three: the soldiers would take up the two hills on each side of the road and the villagers would go to the farther end of the road to block the Japanese from escaping. The air was chilly, and everyone started to do some stretching. While watching his soldiers warm up, Sergeant Fang stood there and reminded everyone that no one should fire until Captain Yin fired the first shot. He asked everyone to check his weapons and ammunition. In a few minutes, he walked to Da-Ming with a machine gun in his hands. "Hey, Da-Ming, today is your lucky day."

Da-Ming stopped polishing his rifle and looked up.

"I've got you a *Fusil Mitrailleur modèle 24.* Would you like to give it a try?"

"Oh yes!" He was excited. "Wow, it looks like it's in great condition."

"It's a bit old but it should work fine," sergeant added, and gave him several magazines.

After sergeant left, the soldier next to Da-Ming said to him, "Wow, you're going to have some fun today! Don't forget, we're going to rely on you." Da-Ming didn't respond and started checking the weapon. They waited patiently in the cold air. Da-Ming patted the barrel of his new gun. *You take care of us, and we will take care of you.*

Sometime after four-thirty, light appeared behind the east side of the hill. Da-Ming turned and looked up. Only a few stars were visible. In the far distance, he heard the faint sound of roosters trying to wake people. He reached into his left breast pocket and felt the letters from his wife. She was with him. Within moments, the noise of truck engines sounded from the northern direction. *The timing is perfect,* he thought. Sergeant Fang came around again and reminded everyone not to fire until they heard the first shot from Captain Yin.

Da-Ming could see the dust appearing first, and soon the sound of engines was louder, and three trucks with canvas tops rolled into view. Suddenly, the trucks stopped in the middle of the road. Three Japanese soldiers came out from the first truck and walked toward the south with their landmine detectors. Everyone on the hills waited patiently.

Da-Ming was controlling his breathing in fear that the Japanese soldiers could hear him. The soldier next to him was about to sneeze, and Da-Ming gave him a stern look. The soldier pinched his nose, and the sneeze never came out. "What's the matter with you, buddy?" Da-Ming whispered to him. "Every time before a battle, you want to sneeze. Do you want to get all of us killed?"

"I'm sorry, man. I'm just nervous." He looked embarrassed.

"Well, in that case, you should go home then!" Da-Ming shook his head.

The three soldiers came back and waved for the drivers to go ahead. The trucks began moving again, and Da-Ming felt a surge of adrenaline. He kept his index finger on the trigger and aimed at the first truck. He heard the first shot coming out from the opposite hill; suddenly, the rain of fire started pouring down from both sides of the hills. The Japanese soldiers jumped out of the trucks, and some were instantly killed as they came out. They ran for cover behind the large boulders.

To conserve bullets, Da-Ming was firing only three shots at a time. Soon, most of the Japanese soldiers were behind the boulders and started firing back. He saw that the first truck was on fire and did not know how it had happened. In less than twenty minutes, Sergeant Fang told his soldiers to hold their fire and let the Japanese come out from their hideouts.

It did not seem that the Japanese knew how many people they were confronting. The sergeant was right. After two minutes, the olive-green uniformed men started to emerge from behind the boulders cautiously.

"Do not fire. Let them get closer," sergeant whispered.

Da-Ming started measuring the distance in his head: two hundred meters, one hundred fifty, one hundred, fifty. . . .

"Fire!" Captain Yin yelled from a distance, and fired the first shot.

Da-Ming kept his index finger on the trigger this time, swinging his FM24 from left to right. He saw olive-green uniforms dropping in front of him as if they were sandbags. The sound of gunfire echoed in the valley, making the sound even louder. The Japanese soldiers took cover again quickly and returned fire. Da-Ming heard bullets flying near his ears. He took pauses from time to time, making sure not to waste ammunition.

"I am out of ammo!" the soldier next to him shouted out.

Da-Ming turned around and stared at the soldier.

"Don't worry, those guys down there don't understand a word of Chinese."

Da-Ming saw three more olive-green uniforms come out from hiding. He pressed his index finger hard but got no response. On his left, the sound of his comrades' gunfire started to become sporadic. Within a few seconds, more olive-green uniforms started charging uphill toward them. Cautiously, they moved closer and closer.

Da-Ming saw three dead bodies on his right, and he remembered talking to those men last night.

"Come on, Da-Ming! Are you taking a nap? These guys are getting closer!"

"Hold on, my gun is jammed," he shouted back, trying to find out where the problem was.

The olive-green uniforms picked up their pace, charging toward them.

"Hey, hurry up! We're running out of time!" he heard his comrades say again. "Draw your swords!"

Da-Ming could see that some of the olive-green uniforms were new and the faces of the men were young.

"I got it! I got it!" The FM24 started roaring again, and he heard loud screaming within twenty meters from him. He saw bullets rip through the olive-green uniforms as if there were explosives underneath, and the bodies dropped onto the ground, making muffled sounds, puffing the dust into the air. He clinched his teeth and did not let his index finger go until there was no one standing in front of him. He stopped, wiping the sweat off from his forehead with his left arm.

"You must pay for your crimes. You must pay," he whispered to himself. As he was switching to a new magazine, he heard a second truck engine. Before he realized what was going on, the truck drove full speed down the road toward the south. He heard the light gunfire coming from the village fighters. Their bullets made holes in the canvas top, but the truck kept going. Since no one could see inside the canvas cover, it was hard to tell if there were any soldiers inside or not. He saw the olive-green uniforms charging on the opposite hill where the gunfire was less intense. Soon, most of them managed to reach the top. He saw soldiers from both sides fighting with their hands. One of the Japanese officers raised his Samurai sword, but before he could come down with his sword, someone stabbed him from behind. Da-Ming watched as he fought very hard to stand up, until slowly, his legs gave in.

Soon he saw everyone on the opposite hill go down. Within seconds, silence returned to the valley. The smell of gunpowder permeated the atmosphere, and dead bodies were strewn everywhere. Da-Ming turned his head from left to right and saw his comrades' faces covered in black. He made eye contact with a soldier on his far-right, and both nodded at each other without saying a word.

Suddenly, over the soldier's right shoulder, he saw an olive-green hat appearing from a distance behind a large boulder. He turned his gun and aimed at the rock. The hat was gone. He signaled to the soldier that he'd made eye contact with a moment ago to move back so that he could have a better view. He waited patiently. Within one minute, the whole olive-green uniform came out and started running uphill. He calculated the distance, the man's running speed, and the velocity of his bullet. He aimed ahead of the soldier and squeezed the trigger. The soldier's body made a swift twist in the air and then fell to the ground with a slight bounce. He did not get up. The soldier on Da-Ming's far-right gave him a thumbs up.

He stood there in silence and looked around for a moment before he climbed out of his ditch. His surviving comrades came down from the hills and walked around the battlefield. Da—Ming walked slowly to the body of the last Japanese soldier he had just killed. The soldier was lying there motionless, the blood on his chest gradually percolating through his uniform. Based on how new his uniform looked, the soldier must not have been in China very long.

Under the soldier's hat, Da-Ming saw a young peaceful face with smooth skin. He bent over and patted the soldier's pockets and felt something in the upper left pocket. Inside, he found a wallet. He opened the blood-covered wallet and saw two photographs: one looked like the soldier himself in the same uniform and the other was an image of a family. The man standing on the right was the soldier. On his left stood a young woman, who was wearing a kimono. In her left arm, she was holding a child, a girl who looked to be about fourteen months old. Da-Ming looked at the back of the photograph: *Tokyo, May 2, 1939.*

He checked the wallet again and saw both Japanese and Chinese currencies. He put everything back in the wallet and put the wallet back in the dead man's pocket. "You should have stayed with your family," he said to the dead body as he sat down on a large boulder. He imagined that the dead soldier would return to Japan and be reunited with his young wife and lovely daughter.

He reached inside his breast pocket and took out Mei's letters. He opened one of them and started reading, but within a few seconds, he couldn't continue. His vision was blocked by the moisture coming out from his eyes. He put the letter back and stood. He swung the FM24 onto his right shoulder and began walking toward his comrades.

Despite the heavy casualties, Captain Yin was very pleased with the battle. He did not blame the village fighters for not being able to stop the escaping truck; instead, he praised them for their bravery. He had his soldiers hand over the weapons they'd captured from the Japanese soldiers to the village fighters and asked everyone to take it easy for the rest of the day.

During lunch, Sergeant Fang came to Da-Ming and said, "Hey, young man, it looked like everything worked out all right with the FM24. I'm sorry it got jammed. I think it just needs some cleaning. If you like it, you can keep it."

"Thanks, Sergeant. I had my hair up for a moment when the Japanese were closing in, but I am glad it all worked out." He wanted to add that they got lucky this time, but he didn't. He ate his steamed bun slowly, thinking about the young Japanese soldier he had killed at the end of the battle. He was surprised that he couldn't stop thinking about him because he had killed many Japanese soldiers before and had never given it a second thought.

They deserve to die.

He decided to take a short nap after the meal. When he woke up, he saw that most soldiers had left, though there were a few still in the room sleeping. From his small messenger bag, he took out a notebook and a pen. The hard backing of the notebook provided a good surface to write:

Mei,

> *We left Changsha and fought a battle early this morning. I am not hurt, but many died. The captain claimed victory, as most Japanese soldiers from the three trucks that we ambushed were killed. I usually feel good after each battle, but not today. I killed a young Japanese soldier, who was the last one to be killed. I went to see his body and was surprised to find how young he was. He was handsome and had smooth skin, almost like yours. Sorry for the inappropriate comparison. I bet he hadn't been in China for very long because his uniform looked new. When I bent over to check his pockets, I could still smell mothballs from his wool jacket. What I found difficult was that I discovered his family picture, where I saw his young, beautiful wife and a baby daughter who looked about fourteen months old. Looking at his peaceful face, I have asked myself many questions but cannot find any answers.*
>
> *I wish you could understand how I feel at this moment. I am very sad right now. This is the aspect of war that I did not prepare for. I only thought about the atrocities that have been committed by the Japanese*

soldiers. I suppose getting even is the answer. I don't know. The ugly truth about battle is that if we don't kill them, they will kill us. Please don't think badly of me. I just have to do this until all the Japanese are out of our motherland.

How are you feeling now? I hope Mr. Lee has been taking good care of you. From what you have told me, he sounds like a good man. I also hope that your classes have been going well, especially your English class. You are going to have to teach me some when I get back. You can't write me, but I will let you know when I find out about our next long stay.

Da-Ming
March 12, 1941

32

May had finally arrived in Shanghai, Mei's favorite month. The air was gentle and mild. She enjoyed watching the flowers in and around the French Concession, and she often took detours whenever she went out to discover new blooms. After donning drab colors all winter, women started to put on brighter colors. Mei wanted to do the same so that she would be regarded as one of the city's people. Even though she only had a few blouses, she tried to keep them clean and pressed. The two new ones that she had just got from her mother she thought should be worn on special occasions only. Since she had classes every morning, she needed to wash her clothes more often so that she would always have clean clothes in front of her classmates.

One Sunday after class, she wanted to have a look in a nearby bookstore that used to intimidate her. She felt more confident now. In the literature aisle, she easily picked out a book and started reading it without much effort. She was proud of herself. After putting the book back on the shelf, she walked toward the farther end of the aisle, and a tall man approached her from the other end.

"Mrs. Zhou, is that you?" He sounded excited.

Mei stopped and looked up at the familiar handsome face. "Captain Aoki?"

"Yes. It's me. I'm so glad to see you here!" His face was animated. She started to turn away, and Captain Aoki came around to her quickly. "It has been a while since I last saw you. How have you been?" He walked closer to her and lowered his face.

"I . . . have been . . . all right. And you?" She regretted her reply right away, but it was too late to take it back.

"Fine! I have been fine." He took a quick look at the surroundings, perhaps as a soldier's habit, and then turned back to Mei. "I don't suppose we should talk in here. I think people are reading. I have some time before I need to head back to my base. How about we have some tea together? I know a teashop not far from here." He checked his watch.

Tea with a Japanese soldier! Mei couldn't believe her ears. She stood there, indecisive. Her instincts told her that she should tell him that she needed to get back to Mr. Lee's house soon and to thank him for inviting her. But then again, she was curious about this polite, handsome young man. She had never met a foreigner before, and it wouldn't be a bad idea to learn something about his country. But most of all, she didn't sense any danger, unlike the first encounter she'd had with him. In the worst case, Captain Aoki would use a soft interrogation tactic to find out if she was a communist. If that happened, she could deny it. And it would be up to him to decide her fate. *I'd either be a traitor or a hero.* She saw her fingers fidgeting on the corners of her blouse, almost the same way as when she'd first met Mr. Lee. "I guess I can give it a try." She couldn't believe her own ears.

"That's wonderful. Follow me!" Captain Aoki led Mei toward the front door of the bookstore and pushed the door open to let her walk out first before he followed her.

He is a gentleman, she thought.

The teashop was crowded on a Sunday. The good weather had attracted many customers. Luckily, when they walked in, another couple was about to leave. They waited for a short moment while the waiter wiped the table clean for them. Upon sitting in their chairs, Mei looked outside the window, where she saw a mother buying some candy for her son from a street vendor. In her mind, however, she was preparing herself for the potential questions that Captain Aoki might ask. The waiter came back, and Captain Aoki ordered a pot of Wulong tea and two small plates of snacks. One plate was mixed nuts, and the other was dried apricots.

"Thank you for joining me today, Mrs. Zhou. I thought perhaps we could get acquainted with each other. I'm sorry that we met under such an awkward circumstance. I was just doing my job."

This sounded like a statement, so she didn't have to answer it. Captain Aoki proceeded to pour some tea into her cup.

"As I mentioned last time, I am from Yokohama. It's a nice city, although it's not as cosmopolitan as Tokyo. You see. . . ." he took out a postcard from his right pocket, "I always carry a postcard of my hometown with me. It reminds me of where I came from, and it makes me feel less homesick." He pointed to a small building near the waterfront. "Do you see this small building?"

Mei had to lean over to look at the aerial view of the postcard. It was a sepia-toned image of the city harbor. She saw buildings and trees on the left side of the photograph, and on the right was the ocean with a few boats floating on it. In the lower right corner, the word *Yokohama* was prominently printed in an italic typeface.

"My father owns a fishing business, and this is where it is. It looks small from the air."

"Did your father want you to be part of his fishing business?" Mei saw no harm in asking the question.

"Yes, he did and still does. But I couldn't join him because I wanted to see China."

"Is that why you are here in Shanghai?" Her curiosity betrayed her.

"Well, yes. I joined the army because I wanted to serve the Emperor. I have always been very interested in Chinese culture, and I wanted adventure . . . but. . . ." He sounded enthusiastic at first before stopping. She waited. Captain Aoki gave a regretful sigh. "I didn't know we were coming here to kill people. I was too naïve." He had a sad expression on his face.

Mei imagined what it would be like if he had his uniform on. It would be awkward, not to mention that people would regard her as a traitor. He was lucky that his fluency in Chinese made everyone believe that he was a native speaker. She thought for a moment and said, "War is wrong. Killing people is wrong."

He nodded and then picked his teacup up slowly. "I agree, but I can't stop it. I wish I could."

"Have you ever killed anyone?" She meant Chinese. Feeling agitated by her own question, she decided to look him in the face. This could help her determine whether this conversation should continue or end.

"I have not," he said clearly and with certainty. "I hope I never have to. My main job is to secure the city, and I spend most of my working hours going around the city streets and making sure that everything is in order. Our presence on the streets, regardless if people like it or not, can be a deterrent for any potential problems." He took a sip of his tea. "I have friends who have gone into battle, and some are already dead."

Mei was about to say that she was sorry to hear this but realized it would be wrong. For those who had Chinese blood on their hands, they deserved to die. *Yes. They deserved to die.* There was also a possibility, however, that Captain Aoki's friends might be just like himself; they didn't know they would be going into battle, and they might even have families at home. She couldn't find good answers for her confusion. She decided to keep her eyes on the teapot, putting a few nuts in her mouth to keep her calm, hoping the captain would break the silence.

"What was growing up like in Suzhou?" the captain finally asked, changing the topic.

It was a better subject, not that she really wanted to tell a Japanese captain about herself. "I have always worked. As a young child, I had very limited schooling because my parents couldn't afford it. I spent a lot of time at home helping my parents with chores. My father taught me how to cook, and I enjoyed that." That was more than she needed to say. She felt like she was being interviewed again by Mr. Lee.

"What is Suzhou like?"

"Well, the city is small, and it has many little canals. Most buildings have white plaster walls and dark-gray roofs, characteristic of a southern city."

"That sounds very picturesque." He was squinting his eyes as if trying to imagine what the city looked like. "I don't recall seeing this type of architecture since I have been here."

"Yes. It is. The city is also famous for silk production as well as man-made gardens, built according to *Fengshui* and *Taoist* principles."

"I see." Captain Aoki nodded. "I have heard the term *Fengshui* before but never knew what it meant."

"It stands for wind and water. My father once told me that *Fengshui* is very important; it has to do with how *qi*, or breath, travels. If the air travels freely around you, your health will be good. So, when you arrange your home, it's better not to have your furniture blocking the *qi*."

"This is fascinating!" He paused for a moment, seeming to ponder what he had just heard. "So, how do I get good *qi* then?"

Mei shook her head. "I'm not an expert on *Fengshui*, but I guess it's better to keep what you have simple."

Captain Aoki nodded pensively and then said, "It sounds like the idea of Zen in Japan. The Chinese word for it is '*Chan*.'" He used his right index finger to write the character on the wooden table. "It's a school of Buddhism." Captain Aoki took a sip of his tea.

Mei was intrigued. She put her teacup down, waiting to hear more.

"I'm sorry to change the subject, but Suzhou sounds like a beautiful city. I would definitely like to visit it someday." He paused again and then said, "You said earlier that you didn't have a chance to go to school when you were young, so what were you doing in a bookstore today?"

"Oh, I have been taking classes at an adult school. When you saw me earlier, I had just come from my classes. Before that, my husband used to teach me reading, and so did Mr. Lee. So I've been making a lot of progress." She suddenly realized her fear toward Captain Aoki had practically disappeared.

"I see. You seem like an intelligent woman. So, what do you like to read?" Captain Aoki had a curious look on his face.

"Well, besides my school work, I like to read. I try to read novels, which help me build my vocabulary. I sometimes read newspapers, which are a bit harder. I don't enjoy reading them because there is too much sad news every day."

He nodded. "I know what you mean. News can be depressing sometimes, especially during war times."

"And I am also learning English." She didn't have to mention this but wanted to make her conversation interesting.

"English?"

She nodded. "Shanghai is a big city with people coming from all over the world. I think it would be very useful to learn the language."

"It's very true. But for me, I want to better my Chinese first. Maybe someday I'll have a chance to learn another language." He looked at his watch, and an expression of regret settled on his face. "I'm afraid I should go soon." He waved at the waiter to indicate that he wanted to pay the bill.

"Thank you for the tea, Captain Aoki."

"I'm so glad I bumped into you today, Mrs. Zhou. May I ask you if you have time next Sunday?"

"Next Sunday?" She felt almost excited. She knew she would need to check with Mr. Lee, and right away, she realized that if Mr. Lee found out that she was going to have a secret meeting with a Japanese soldier, he not only would be angry at her, she could also lose her job. She did not know how to respond.

"I wonder if you wouldn't mind accompanying me to the Jade Buddha Temple. I've never been there and am very curious about it. I've read about it in the past but would like to see it for myself." He sounded enthusiastic.

"I . . . can try. Where would you like me to meet you?" She couldn't believe her ears.

"Great! How about at the same bookstore around the same time?" He looked overjoyed.

She nodded, and they both stood and walked out of the teashop.

• • •

Sitting on the edge of her bed, Mei saw herself in the small mirror above the dresser. She wondered if the person in the mirror was the same person she'd once known. She looked down and saw her fingers shaking.

Da-Ming is away fighting the Japanese, and I am here befriending a Japanese captain? What kind of a wife am I? The newspaper headline she'd read just a few days ago kept coming into her mind: *All Traitors Will Be Shot!* Yes, she was among the traitors and would be shot, she told herself. The thought of it sent an ominous chill up her spine.

It had become obvious that her meeting with Captain Aoki was not optional. If she didn't show up, he could track her down, as he knew where she lived. She covered her face with her hands.

Let next Sunday be over as soon as possible.

33

In the early afternoon on the following Sunday, Mei and Captain Aoki arrived at the Jade Buddha Temple. She was excited about visiting the temple, and her curiosity seemed to have erased her nervousness and worries.

Captain Aoki seemed thrilled to have Mei in his company. "To be able to visit a cultural site with a local friend is something I had never dreamed of," he expressed. As they entered the courtyards, they were embraced by the fume of burning incense. They saw people holding incense in their hands, smoke rising above their heads and permeating the entire space around them. Upon entering the Grand Hall, they saw the beautiful statues of *Amitabha* and *Bhaisajyaguru*, flanked by eighteen *Arhats*, nine on each side of the room.

Mei and Captain Aoki walked quietly around the room, and from time to time, they read the descriptions and stories posted in various parts of the room. When they came out from the Grand Hall, they found an empty bench in the courtyard and proceeded to sit.

"This is a very interesting temple." Captain Aoki looked around the courtyard. "It reminds me of the Asakusa Temple in Tokyo, which is also a Buddhist temple. Its formal name is Sensoji, and it's the oldest temple in Tokyo."

"What's the history of the Sensoji Temple?" Mei asked.

"Well, I know it goes back to the early seventh century. If I recall the story correctly, one day, two brothers fished a small statue of Kannon, the goddess of mercy, out of the Sumida River. They put the statue back in the river, but it kept coming back to them. As a result, they built a temple there. So Sensoji Temple is indeed a Kannon Temple. I think the Chinese words for it are *Guan-yin*."

"Legends are always interesting." Mei was fascinated. "I think both our countries have many interesting legends."

"To say the least. Even though Buddhism originated from India, its influence has enriched the entire Asian continent." He looked as if he were in deep thought.

It was around noon and some clouds arrived, bringing drizzling rain. Captain Aoki suggested that they go into a small restaurant nearby. Mei liked the idea because she was feeling hungry. Captain Aoki walked in first, and she followed him inside. The restaurant was not crowded. She heard most customers there speaking in various dialects, most of which sounded like they came from the north. After looking at the menu, they decided to order noodle soups.

"Are you a Buddhist, Captain Aoki?" Mei asked the first question.

"No, I'm not. I'm just interested in some of its beliefs."

"Can you give me some examples?"

"Well, I'm still learning, and there is a lot in Buddhism that I haven't learned yet. Presently, I'm fascinated by its *Five Attributes* and the concept of *Emptiness*."

"And what are they?"

"*The Five Attributes*, or *Khandha*, include form, consciousness, feeling, perception, and formation. These are considered the ultimate referent in the Buddha's explanation on suffering, and understanding them is essential for understanding the *Four Noble Truths*, which is related to the concept of suffering."

He paused for a moment to trace his thoughts while the waiter put the food on the table.

"The concept of *Emptiness* is also very intriguing. A Buddhist believes that *Emptiness*, or *Sunyata*, signifies that everything one encounters in life is empty—empty in the sense that they are not tangible, like air or time, but they are also interrelated and mutually independent, and nothing is wholly self-sufficient or independent. Well, I don't know if this makes sense to you. Like I said, I am still learning."

"I think it does, Captain. My knowledge at this point is very limited and not advanced enough to understand the complexity of various types of thinking, but I think many beliefs are also interrelated."

"That's true. Cultures do go beyond country boundaries and influence each other. When I was in high school, I had an interest in Confucianism but never had a chance to study it. It must have deep roots in Chinese culture. Can you tell me something about it?" He looked eagerly into Mei's eyes.

"You did? Unfortunately, my schooling is very limited." She felt herself blushing. "As I said, my parents didn't have enough money to send me to school. However, I do recall my father was very much into Confucianism, and I think he and my mother raised me under Confucius principles."

"How so?"

"Well, you may or may not have heard the idea of *filial piety*, which is one of the virtues to be held above all else. It is the idea of respect for parents and ancestors. My father used to explain to me how family members should relate to each other under this principle. Basically, as far as I understand, it means that the older members of the family should show kindness toward the younger members, and the younger members should show *filial piety* in return. It is also important for the young to take care of the elderly. It's a social obligation."

"It sounds like the family bond is based on this principle. Am I right?"

"I guess you can say that."

"Do you know anything about the idea of *Ren*?"

"Only superficially. Even though it's only one word, I think there are many interpretations of it."

"And what would be yours?" He smiled at her.

"From my limited knowledge, which came mainly from my father, *Ren* can be interpreted as *Complete Virtue* or *Humanness*. The word itself also means benevolence, if I recall correctly."

"So, how can one obtain *Ren*?"

"My father said Confucius wants all of us to have *Ren*. He once quoted him as saying, '*He who seeks it* [meaning Ren] *has already found it*.'"

A smile of comprehension came to Captain Aoki's face. He nodded quietly and said, "It sounds so simple, and yet it's very profound." He gazed at the table for a moment, and then added, "When I go back to Japan, I would like to study Confucianism. It's so interesting!"

"I wish I could be more helpful on this topic. My understanding of Confucianism is very limited and may not be accurate. So please don't quote me on anything I have said."

"You have taught me a lot today, Mrs. Zhou. For that, I want to say thank you!" He then looked at the food and said, "I don't want to be rude but I think our noodles are getting cold."

After finishing their lunch, both Mei and Captain Aoki went out to the courtyard again. They sat on a bench, watching visitors go by. After a few minutes, Captain Aoki took his postcard out again. From his left breast pocket, he pulled out a pen, wrote something on the back of the postcard, and gave it to Mei. "Here, I would like you to have this."

Mei took it and read what he wrote. Written in Chinese *kanji* was his full name and his home address in Yokohama.

"When the war is over, I would like to invite you to visit me in Yokohama. I would like to show you around. It's a nice city. Besides, my parents would be delighted to meet a friend from China."

Mei was touched when he used the word "friend" because she'd never had any. When she was young, she'd always had to work. Whenever the children from her neighbors' houses came to ask her to play with them, her mother would tell them that Mei had no time to play. She was convinced at an early age that life was all about work, and the concept of playing with other children never existed. As she got older, the amount of work increased. After her wedding, her parents were reluctant to let her go because they didn't want to lose a good worker. Since she never had any friends, she had no idea what friendship was and spent most of her limited free time fantasizing about what it would be like to spend time with someone who was not related to her.

"That would be nice. Never in my dreams did I see myself going to another country. I just can't imagine what that is like." She shook her head.

Captain Aoki looked into the sky. "I wish this war would be over soon so that we could get back to our normal lives."

"Do you miss your family in Yokohama?" Mei turned her head toward him.

"I miss my parents very much. They didn't want me to come to China but realized that they had to let me go." He looked at his watch, just like he did last time. "Thank you again, Mrs. Zhou, for coming here with me. Most of all, thank you for your friendship. I am very glad to have met you."

"I, too, have learned a lot from you, Captain."

"I think I may have a work schedule change in the coming weeks, but I will try to get in touch soon. Perhaps you could teach me more about China again?"

"I don't know if that's possible, Captain." She really meant it.

"I understand, Mrs. Zhou. I fully understand the potential danger of our friendship, and I wouldn't do anything to jeopardize your safety. Let's see where life takes us."

"Thank you, Captain. I'm not sure I will see you again." *I should end this "friendship" now.*

Captain Aoki smiled. It looked final. "May I shake your hand, Mrs. Zhou?"

• • •

She had a dream that night. She was a butterfly, and so were Da-Ming, Mr. Lee, and Captain Aoki. She was a small, yellow Swallowtail, with blue eye shadow and orange scales, struggling to fly against the wind. On her left was Mr. Lee, who was a quiet Purple Emperor. He had warm earth tones and dark-black borders on his wings. He was flying slowly but steadily, keeping an exact distance from her as if making sure she was safe. On her right was Captain Aoki, who was a bright Great Orange Tip, flying with energy, his vivid orange wings shining under the bright sun. Ahead of her, flying high and fast, was Da-Ming, a large Birdwing who was glowing bluish green with a black central band. He was fearless and flew with great speed. Suddenly, a dark cloud came and took Captain Aoki with it. She screamed and went after him. Then another dark cloud came and wrapped her inside it. She couldn't free herself and woke up in a sweat.

34

The summer months seemed to go by quickly as Mei spent most of her free time studying. Mr. Lee had been very good about paying Mei's tuition and never disclosing the cost to her. All she had to do, he said, was to do well at school.

She had not seen Captain Aoki since their last encounter in May. From time to time, she wondered about him—what he had been doing and if he was still in the city. At one point, she feared that he might have been sent to battle and perhaps either been wounded or even killed. The thought of it scared her. After all, he regarded her as a friend. In fact, he was her only "friend," a friend who she could only see in secrecy and never mention to anyone. She hated herself for thinking about him and concluded, more than once, that it would be best if she never saw him again. The thought of that saddened her.

One day, as Mei was just finishing cleaning, Mr. Ma brought a letter to her. It was from her husband. Without taking it to her room, she opened it in the kitchen.

Mei,

> *I am coming home next Wednesday. At this point, it looks like I should be able to take the afternoon bus from Wuhan, and it should arrive in Shanghai in the late afternoon. I don't have the bus schedule, but it is the only bus for the day. Could you meet me at the bus station?*
>
> *Can't wait to see you.*

Da-Ming
September 15, 1941

She almost jumped from the kitchen floor in her excitement. It had been a long time since her husband had left, and she wanted to see him badly. She wanted to know everything that had happened to him. Sitting in her chair in the kitchen, she imagined what he would look like. He must be unshaven, malnourished, and thin. The food provided by the army couldn't be very good. Besides, most likely there was never enough food, and meat was a rarity. The soldiers must be lucky to get turnip soup, which consisted of a few slices of turnips in thinly cooked soy broth. He must be exhausted from all the traveling and the battles. Worst of all, he never knew where he was going to sleep at night.

After dinner, when Miss Wong left the dining room, Mr. Lee helped Mei clear the dining table. After she wiped the dining table clean, she thought it might be a good time to bring him the news about the return of her husband. "Mr. Lee, I have a letter here from my husband." She couldn't contain her excitement, pulling the letter out from the envelope. "And he is coming home!"

As usual, Mr. Lee did not react quickly. He stood there with his familiar calm, smiling. "That is good news, Mei, very good news. You must be very excited."

"I can't wait to see him." She tried to contain her joy.

"Do we know if he is coming back to stay or just to visit?"

Staring at the letter, she said, "He doesn't say, but I hope he is staying because it has been a year. That's what he promised."

"True. A man should always keep his promises."

"So, do you think I could. . . . ?" She hesitated to finish her sentence.

"Yes, Mei. Upon his arrival, I would like you to take a few days off so that you and your husband can spend some time together. I am sure you two miss each other very much."

"Thank you, Mr. Lee!" She folded the letter and put it back in the envelope. "But what about you, Mr. Lee? There are chores to be done around the house, and Miss Wong may need help too."

"Don't worry, Mei. We will manage. In case you haven't heard, Lily just got a new kitchen. So, it looks like this could be a good time for her to learn to cook something for us! It will be a test of her culinary skills!" He laughed wholeheartedly.

Behind his laugh, Mei sensed his concern; his facial muscles were noticeably tense, and she could see sadness through subtle movements at the corners of his mouth. She realized the importance of her being here for him. "I promise I won't be away too long, Mr. Lee. I think I'll only need a couple of days. As soon as my husband goes back to work, I'll come back here."

"That's very kind of you, Mei. Remember when you were away visiting your parents during the Chinese New Year? We were here by ourselves, and none of us lost an ounce, sad to say. I think all of us here have been over-nourished by your extraordinary cooking. I can assure you some fasting could do us some good!"

"That wasn't my plan, Mr. Lee." She giggled.

"I know." He put both his hands together. "Anyway, I am happy for you, Mei. Promise me that you won't think about this place when you are with your husband, and enjoy your time together. And I will see you whenever you are ready to come back."

35

"The eggs are delicious, Lily! This could be a new chapter for us. You cook and—"

"Don't get used to it, De-Chang." She looked at her new appliance. "I just wanted to test out my new stove. It's amazing how efficient it is, and I really like the workmanship."

"You can't go wrong with *Miele*. The Germans know what they're doing."

"Evidently."

"I think you should cook more often, especially since you have this brand-new kitchen. Don't you think so?"

"I believe I have told you this—I *do not* cook."

"But it could be fun!"

"The fact of the matter is," she took a sip of her coffee, "if I put my mind to it, I can do almost anything. It's just that I have no interest in cooking."

"That's too bad. I happen to like to eat!"

"I know you do, and so do I. That's why we hired Mrs. Zhou, right? Besides, women in my family don't cook. My mother certainly never did, nor did my aunts and cousins. Why bother to cook if you have housekeepers and chefs?"

"I suppose that's a good enough reason. It's just a shame that you have this gorgeous kitchen and—"

"Hey, if you want to bring Mrs. Zhou here, I don't care, except I am not home that much. You know that."

"Could we sit on your sofa?" He wanted to get closer to her.

Lily picked up her coffee cup and walked quickly on her bare feet to the velvet red sofa. She put the cup on the coffee table and then tucked her feet in under her thighs. "Thank you for the suggestion, De-Chang. This happens to be my favorite spot in the morning when the sun comes in, although I don't do this often because I sleep late. I just can't imagine those who have to get up early every morning to go to work. It must be a real pain."

"I think most people on this planet do just that, and no one complains." He stood there, debating how close he should get.

"I knew you were going to say that, but I'm not most people. Why don't you sit next to me, right here?" She patted the cushion next to her.

With precision, he cautiously landed himself exactly where her hand had patted.

"That's nice. Can I use your shoulder as my pillow?"

Before he realized what Lily was asking, he felt her head on his left shoulder. He could smell the flowery scent of her shampoo.

"Your shoulder feels a bit bony," she said, adjusting the position of her head. "I suppose you could put on a couple of pounds. Still, you make an excellent headrest, I must say. I like a man with wide shoulders. Could you just lower yourself a bit? There you go."

He felt his heart pounding again, almost the same way it had when they were at the Beethoven concert together quite a while ago. He debated about whether he should use this opportunity to get closer to her, but right away he told himself that he should not make any foolish moves without her permission. "Lily . . ." he said hesitantly.

"Is there something wrong?"

"No, Lily. No."

"Were you going to ask me something?"

"You see. . . ." He rubbed his nose to reduce his nervousness. "We've been engaged for some time, and—"

"Are you worried about me abandoning you?" She adjusted herself and replanted her head on his shoulder.

"I'm not, and I still think you . . . love me."

"Don't be silly, De-Chang. Why do you sound so hesitant?" She sat up. "Let me have a sip of my coffee." She took a swallow and then put her hand on his left thigh. "Are you all right?"

"I am, Lily. I am." He was not all right.

"You seem quite tense all of a sudden," she said casually, entirely in control.

"I do?"

"So, what are you trying to say then?" She sounded prepared.

"I. . . ." He put his hand through his hair. "I sometimes wonder—"

"Wonder about what? Do you get into your *romantic reveries* sometimes?" She giggled. "Sorry, I'm just kidding."

"I wonder if I could. . . ." he felt Lily's eyes on him. "Hold you," he finished.

"Oh, my goodness! You are such a bookworm! Of course, you can." She turned around quickly, and within a fraction of a second, he felt the warmth of her back through her silk pajamas on his chest. Feeling suddenly frozen, his heartbeat racing, he didn't know where to put his hands.

"I thought you wanted to hold me. Where are your hands?" Lily asked impatiently.

"I didn't know if I could. . . ."

"Just a few minutes, okay? Wait a minute. You're holding me too tight."

"I'm sorry. . . ." He felt as if his hands were no longer his, but since he was only given "a few minutes," he knew he had to seize the moment. His hands wrapped around Lily's thin body mechanically and joined in front of her chest, not too tight. He felt her warm, soft bosom beneath the smooth silk pajamas. He wanted to remember this moment. He wanted to say something romantic, but nothing he composed in his head sounded natural.

"Actually, I need to go to the bathroom. Sorry, De-Chang." Lily gently pushed his hands away with hers. She got up quickly as if escaping from him. "Could you get me some more coffee?"

Still feeling the warmth from Lily's body, he remained on the sofa alone, looking outside the window, deflated. After taking a deep breath, he got up and headed to the kitchen.

36

The bus station was crowded, as usual. One could never tell the difference between a weekday and a weekend. Standing in the middle of the waiting lobby, Mei wasn't aware of the luggage and bags hitting her from the people who walked by. She watched mothers carrying their young babies on their backs, while the older ones held the corners of their mothers' jackets. Within a couple of yards from where she stood, one young mother who looked older than her age, wearing a faded blue scarf wrapped around her weathered thin face, held a broken, empty china bowl in front of her three children. The kids were on their knees and had their heads on the cold ground, begging for food. They kept repeating their words, which became like a chant. She couldn't tell which dialect they were speaking.

Mei walked over to the mother, pulled out a coin from her blouse, and put it into her hand. As she walked away, she heard the young mother say in Mandarin, "You must be my sister; you must be my long-waited-for sister."

Mei looked into the teashop and remembered the day when Mr. Lee had come to see her off. It seemed so long ago. The place was still bustling with customers. She came out to the dirt yard and kept looking at the clock above the main gate. Whenever a bus came through the gate, bringing with it dancing dust, she would cover her mouth and check to see if the word Wuhan was on the side of the bus. After seeing more than a dozen buses that were not the right one, she felt tired and frustrated.

Another bus pulled in, and Mei didn't catch the nameplate on it. She reluctantly gazed at it until it came to a full stop. She watched the bus door open, and the passengers struggled to squeeze out with their oversized luggage. Amid the dust, a familiar face emerged in the doorway. He took a quick look around and then stepped down sluggishly, pushing his hat back a bit. When he landed on the ground, he patted his uniform and smoothed it out under his leather belt. He shook his shoulders to adjust the sack on his back.

Mei ran toward him, and within a few feet, stopped and made eye contact. It was indeed him, her husband. They stood there like frozen trees until she rushed into his arms. She felt tears running down her cheeks, wetting his shoulder. When she moved back a bit, she looked at his seasoned, thin face, no longer innocent. There was a healed scar on his left cheek, below which she saw a forced smile. He adjusted the leather strap of his rifle on his right shoulder, and the two of them walked out of the bus station.

● ● ●

Although it had been a year, the small apartment was unchanged except for the unwelcome dust on the furniture. Mei looked at Da-Ming silently while he placed his sack on the floor.

"I need to take a bath, if you don't mind." He sounded exhausted.

"I'll get the hot water ready right away." Mei ran into the kitchen to start some hot water.

While he waited, he stood in the small room and looked at the familiar surroundings. The bed appeared to have a clean sheet on it with two pillows neatly laid side by side. There was a tablecloth covering the old wooden table, and the two familiar chairs were pushed under it. He removed his rifle from his shoulder and leaned it against the corner of the wall. He took everything off his back, and then, finally, he removed his belt.

When Mei walked in the room to tell her husband that the water for the bath was ready, she found him sleeping on the bed and snoring, still wearing his uniform and boots. She removed his boots and pushed his legs over a bit so that he would be more comfortable. Then she sat on the bed with her hands in front of her, not knowing what to do next.

Da-Ming didn't get up until the following afternoon. Mei wasn't home. He went to the washroom, and since the water was cold, he had to wash quickly. When he looked into the broken mirror, he was surprised to see how much he had changed. His face looked thinner and rougher. His facial hair was uneven because he could never get a proper shave on the battlefield. His hair was messy and long. "I need a haircut," he said to himself.

When he came out of the washroom, he saw that Mei had returned. She had bought some vegetables and a small piece of lamb. During dinner, they ate quietly. Mei kept looking at her husband, and she couldn't tell whether he was still tired or if something was on his mind. After a while, she broke the silence. "Fighting a war must be very difficult."

He nodded but did not speak as he chewed his food slowly.

"How is your health?"

"I'm all right. Glad to be alive," he said coldly.

Mei was hoping to hear more from him but sensed he didn't want to say much. "Perhaps we could go for a walk later?"

"Sure."

Feeling encouraged, she started eating. In her head, she wondered what was going on with him. The person she remembered was energetic, loved to laugh, and never hid anything from her. She remembered how optimistic he had been when they first moved to Shanghai. When she was worried about him finding a job, he tried hard to convince her that he would find work—and not just any work but something he would enjoy. He had been right. He enjoyed working for Manager Wang and had learned a lot about various types of weapons. He'd enjoyed his work so much that he never left the plant early. Mei also knew that he was a social person and had friends at work. He liked his chess matches so much that he often lost track of time.

After dinner, as they walked outside, the air felt cool. Da-Ming wrapped himself tightly in his light jacket. Mei, as usual, put her arm through his. She was happy to feel his arm again and have him next to her. "You've been very quiet since you've been back," she said in a concerned voice.

"I'm just tired, that's all."

"You can have all the time you need to rest. Mr. Lee has given me permission to take some time off so that we can be together. I want to take care of you." She put her head on his shoulder and wrapped her arms around him.

She felt his hand in hers. He kept his gaze in the distance. "Mr. Lee must be a great person."

"He is. I meant to tell you that he's also paying for my school."

"His generosity knows no boundaries." There was no enthusiasm in his voice.

"You don't seem very happy for me. . . ."

"I am, Mei. I'm very happy for you." His words sounded hollow, though, as if he just said them out of obligation. "Actually, what I was going to say was. . . . well, when I first saw you at the train station . . . well. . . ." He looked at her closely. "You look different."

"Me, different? How?"

"You look like a city girl now. Yeah, a city girl. That's what I mean."

"You think so? What does a city girl look like?"

"I guess the hairstyle or maybe the clothes."

"As far as I know, I have never thought about my hairstyle, and I still wear the same clothes I brought from Suzhou."

"Perhaps it's the way you carry yourself, which seems different."

"It's funny you say that because I used to never think too much about my own appearance. I guess I do now."

"You look great." He sounded sincere, but she felt no warmth.

"Do you still want me?" She pulled his sleeve, and he stopped walking. "Can you look at me?"

"Don't be silly, Mei. Of course I do. You're my wife." He looked at her and then looked away. "I don't know what has gotten into your head."

"If that's true, perhaps we could. . . ."

"Come on, Mei. I'm tired. I really am."

"I know, but I want my son. I do." *There. Short and to the point.*

"I know. I know. Can we talk about this later? I have a lot on my mind right now." He sounded agitated.

"I know it hasn't been fair to you," she said, feeling guilty. She held his arm tighter. "You were fighting in battles, and I was enjoying the good life in the big city, but. . . ."

"It's all right, Mei. You were also working to pay off our debts. So you were making sacrifices, too." He wrapped his arms around her. "I know this has been hard for both of us, but once the war is over, life will be better. I promise. Let's go home."

●　●　●

Da-Ming had been back for days, and every day he remained subdued and spent a lot of time staring out the window. Whenever Mei asked him if there was anything wrong, he would merely shake his head. She had thought that once he came back, all her worries would be gone. She was wrong.

One day after dinner, seeing him more relaxed, her patience came to an end. "I've been meaning to tell you that it has been a year since you left, and well. . . . when you left to join the army, you said it would only be a year of service."

"You're right. I haven't thought about that much. Time certainly went by quickly." He sounded surprised.

"Are you done?"

"Done with what?" He seemed irritated.

"With the army." She lowered her face to look at him. "Are you going to stay and go back to the factory soon? I'm sure Manager Wang has been expecting you." She felt anxious, her heart palpitating.

He was silent. Even though it was only a couple of minutes, it felt like hours to her. She put her head next to his.

"Well," he finally said, not looking at her, "I wish I were done. I wish I could say that." He shook his head. "I *have* to go back. My comrades need me, and I need to—"

"But you promised!" She raised her voice, grabbing him by the collar. She was surprised by the volume of her voice. "What about us? What about. . . . ?" She couldn't finish the sentence because her lips started trembling.

He once again put his arms around her shoulders. "Look, Mei. This war has been very difficult, and the Japanese are not easy to fight. Their soldiers are much better trained than ours. I wish I could tell you when I'll be done. I want to keep fighting until they are out of our motherland." He sounded very determined, as always.

"So, when are you leaving again?" She wiped tears from her face, preparing herself for the news.

"Next Tuesday, but this time I'm taking the bus, not a boat." He smiled at her awkwardly. He moved closer. "I did miss you and always will. I always carry your letters with me. You see. . . ." He took out her two wrinkled letters from his uniform. "Your letters give me the strength to fight, and I want to—"

Mei put her hand on Da-Ming's mouth. She could no longer control herself; she put her head on his chest and let all her emotions out. She buried her head in his shirt, and the soft fabric muffled the sound of her crying. She felt his hand stroking her hair.

Da-Ming's short stay went by quickly, and once again, Mei was helping him pack for his long bus journey. This time, she was better at it. She knew what he needed. As she was making steamed buns again for him, she remembered the first time she had seen him off in the dark, chilly evening. She still remembered the little boat he rode on and how excited he'd been.

When they arrived at the bus station, she felt as if he had never come home. They sat on the cold bench in the waiting area, and neither of them could come up with anything to say. She kept looking at him as if she were afraid that she would forget what he looked like. He looked back at her occasionally and checked his watch often. Finally, it was time to leave. He stood up first, and she followed. With her arm in his, they walked slowly to the bus door. He turned around and looked at her pensively. "I will write you, Mei."

"Promise me you will be careful." She looked at him wistfully, waiting for confirmation.

"I promise." He grabbed her palm and put it on his face for a few moments and then went inside the bus.

She stood motionless as if she had been nailed to the ground.

Within minutes, the engine started, and the driver closed the door. Behind the dirt-covered window, she saw his face looking at her. As the bus started moving toward the gate, she raised her hand to wave at him. Before long, she could no longer hear the engine, and all she could see was the dust above the horizon.

37

"I heard from Manager Wang that your husband has gone back to the army." Mr. Lee's voice sounded unusual. Hearing no immediate response, he asked, "Are you feeling all right, Mei?"

"I . . . am not, Mr. Lee." Mei stopped drying the last dinner plate. "I thought for sure he was going to stay and resume his old work. I guess Manager Wang must be disappointed."

"We all are. Your husband was an excellent worker, and I think he was about to be promoted if he had stayed."

She felt the growing anger inside of her but did not want to show it. "Mr. Lee, I'm getting tired of apologizing for my husband."

Mr. Lee walked closer. "As much as we are disappointed to lose your husband, his reason for leaving us is admirable and not for selfish reasons, I'm guessing. Once the war is over, we will have him back, right?" He took a sip of his tea. "He has to come back because you are here waiting for him."

"I hope so. But it just seems that he only thinks about what he wants to do."

"Mei, it may seem that way, but I'm sure he cares about you. Men sometimes have trouble expressing and articulating their feelings. But he writes you nice letters, right?"

"True, Mr. Lee. He does write nice letters."

"Let's look at it this way: your husband is our hero. None of us here has the courage that your husband has. He's making the sacrifice for all of us; he is risking his life for all of us to have a better life—a life with dignity without being bullied by foreign powers."

"It's just . . . very hard. Although I can . . . see that, Mr. Lee . . . I. . . ." With blurred vision caused by her tears, she saw her shaking hand barely able to hold the dinner plate.

Mr. Lee took the plate from her shaking hands and put it on the kitchen counter. He then gently placed his hand on her shoulder. "I know this has been very difficult for you, Mei. I know that. And I'm sure this hasn't been an easy choice for your husband either." His hand remained on her shoulder. "He will write you. I am sure of that."

"I worry about him . . . because he is not . . . always careful," she said between choking tears.

"Let's hope for the best. That's all we can do right now." He turned around, ready to go upstairs. "If you need me, Mei, do come get me, all right?" He left the kitchen quietly.

• • •

That night, it took her a long time to fall asleep, and then she kept waking up. Instead of staying in bed and waiting for the sun to come up, she decided to go to the laundry room to get some washing done.

By the time she finished all her washing and walked into the kitchen to get the hot water ready for Mr. Lee's tea, he was already there, drinking his white peony with his newspaper in front of him, sitting in the small chair where she usually sat every day. He was obviously waiting for her. "I'm sorry, Mr. Lee. I seemed to have lost track of time," she said, smoothing her hair. "I was just getting some washing done."

"Good morning, Mei. I guess you didn't sleep well last night?"

"No, I did not." There was no need to pretend.

"Let's hope all goes well with your husband."

She did not answer but decided to sit down across from Mr. Lee, whose presence seemed to have a calming effect on her.

Mr. Lee put his teacup on top of the newspaper, and his smile appeared. "Mei, I have a proposition, which I think could cheer you up."

Although she was not in any mood for any "proposition," she knew she should hear him out. It was her job. "Forgive me, Mr. Lee. My mind is not quite together lately. You were saying . . . a proposition?"

"Yes. I was wondering if you would be interested in accompanying my stepmother on a trip."

"A trip?" She was surprised, unsure if she had heard him right.

"You see, Mei, my stepmother has always wanted to visit Beijing but I can't really let her go on her own in case something happens."

"I see, Mr. Lee."

"She has asked me to go with her, but I'm tied up by my work now. So. . . ."

"What about Miss Wong? She seems to have a lot of free time." She immediately regretted her words. "I shouldn't say that, Mr. Lee. I'm not in a position to say that. I don't really know what Miss Wong does." She added, "Forgive me."

"You are actually right. She *does* have a lot of time on her hands, except there is one problem."

"A problem?"

"Yes. You see, I don't think my stepmother likes Lily," he said calmly, with no hint of regret.

"I am very sorry to hear that, Mr. Lee." She paused to think about Miss Wong. "Actually, I wish I were more like Miss Wong. She is so smart, beautiful, and. . . ."

"But my stepmother has said that she likes *you* very much."

She was very surprised. "Me? I am nobody. I'm just a housekeeper from Suzhou." She had to laugh.

"It's true, Mei. I'm being serious about this." Mr. Lee locked his eyes onto her face. "My stepmother said many times to me that she liked you from the very first time she met you."

"I . . . am very flattered and am trying to recall the first time I met her. . . ." She began rubbing her fingers. "Oh yeah—the night I cooked something when she was here with Miss Wong."

"And you also bought the moon cakes for us, with some trouble, of course."

"Ah yes, I remember that. She was a very nice lady."

"So, should I tell her that you are available to join her?"

"Join her?"

"For the trip to Beijing?"

"Oh yes. Sorry, I'm a bit slow comprehending this morning." She shook her head, scratching her forehead. "If she doesn't mind. I mean Mrs. . . ."

"Frau Elke—that's what she prefers to be called."

"F . . . rau . . . E . . . l . . . ke." It was the longest two words she had ever pronounced.

"Yes. That's perfect. It's a German name. 'Frau' simply means lady or woman in German. All right, I guess that settles it!" Mr. Lee put his hands together. "I will have Mrs. Shen make the travel arrangements immediately, and you both will be leaving this Saturday. Will that be okay?"

"I will do whatever is needed to make Frau Elke comfortable, Mr. Lee. It's my job." She nodded repeatedly.

"Good. To make it easy for my stepmother, we are going to pick her up from her apartment, and then we'll go from there to the train station. Let me know if you need anything before we go, okay?"

"Thank you, Mr. Lee. I mean, thank you for trusting me as your mother's travel companion."

"No, thank *you*, Mei. She will be very thrilled!"

• • •

Saturday was a cloudy day. Mei sat in Mr. Lee's office with her small suitcase next to her, holding a teacup from Mrs. Shen. Never in her dreams had she thought she would have the opportunity to visit Beijing. It had never been realistic for her to think about visiting the northern part of China because it was too far. She had heard about the Great Wall from her father and imagined what it looked like: high and long with large bluish-gray stones. She put the teacup down on an end table and took out the letter she had received that morning from her husband.

> Mei,
>
> Yesterday the Japanese ambushed us, but I escaped unscathed along with a few of my fellow soldiers. Someone among us must have given the Japanese our itinerary and route, but we couldn't find out who that person was. That made me very angry. Sergeant Fang was also upset, and we have told him that we will do our best to find this person before we get ourselves killed.
>
> I hope you weren't too angry with me when I told you I needed to come back. I couldn't leave my brothers behind and enjoy life in the city. I was too naïve when I told you that I would join the army only for one year. It was not very realistic because no one could predict the length of the war. I thought I would be excited to see you, but all I could think of was the battles. Please forgive me. I wish I deserved you.
>
> We have killed many Japanese over the last few weeks, and I try not to think about it too much. All I want is for them to leave our country. But if they don't want to leave, we have to make them. There is no other way.
>
> The mail service in the army is very inconsistent

because of the war. So it's very hard to send letters and
even harder to receive them. I will try to write as often
as possible. Don't worry about me.
        Hope you are well.

Da-Ming
December 29, 1941

The office door suddenly opened, and Mr. Lee, Mrs. Shen, and an older European man walked in urgently. Mei quickly put her husband's letter back inside her bag.

Mr. Lee's face was puzzled as he spoke to Mrs. Shen, "So when did this road blockade start?"

"Only about half an hour ago, when you and Herr Meyer were in the meeting."

"But we don't have much time left, and we still need to go get my mother before we catch the train."

"Those checkpoints will definitely slow you down," Mrs. Shen stated with certainty.

Mr. Lee put his hand under his chin. "This is very hard. Let me think," he said, checking his watch.

"I have an idea," the older European man said. "Why don't we take my car?"

"*Your* car?" Mr. Lee turned to look at him. "Does it make any difference?"

"Yes, it does. I keep my party flag on my car always. It's like my passport whenever I need to pass the Japanese checkpoints. It's faster that way."

"That's not a bad idea, Mr. Lee," Mrs. Shen nodded.

"All right. Let's try that. We're running out of time." Mr. Lee walked quickly to Mei. "Sorry for keeping you waiting. The meeting took longer than I thought. I have someone to take us to the train station. Come and let me introduce you to him." He bent over and grabbed Mei's suitcase and directed her toward the European man. "Herr Meyer, this is Mrs. Zhou. She is my mother's travel companion."

"*Hallo, schöne Frau*, I mean Mrs. Zhou." He smiled and offered his hand. "Mr. Lee has mentioned you a few times."

"It's nice to meet you."

"It's a pleasure to meet *you*! I have heard from Frau Elke about your extraordinary cooking. Perhaps someday I could invite you to cook at my place?"

"We better get going," Mr. Lee interjected.

38

The train ride was expected to last roughly twenty hours. Though it was a long ride, she didn't mind. She was on her way to visit the cultural capital, and she could hardly contain her excitement. Thanks to the soft seats that Mrs. Shen had purchased for them, the journey was comfortable. During lunchtime, both Mei and Frau Elke sat in the dining car, enjoying the food and the scenery outside the window. Among the lush green, farmers, with the help of oxen, worked in the rice fields, which were accentuated by the women's bright-colored scarves. In the distance, villages stood quietly next to small rivers. Occasionally, they saw commercial vehicles next to the railroad on the dirt road.

Frau Elke seemed to be in good spirits. "I have been meaning to ask you, Mrs. Zhou—do you like working for Mr. Lee?" she said, holding her post-meal coffee, her large blue eyes warm.

"Yes, I do. He is a nice person. And by the way, Frau Elke, please call me Mei, if you don't mind."

The German woman nodded with a smile. "Mei. I like the name."

Mei had her teacup next to her. "Mr. Lee has done a lot for me and my husband. Because of him, my husband was able to have his surgery and I have been able to attend school. We just don't know how to repay him." Her answer was longer than she thought it would be.

"I am glad he has been able to help. I know he gets a lot of satisfaction from helping people." Frau Elke had a proud expression on her face. "He was a good child from the very start, and it was easy for me to raise him."

Mei nodded, sensing there was more to come.

"He was always very focused and did very well at school. I sometimes feel he is like a German boy."

"What do you mean by that, Frau Elke?"

"Well, he is very disciplined, and I think that fits his personality very well. He is very much like his father, who was also very disciplined." A waiter came by, and she asked for more coffee.

"Was Mr. Lee Senior also very kind and generous? He must have been."

"Yes, he was. He was a wonderful man, and I miss him very much." Frau Elke showed a subtle display of emotion, blinking her eyes, the corners of her mouth gently squeezing upward. "Thanks to him, I never have to work again." Frau Elke took a sip of her coffee. "I suppose all mothers like to talk about their sons and their families, but in case you haven't noticed, my son is not a big talker."

Mei paused for a moment. "I have sensed that Mr. Lee doesn't waste his words."

"That's a good way to put it, Mrs. Zhou. He is the same way with me sometimes, and I wish he could. . . . I don't know how to say it. . . ."

"Show more emotion, perhaps?"

"Exactly. I was searching for that word, emotion. Anyway, I suppose his lack of emotion is partly my fault."

"I . . . don't quite follow, Frau Elke. What do you mean?" Mei put her teacup down and looked into Frau Elke's eyes.

"You see, Mrs. Zhou—I mean, Mei," Frau Elke glanced at her coffee cup, "I have never given him the encouragement for that." She shook her head. "If I had shown more affection around him, he might have been different."

Mei nodded, unsure how to respond.

"As you have sensed, Mr. Lee likes to keep his feelings to himself. His father was kind of the same way, and I respect that. Perhaps many Chinese men are like that. Quiet." She paused. "There is also the concept of 'saving face' in Chinese culture."

"True. Perhaps he also doesn't want his feelings to affect others?"

"Perhaps." Frau Elke nodded. "But he has been wonderful to me, just wonderful. His actions show more than his words can ever articulate. I have been very lucky."

"Me too." Mei nodded firmly. "Both my husband and I are very grateful."

"Speaking of your husband, do you know where he is now?"

"I don't know, Frau Elke. I wish I did, but it wouldn't make any difference."

"What do you mean?" Frau Elke asked, a concerned expression on her face.

"He is fighting the Japanese somewhere. And that's what he wanted to do." She wanted to say more but decided not to.

"I see. He is a hero. I pray for his safety." Frau Elke patted Mei on her hand. "Shall we go back to our cabin?"

Both Mei and Frau Elke spent the afternoon reading. Mei had brought her schoolbooks with her so that she wouldn't fall behind in her classes. In the evening, the train reduced its speed to allow the passengers to rest comfortably. Mei lay on her bed across from Elke, contemplating the war, her own education, and most of all, her future with her husband. She imagined them having a son soon and how happy they would be. She also imagined what their son would look like, perhaps like his father: dark haired, with a strong jaw and broad shoulders. *He will be strong and brave, just like his father.*

Frau Elke was reading a guidebook about Beijing. From time to time, Mei could hear her making soft nasal sounds as if something she was reading impressed her. Gradually, the constant sound of the train going over each metal rail became something like a sleeping drug. Soon, Mei heard snoring coming from Frau Elke's bed.

The next morning, after breakfast, the train conductor announced that they would be arriving in the capital in less than ten minutes. Frau Elke grabbed Mei hard on the arm with excitement.

Fighting the crowd to walk out of the train station, Frau Elke started looking for a taxi as soon as they came out of the building, while Mei pushed through the crowd with two suitcases in her hands. Luckily, they found a taxi quickly. Without consulting with Mei, Frau

Elke told the driver that they would like to take a detour to Tiananmen Square first before heading for their hotel. Mei was actually very excited about the idea and forgot about how tired she was.

The traffic looked just as bad as in Shanghai. Other than taxis, there were large buses with red-and-white stripes, black government vehicles, bicycles, and rickshaws, which maneuvered through the traffic with nimbleness and speed. Pedestrians were well dressed, but more conservatively than in Shanghai—darker suits and hats for the men and light-gray and warm-toned dresses for the women. Occasionally, children in brighter colors stood out in the crowd. Red was the most common color Mei saw.

When they arrived at the square, Mei was the first to jump out of the car, followed by Frau Elke with her *Leica* in her hand. They both had a photo taken of each other. A middle-aged man in a dark suit walked by and offered to take a photo of Frau Elke and Mei together. Standing next to the German woman, Mei felt a hard squeeze on her shoulder while the man tried to figure out how to use the camera. He said, "Smile" in a victorious voice before he pressed his index finger on the button.

When they arrived at the lobby of the Palace Hotel, Frau Elke asked Mei to pick out some brochures for the daily excursions while she was finishing the registration at the front desk. The staff behind the desk told them that there would be a tour bus going to *Badaling* the next morning, which offered the best view of the Great Wall. They would need to be in the lobby at nine o'clock to catch it. Both of them were very excited.

There were very few tourists on the bus, and the city portion of the bus ride was smooth. As the bus approached the Great Wall, the road became rough, and the driver had to slow down as the road became narrow and rugged. The dirt road wrapped around the hills like a long snake without end. Small country huts perched on the hills, surrounded by carefully raised small patches of gardens that were mainly built for vegetables. Luckily, the uncomfortable ride only lasted less than half an hour.

When they came out of the bus, Mei felt the cool, fresh air, chillier than the air in the city. The tour guide gave the group a short lecture on the history of the Great Wall before he let the people go on their own. Frau Elke put her camera strap over her neck, ready to document her trip. Mei checked her shoes, also getting ready for the climb.

"You know what, Mrs. Zhou?" Frau Elke had a funny look on her face. "I think I underestimated the climbing part of this trip!" She looked at the steep steps ahead, shaking her head.

"Don't worry, Frau Elke. I will help you. That's why I'm here." Mei was also preparing herself for the hills ahead.

"Thank you, Mei. I usually don't think about my age. Only when an occasion like this arises do I have this sudden realization that I may not be fit for this kind of activity anymore. I remember climbing the *Schwarzenstein* in Austria when I was a young girl. It was almost effortless, but time has changed me!"

"That must have been fun!" Mei had no idea where that was.

"It was, but now I think I might be too old for this." She shook her head again. "But here I am. I'm going to climb the Great Wall of China. Please remind me to document this when we get up there. Otherwise, no one is going to believe me!"

"Don't worry, Frau Elke. I am your witness."

Frau Elke took a deep breath, checked the frame count on her camera, and then put her arm through Mei's. "It's too late to change my mind now. Let's go, my dear!"

After the first few minutes, Frau Elke took a short pause. "Actually, the first part of this wall isn't so bad," she said.

"Please hold on to me, Frau Elke. We have some steep hills ahead." It was Mei's responsibility to make sure that the elderly woman returned to Shanghai intact; otherwise, she would have some explaining to do to Mr. Lee. Feeling Frau Elke's firm grip on her arm, Mei was relieved. But before long, Mei could hear labored breathing from the German woman. She purposely slowed down, as Frau Elke had to catch her breath. "Maybe we could walk closer to the side so that you could also get some help from the wall?" Mei asked. She wished she had thought up that idea sooner.

"That makes sense. Thank you, my dear." Frau Elke put her left hand on top of the stones, and this made it easier for her to climb.

When they reached the first observation tower, Mei thought they should take a short break. She suggested that perhaps Frau Elke would like to take some pictures.

"*Das ist wunderschön!*" The German woman finally had a chance to enjoy the view while catching her breath. "You may not believe this, my dear, but this camera gets heavier as I climb higher. Still, I am glad I have it." She started taking pictures. Soon they started photographing each other and letting other people take their picture as well. After a while, they stood side by side, silently looking at the Great Wall snaking over the many hills into the misty distance.

"There is no other place on earth like this," Frau Elke said to Mei over her shoulder. "I think I can do two more towers up, and then I am done. I hope you are not disappointed."

"Don't worry, Frau Elke. I am happy to do whatever you like." She was enjoying the Great Wall herself.

A light lunch was provided when they descended from the Great Wall. The restaurant was located at the foot of the Great Wall, next to many vendors that sold souvenirs. The set lunch consisted of stir-fried pork with garlic and egg drop soup. Although it was nothing fancy, both Mei and Frau Elke enjoyed the simple, flavorful meal. By the time they came back to the hotel, Frau Elke had decided that it would be better to see the Summer Palace the next day instead of rushing to see it today. Mei agreed.

The Great Wall trip seemed to have taken its toll on Frau Elke, who told Mei in the evening after dinner that she just wanted to stay in the room and relax. After washing herself, she sat in her bed reading the tour guidebook. From time to time, she would comment on something she read, but without many references, Mei couldn't quite follow. Before long, her comments stopped. Mei sat by the desk with her English dictionary in hand, trying to expand her vocabulary. Soon, the sound of snoring from Frau Elke made it difficult for her to focus. She put the dictionary on her lap and looked out the window. The trees outside moved about with the wind, and the slow-moving traffic formed a long, golden snake.

• • •

Located in the northwestern part of Beijing, the Summer Palace occupied nearly three square kilometers, most of which was water, and consisted mainly of the Longevity Hill and the Kunming Lake. In 1749, the Qianlong Emperor of the Qing Dynasty commissioned the work for the imperial gardens on the Longevity Hill to celebrate his mother's sixtieth birthday. At sixty meters above the ground, overlooking the Kunming Lake, the hill had many interesting architectural structures, with elegant halls and pavilions, most of which were built in the front of the hill facing the lake. Next to the lake stood the Long Corridor, where the Emperor and his family would come for their walks. It was the official summer residence of the imperial court.

It took both Mei and Frau Elke a while to arrive at the Summer Palace because their taxi driver had car problems. While the driver was fixing the car, Mei sat inside the car and Frau Elke stood on the curb with her hands on her waist. Luckily, it took only ten minutes for the driver to get the engine running again. Once the car was moving, the driver explained what went wrong, but both Mei and Frau Elke couldn't understand what he was saying. The driver must have come from the western part of China, Mei guessed. When they arrived at the main gate of the park, it was closer to noontime. Once they were inside the Palace, Frau Elke acted as if the trouble with the taxi had never taken place, and Mei was relieved.

Near the Benevolent Hall, Frau Elke insisted on buying some snacks, as having a full lunch would take too much time. After the snack, they walked along the Long Corridor, and Frau Elke scrutinized the hand-painted designs above, which consisted of landscapes and small figures dressed in traditional clothing. Before this morning, Frau

Elke had made a plan of what she wanted to do: climb the Longevity Hill first and then have a boat ride on the Kunming Lake afterward. Since neither of them knew how to row, taking the boat tour on the Kunming Lake first seemed to be the default choice.

Painted in Chinese red, the large wooden boat had a flat bottom with benches along the edges of the boat. Two men with their long wooden oars stood on each side of the boat. They walked back and forth, pushing their oars. While en route to completing their loop around the lake, Frau Elke kept herself busy by taking as many pictures as she could, some of which included Mei in them. Mei kept smiling until she felt her facial muscles become stiff.

After having some tea at the Pavilion, Frau Elke walked over to Mei and said, "I didn't realize that there is another hill to climb, as my guidebook has indicated that Beijing is a very flat city. But this one is much smaller than the Great Wall!" She giggled after her statement.

"Well, Frau Elke, you are right. But if we don't get to the top of Longevity Hill, none of us will have longevity. Don't you think?"

Frau Elke laughed wholeheartedly. "All right then, my young friend. We certainly don't want our lives to be shortened. But I need to work on my breathing for the moment." She closed her eyes and extended her hands as if working on a new technique she had just learned in China. Within a few minutes, she proclaimed, "I think I am ready to achieve my *longevity* now!"

Mei walked to Frau Elke and once again offered her arm, and the German woman took it with confidence. Mei kept her pace slow, and luckily, the steps going to the top weren't so steep. Whenever she sensed that the elderly woman was getting breathless, she would pause and point out the beautiful view to her so that Frau Elke would stop and take her pictures, forgetting about being tired.

When they reached the top, Frau Elke said to Mei, while catching her breath, "I never thought my trip to Beijing would require so much climbing. The strength of my legs is not what it used to be. I thought this trip would be cultural sightseeing, not a hiking trip!"

Mei was amused. "Perhaps our next trip together *should* be a hiking one!"

"I don't know, my dear. I would say yes if you had asked me this ten years ago. I just don't have that kind of strength anymore. It's not fun when one gets old."

· · ·

By the time they came back to their hotel room, Frau Elke seemed exhausted. "Mei, there will be no more climbing for me. I don't think anyone comes to Beijing intending to do this much climbing, and my legs are killing me!"

"I promise, Frau Elke, no more climbing—but you're right. I think we have broken the world record of climbing in Beijing!" They both laughed.

Mei looked at one of the brochures and suggested that for the next day, perhaps they could go to *Liulichang*, known as the Antique City. Frau Elke was excited about the idea. For the remainder of the day, they stayed at the hotel. Mei walked around the premises, looking through the gift shops and at the artwork, while Elke stayed in her bed with a book. In the evening, they went to the hotel restaurant and each ordered pork noodles for dinner.

After dinner, Frau Elke went to the front desk to ask the staff for suggestions on what she should look for in the Antique City. The young girl behind the desk suggested that she should be able to find some good jade as well as works on silk of Chinese landscapes or calligraphy. Frau Elke made a note to herself and was looking forward to her next excursion in the Antique City.

Liulichang was a relatively small area in the southern part of the city center. Consisting of antique shops and second-hand bookstores, the area attracted people from everywhere. Frau Elke seemed surprised to see the many foreigners frequenting the narrow streets. Because of her earlier preparations, she and Mei walked into a shop that sold jewelry. She picked out a few pieces for herself and then asked Mei for her zodiac sign. Mei told her that she was a sheep. Frau Elke asked the store owner to bring all the jade pieces that were carvings of sheep. Mei was embarrassed and asked Frau Elke not to buy her anything, but who could change the mind of a German woman? At Frau Elke's insistence, Mei reluctantly chose a small jade sheep. It was carved on a semi-transparent piece of white jade. Frau Elke put it on Mei's neck and smiled at her. "It looks beautiful on you!"

"Thank you very much, Frau Elke." Looking at the jade, she said, "I am not used to people giving me gifts. I don't think I did anything that deserves a gift."

"That's nonsense, my dear young friend. You cooked for me, and now you are my travel companion. This is my way of saying thank you."

"You are very kind, Frau Elke. I will always remember your kindness and generosity." She gave the German woman a bow.

"It's just a very small gift, my dear, and it's my pleasure. In fact, I learned my generosity from the Chinese. Don't forget that I married a Chinese gentleman who was the most generous person I have ever met."

The next street was where *Rongbaozhai was* located. Known for its high-quality artwork, the store specialized in selling reproductions of traditional Chinese paintings, calligraphic works, and original works by contemporary artists. The reproduction process was done using the same material, such as black and colored ink and paper, and the printing plates were made of wood. When the printing was finished, an untrained eye couldn't tell which one was the original and which was the reproduction.

As soon as Frau Elke walked inside the shop, she had her eyes fixed on a Ming-style landscape. She said she liked the warm tone of the silk background and the atmospheric appearance of the landscape. Above the mountain was a short passage of writing that described the mood of the artist as well as the peaceful scenery. She asked the shop assistant to roll it up and put it in a tube for traveling.

With only one day left, they went to *Wangfujing*. Mei's duty was to accompany Frau Elke, who wished to buy a few gifts for herself and her stepson. In a men's clothing store, she found a dark-blue bowtie for Mr. Lee. In the evening, Frau Elke wanted to go to a Western restaurant that she'd found in the guidebook. Mei was embarrassed when a tall waiter in a tuxedo pulled out the red upholstered chair for her to sit in. She felt small and uncomfortable. Upon sitting down, she stared at the skinny crystal glasses that Frau Elke had ordered, not sure what was in them.

"Here's to us." Frau Elke raised her glass. "Thank you again, Mei, for coming with me."

Mei reluctantly picked up the surprisingly heavy glass. "Thank you, too, Frau Elke, for everything. And I also want to thank Mr. Lee." She took a small sip; the drink was slightly sweet.

"I am glad we finally got a chance to get to know each other a bit, and I hope I haven't been too much of a burden to you."

"Burden?" She felt her face getting warm, and she put the glass down. "Frau Elke, I want to make sure that I have been doing a good job so that Mr. Lee will be happy."

"You are very sweet, Mei." She raised her glass again. "And Mr. Lee is happy all right. I haven't seen him happier since he hired you. So thank you."

"Frau Elke?"

"It's true. I can see the joy on his face whenever he talks about you."

"Talks about *me*? I'm just a housekeeper and a cook." She felt a bit uneasy. "I just want to do a good job. I remember burning the rice one night. That was very embarrassing. . . . I thought he was going to fire me."

"Mei, I have a feeling that you have some amazing qualities that you don't even realize."

"You are very kind, Frau Elke. But really, I am nobody, and. . . ." she hesitated for a moment, "and I wish I was more like Miss Wong. She is so smart, beautiful, and educated."

The tall young waiter came back and handed out the menus, first to Frau Elke, and then to Mei. "Our special tonight is baked fresh rainbow trout, which is served with sautéed leek with mushrooms and a whole-grain medley," he said.

"That sounds good. Why don't we just have that? What do you think, Mrs. Zhou?" Frau Elke sounded formal, ready to give the menu back to the waiter.

"Let's do that, Frau Elke." Mei tried to sound formal too, noticing the awkward expression on the waiter's face after she said "Frau Elke."

After the waiter left, Frau Elke resumed her topic. "I understand that you admire Fräulein Lily." She cleared her throat and shook her head. "The truth of the matter is that she has been a puzzle to me, and I don't know how she got into the picture with my son. But you are right. She *is* smart and pretty, but appearance is not everything." She sounded as if she had been waiting to say this for a long time but had never had the opportunity until now. "Maybe it *was* her appearance that caught my son's eyes. And of course, I don't deny the fact that she is intelligent. Do you recall the night that you cooked for us?"

"Yes, I do," Mei said, still processing the long statement from Frau Elke.

"Did you hear our discussion?"

"No. I'm sorry, Frau Elke. I didn't." It was the truth. She'd heard nothing from the kitchen.

"Well, we had a little confrontation that night, and I probably embarrassed my son, who seemed worried about us pulling each other's hair out!" Frau Elke seemed amused rather than upset at sharing her story. "To make a long story short, my dear, we don't seem to see eye to eye on many things."

"I'm sorry to hear that, Frau Elke. But I'm in no position to discuss her." That seemed like the right thing to say.

"It's quite all right. You're correct—you are not. But I *am*. It was quite a while ago. But time can change things. We will see what happens to the two of them." Frau Elke turned her head away as if trying to reflect on something. "I hope you don't mind me saying this, my dear, but I was actually hoping that my son would find someone like you." Frau Elke's warm gaze shifted to Mei, who suddenly felt a surge of heat coming up to her face.

"Thank you, Frau Elke, I am . . . very flattered, but I. . . ." She looked back at Frau Elke, whose gaze remained unchanged. "I think both Mr. Lee and Miss Wong look great together. Besides, someone like me who doesn't have the elegance, education, and status that Miss Wong has, well . . . I think it would be a mistake for Mr. Lee to find someone like me—poor, uneducated, and unsophisticated."

Frau Elke quickly responded, "First of all, don't underrate yourself, my dear. And second, I do agree that Fräulein Lily and my son seem like a perfect match, at least to outsiders. But again, I don't really know what's going on between the two of them because no one tells me anything. So far, he hasn't talked to me about their wedding plans. So something is not right, as they have been engaged for quite a while." She sounded frustrated and grabbed the crystal glass, emptying the remainder of its content in one gulp.

"Don't worry, Frau Elke." Mei wanted to comfort her. "I trust Mr. Lee has everything under control."

"You are right, my young friend. I just have to trust my son."

The food arrived, and Frau Elke raised her wine glass. "Here's to the victory of China and the safe return of your husband! And I hope I get to see you more often."

39

Mei,

Time has gone by faster than I thought it would, and I feel ashamed to have you waiting this long for my return. However, I still do believe that a man should keep his promises; it's just that the war makes everything difficult. I am getting tired of asking for your forgiveness. So upon my return, whenever that time is, let's plan to have a family, all right? Don't be angry with me.

My general health has been good, despite the hardships from poor living conditions and lack of nutrition. I think I am getting better at taking care of myself; I learned a better way to get more rest. Instead of trying to get a full night's sleep, which is rare, I try to get more short naps whenever it's possible. This way,

*I feel less tired, and it makes my appetite better too.
Aren't you proud of me?*

*It sounds like you have been doing very well in the
big city, and I am very impressed by the progress you
have been making at school. Your writing is
sophisticated, and I am amazed by your new
vocabulary; many of the words you have been using I
have never heard of.*

*While you are getting sophisticated and perhaps
even elegant, I imagine, I think I am getting older
much faster than I would have liked; I no longer look
as good as you remember. War does that to you.*

*Tomorrow, we will be going on a long journey, and
I don't know when I will be able to write you again. I
will definitely let you know as soon as I find out when
and where our next long stay will be.*

Please take good care of yourself. I know you will.

Miss you,
Da-Ming
April 7, 1944

As always, Mei put his letter in the top drawer of her dresser, where
she organized his letters in a bundle with the most recent ones on top.
She smoothed her hair before she walked into the kitchen, where Mr.
Lee was getting some hot water for his tea.

"Is everything all right with your husband?" He seemed used to
asking the same question.

"I think he is. They were getting ready to leave again, so I can't
write him until he finds out where his next long stay will be."

Mr. Lee kept his eyes on the floor. "War is like that, but at least he
is all right."

"I worry about him." She sighed.

"But there is some good news, Mei."

"Good news?"

"Yes. You probably haven't read today's paper yet. The Japanese Imperial Army is not doing very well; they are losing a lot of ground."

"That *is* good news, Mr. Lee." She was very pleased. "I suppose this could mean that my husband will be coming home soon."

"*That* we don't know, but I sure hope so. The prediction is that the Japanese may not be able to hold on to Shanghai much longer."

"Their days are numbered." She suddenly thought about Captain Aoki, whom she had not seen for a very long time.

"Yes, you can say that," Mr. Lee replied with a smile. "I hate to change the subject, but. . . ."

The sound of high heels echoed toward the kitchen. Within seconds, Miss Wong, in her light-blue satin *qi-pao*, appeared in the kitchen doorway, her matching light-blue leather purse under her arm. "I hope I am not interrupting anything." The scent of her flowery perfume reached several feet to Mei. "Just want to let you know that I won't be home for dinner."

"Thank you, Miss Wong."

"And is there a number where I can reach you?" Mr. Lee asked in his customary, almost obligatory voice.

"Oh, I will be at the White Orchid Café. You have their number, don't you? And I'll have both of my legs intact upon my return, whenever that might be. So don't worry." She swung her hips sideways a bit and then checked her pearl earrings with her fingers, which were encased in white-laced gloves.

Mei was surprised that Mr. Lee did not know where Miss Wong was going. Frau Elke was right; the dynamics of Mr. Lee and Miss Wong's relationship seemed unusual.

"I will let Mr. Ma know not to lock the gate." There was a sense of disappointment in Mr. Lee's voice. He was not looking at Miss Wong.

"You do that, De-Chang." Miss Wong made a quick spin on her high heels. "Okay, I am on my way, and I am sure you two have a lot to discuss." She dashed in her quick steps toward the front lobby.

"Just wait a second. I need to go close the door after her." Mr. Lee put his teacup down and then left the kitchen.

Mei remembered Mr. Lee telling her that Miss Wong tended to leave the door open whenever she left. How strange this all was, she thought. There was no good answer for it.

Within seconds, Mr. Lee rushed back to the kitchen. "Where were we? Oh, yes. I meant to ask you about your school."

"We have just started reading the *Three Kingdoms*. It's very hard." Mei remained in the same spot.

"That's a long novel with several volumes. And yes, classical Chinese is not easy, but it will help you to understand some of the modern expressions, which draw references from the ancient expressions. I think you are going to enjoy the book very much."

"I think I will, and the teacher is excellent."

"And is this Professor Meng?"

"Yes. Do you know him?"

"I do. He used to teach at St. John's when I was there. After his retirement, I think he wanted to do some part-time teaching. So I am very glad you have him as a teacher. And what about your English class?"

"Ah, yes. We are reading Thomas Hardy's *A Pair of Blue Eyes*. It's been very slow progress for me so far."

"That's a nice story about two men interested in the same woman. I believe that's Hardy's third novel but the first to bear his name."

"You know everything, Mr. Lee!"

"Not really, but for a while, I was very interested in his novels."

"So—" Before Mei could finish her question, she heard the sound of the front door opening, and Mr. Ma rushed in.

"I am sorry to disturb you, young master and Mrs. Zhou, but I have here a note from a messenger for Mrs. Zhou. He said it's urgent."

Mei took the note and opened it immediately. She thought it might be from her husband.

> *Mrs. Zhou,*
>
> > *I am leaving for Yokohama tomorrow. Could you meet me at the corner between Huaihai Road and Songshan Road at five this afternoon?*
>
> *Thank you.*
> *Captain Aoki*

She closed the note and put it in her blouse pocket, feeling her heart beating fast.

"Is everything all right, Mei? You look like you've seen a ghost or something." Mr. Lee looked puzzled.

"I. . . . I'm fine." She checked the clock on the wall, which was showing four thirty-five. "I have to be some place." She saw her hands shaking.

"Right now?" Mr. Lee's eyebrows went up.

"Yes." She smoothed her hair and her blouse. "I'll be right back, Mr. Lee. I promise it won't be long." She tried not to show her nervousness.

"Should I assume you know where you are going?"

Mei nodded quickly.

"Be careful."

"Thank you, Mr. Lee." She felt his gaze following her as she rushed out of the house.

40

When she arrived, she saw three Japanese soldiers standing in front of a gift shop. Two of them were looking at the store window, and the taller one kept checking his watch. It took her a couple of seconds to recognize Captain Aoki. She walked over cautiously, hoping he would catch her eye.

"Ah, Mrs. Zhou. Long time, no see. Thanks very much for coming. I am sorry for the short notice." He removed his hat and smiled at her. "I think the last time we saw each other might have been two years ago. How have you been?"

"I have been . . . fine," she replied, feeling nervous. "Are you leaving tomorrow?"

"Yes. My father is ill, and the military told me that I should go home. I may or may not come back to China, but I didn't want to leave without saying goodbye."

"I hope your father's illness is not life-threatening."

"Hard to say at this point. Things change, and I wasn't prepared to leave, as I have been enjoying the city." He looked down at her as they walked side by side. "I will miss our time together, and I thank you for being my friend. I wish we'd spent more time together." There was a mixture of joy and sadness in his eyes. "I certainly hope you can come to Yokohama to visit me when the war is over. I promise I will show you around."

"I will try, Captain." Although she meant what she said, she knew it would not be possible.

"I enjoyed our chats very much, and thank you for sharing Chinese culture with me. I feel I have learned a lot from you."

"Me too."

He looked around and sighed. "China is such an interesting country. It's a shame that we are at war. When I return, I want to come back as a visitor rather than a soldier. Perhaps then you won't feel as awkward and can teach me more about China?"

"I am glad you like China, but I have a lot of learning to do myself, Captain."

"We all do." He nodded politely. "You seem a bit nervous tonight. Are you worrying about something?" He turned his head toward her.

"I have this strange feeling . . . and I'm usually not like this." She looked around aimlessly, not sure why, rubbing her sweaty hands on her blouse.

They walked slowly toward a side street, and the two other soldiers followed not far behind them. The street was quiet; no one other than the four of them were out. They walked a little further, and Captain

Aoki stopped to check his watch. While he was doing that, Mei walked a few steps ahead of him.

Suddenly, several men in black masks emerged from nowhere and walked stealthily and swiftly toward the Japanese soldiers. Mei heard a few short hollow sounds like knives poking into watermelons, dull and fast. She turned around and saw the two soldiers lying on the ground. A man in a black mask walked toward her and asked, "Are you all right, Miss?"

She nodded but couldn't utter a word. Within seconds, the black masks were gone. Recovering from the shock, she looked for Captain Aoki and saw him struggling to stand straight, his left hand searching for support. Mei moved next to him and let his arm rest on her shoulders. She felt the entire weight of him land on her small body, and she couldn't carry him. Quickly, she lowered herself onto the ground with the captain. She saw blood soaking through his clean uniform in front of his chest. When she looked at his face, she saw a puff of dark-red blood oozing out slowly from the corner of his mouth. "Captain," she cried. She was trembling uncontrollably.

"I . . . am very . . . sorry . . . Mrs. Zhou . . . I'm afraid . . . I won't . . . be able to . . . show you Yokohama."

"Captain Aoki!" Tears blocked her vision, and as they dropped onto his uniform, they mixed with his blood. She used both of her arms to support his head and shoulders.

"Please . . . run . . . before . . . the soldiers . . . catch you. Run!" His eyes were nearly closed. He tried hard to form a smile. "Thank . . . you for . . . being . . . my friend." He choked out a gurgling cough before finally closing his eyes peacefully.

She looked around and saw a small briefcase next to Captain Aoki's body. She grabbed it and put it under his neck, reluctantly lowering his head onto the briefcase. She wanted to scream for help but realized that if either the Chinese or the Japanese caught her, she would be dead. She would be beheaded for killing an imperial soldier or shot for being a traitor.

With no time for hesitation, she ran. She ran as fast as she could, all the way back to Mr. Lee's house, not realizing she had bloodstains on her blouse. When she entered the house, there was no one there. For a brief second, she caught a glimpse of herself in the front lobby mirror and saw the blood. She rushed into the washroom and took off her blouse. With tears still coming down, she washed the blood out as quickly as she could and hung the garment on a hanger. She returned to her room and put on a clean blouse, then went to the bathroom to fix her hair before returning to the kitchen. A short note on the kitchen counter was waiting for her.

Mei,

I hope all went well and that you are safe. There's no need to make dinner for me. See you in the morning.

Lee

She had lost her appetite for dinner and went back to her room. After closing the door, she sat in her chair and opened the dictionary where she had put the postcard from Captain Aoki. She held the postcard in her still-shaking hand and stared at it, imagining

Captain Aoki's parents coming out from their house to welcome their son back.

But he's not going back.

Unlike his fellow soldiers, he had come to China for very different reasons and had died for the wrong reason. His uniform had betrayed him. He should have worn the suit that he'd worn during all their other meetings.

It's too late for that now. Our friendship is finally over.

41

After a short pause, he knocked on her door.

"Mr. Lee? I must have lost track of time." Mei closed the book in her hand. "Is it time for me to—"

"No worries, Mei. I'm sorry to disturb you. I came to tell you that Mr. Ma is not going to be home today." He checked his watch to hide his nervousness. "So instead of cooking, I thought perhaps we could go out to get some steamed soup dumplings?"

"Sure. . . . but what about Miss Wong?"

"She's not coming today. She just called me a short moment ago. So I'm heading to my office now. Could we meet back at the house, say around 5:30 pm?"

"Soup dumplings are my favorite!"

• • •

"Thank you for the delicious treat tonight, Mr. Lee. I really like this restaurant, and the filling of the dumplings was so flavorful, with just the right amount of crab meat and pork."

"And the juice in them was tasty, too," he happily added. "I'm also glad we have, an opportunity to chat, as I've been busy with work and you with your school—plus housework."

"Thank you, Mr. Lee. I hope I have been doing a good job at the house. I know I've been occupied lately, but my main worry is my husband because I have no idea where he is now."

He was silent for a short moment. "I guess it's important for the military not to disclose their maneuvers; hopefully, we will hear from your husband soon." He decided that this would be the right time to ask Mei something he'd had in mind for a while. "Mei, I remember you had to run out one night after receiving a note. Although I prefer not to know the contents of that note, should I assume that everything is okay?"

"Yes, Mr. Lee. It's interesting that you remember it." She looked like she wanted to end the topic.

"Good. I am glad all is fine. As you know, we are at war right now, and I don't want anything to happen to you. It makes me worry that—"

"I'll try to be careful, Mr. Lee," she interrupted.

"Okay. Could we go out for a walk?"

She nodded, and as they walked outside, he saw her take a deep breath. "Ah, the evening air is so soothing," he said. "Oh look, Mei!"

He pointed to the orange-pink clouds in the distance. "The early evening clouds are always beautiful."

"I agree, Mr. Lee. They remind me of the scenery passage that you read to me when I was sick."

"That's right! I like that little book. You have an amazing memory, Mei."

"Sometimes I feel like memory can also bring distress."

"True, Mei. True." He nodded, and at the same time, he purposely made his strides smaller. "Do you have plans for when the war is over?"

"I had hoped that my husband and I could have a son soon. I feel I'm ready to have a family. I can hardly wait. What about you, Mr. Lee?"

He was taken by surprise. "I am not sure yet because I rarely see Lily, and we haven't really talked about our plans yet. Life seems to have a lot of uncertainties, and the war only makes everything more complicated."

"I feel raindrops, Mr. Lee," Mei said, changing the subject.

He looked up and saw large dark clouds moving in. "The weather here sometimes changes fast," he said. Within a few minutes, the rain started to pick up. "We probably should find a place for refuge where we can wait for this rain to stop so we won't get soaked trying to get home." He removed his trench coat and covered both of them with it.

"There's a little tree," Mei said, pointing. They rushed under the tree as the rain began to pour. Soon, the wind started to pick up.

He saw Mei begin to shiver. "May I keep you warm?" He needed her permission and moved closer to her after seeing her nod. He could smell Mei's scent, very different from Lily's—light and earthy rather than flowery. The memory of watching Mei sing from the kitchen doorway when she was ironing his shirts came back. He missed that moment; at the same time, he regretted it had happened. He felt abashed at having stalked her even though it was unintentional. He felt ashamed to have fallen in love with a married woman while he was engaged to Lily.

"Shall we go home, Mr. Lee? The rain is getting lighter."

Her voice brought him out of his trance, and he nodded.

42

Letters from Da-Ming remained erratic, but she still received at least one every four to six weeks. The best ones were usually one to two pages long, telling her details about what he had been doing, but often they were just three or four sentences. She was disappointed when that happened, but she had stopped blaming him. It was hard to tell if he was too lazy to write or if the battles had prevented him from writing. It could have been both factors.

She was pleased that the news started to sound more positive, especially toward the second half of 1944, even though there was no indication that he was coming home soon. Between March and June in 1945, however, she received nothing. She became anxious, as she thought he might have been killed in a battle. She began to ask Mr. Ma several times a day to check and see if there was any mail for her, until finally the older gentleman said, "Mrs. Zhou, I know this has been very difficult for you, but as soon as I see anything for you in the mail, I will jump on my old feet to deliver it straight to you!"

Finally, on the 25th of July, Mr. Lee showed up in the kitchen with a pensive look on his face. "I have just received a telephone call from Dr. Liu that your husband is in the hospital." His voice sounded low and concerned.

"He came back?"

"That is correct. Your husband was injured in a battle and was brought to a local hospital, and he requested to see Dr. Liu, who once saved his life."

"Can I see him tomorrow?"

He hesitated. "Yes. . . . but you need to prepare yourself."

"What do you mean, Mr. Lee? Is he all right?"

"Well, like I said, he is injured, and I think it's quite serious."

"I have always asked him to be careful. Always," she yelled. Within seconds, her anger turned into sadness. "He must have hurt himself badly." She lowered her head, her vision becoming clouded by her tears.

Mr. Lee remained in the same spot. "Dr. Liu is expecting you tomorrow. I can drop you off at the hospital in the morning when I go to work."

Mei nodded, unable to continue the conversation. Mr. Lee hesitated; he seemed to want to say something or do something but did not know what. He sighed quietly and then walked upstairs.

• • •

"Good morning, Mrs. Zhou." Dr. Liu looked the same, except with less hair. "I didn't think we would meet again, not that I didn't want to see you." He had the same warm smile. "I was actually hoping to be able to try your cooking one day, but I guess the war made everything difficult."

"True, Dr. Liu. I wish we had met under a different circumstance."

"Me too. Now, back to business." He sighed. "Your husband was hit by some shrapnel. My guess is that the bomb exploded not far from him."

She immediately stood, her hands moving about on her blouse. "I'm ready to see him."

"Let me take you to his room. It's the same room he was in last time, but Mrs. Zhou," Dr. Liu moved a bit closer, "you need to prepare yourself."

When they walked in, there was only one bed in the room. The room looked as clean as ever, and the familiar windowpanes were open to the front. She recalled once observing the yard below from the same spot. Da-Ming's eyes were wrapped in gauze and so was his chest. She saw his strong hands on top of the blanket moving from time to time. She walked to him quietly and squeezed his fingers.

"Is that you, Mei?" The corners of his mouth moved up slightly.

"Yes, Da-Ming. It's me." She tried to hold back her tears.

"It's nice to hear your voice, so soft and sweet." He sounded relaxed and peaceful.

"I am . . . here." Her voice trembled.

Dr. Liu leaned over to Mei and said quietly, "He seems all right now, but come see me before you go." He then left the room.

When the doctor left, Da-Ming ran his fingers about Mei's face and her hair. "I can tell that you are more beautiful than ever! Your hair must be very stylish."

"Da-Ming, are you in pain?" She ignored his compliment.

"Wow, *you* are what a city girl looks like, I guess."

"Are you in pain?" Mei asked again.

"Unfortunately, I am." Mei saw his face twitching. "It's my fault, Mei. I should have been more careful. I didn't see the big shell coming at me. I just didn't. I only remember the loud sound, and then everything went dark."

Mei couldn't respond. She lowered her head onto Da-Ming's chest, wiping her moist cheeks.

"I am so sorry." He added, "Please forgive me."

"Shhh. . . . please don't talk anymore." She sat next to him quietly for a while, holding his hands in hers, until his fingers stopped moving. "I'll be back tomorrow, okay?"

He didn't reply, and she heard his labored breath emitting soft snores. She got up softly and went downstairs to see Dr. Liu.

"What kind of injury does my husband have, Dr. Liu?"

"Well, we found quite a few pieces of shrapnel in his chest. His eyes also sustained severe damage. He lost a lot of blood. When we examined the damage done to his body. . . . well, let's just say it's a miracle that he's still alive."

"What do you think of his chance for survival?" she asked, fearing the worst.

Dr. Liu hesitated. He gave a deep sigh, shaking his head. "I want to be honest. It's very slim, Mrs. Zhou. I don't want you to get your hopes up. We will try all we can to keep him alive as long as possible, but. . . ." He looked down. "This is the part of my job that I don't enjoy. You need to prepare yourself, Mrs. Zhou. I am very sorry."

• • • •

Mei went to the hospital every day. On the eleventh day after Da-Ming's return, Dr. Liu asked Mei to come to his office. "Mrs. Zhou, time is not on our side, and I need you to ask your husband something very important before it's too late."

"Yes, doctor?"

"When you get a chance, you may want to ask your husband where he would like to be buried. This would bring some comfort to him—and to you," Dr. Liu said kindly but solemnly.

"I will do that, Doctor." Suddenly, she could no longer keep herself calm. "How could he do this?" she cried. "How could he?" Soon, it was hard to breathe. "What about me? How . . . am . . . I going to . . . go on? It's . . . not fair. It's not fair at all!"

Dr. Liu came around the desk and took her hand. "Mrs. Zhou, your husband will be remembered by all of us as a hero for our country. His courage and determination will be admired by generations. You should be very proud of him."

"I am, but, but he is abandoning me. Isn't he?"

Dr. Liu sat there in silence, still holding her hand.

"I've been waiting for him for all these years so that when he came back, we could have a family. He promised. He promised!" She wiped her tears and waited until her breathing was even. "I think I'm ready to see him now." She got up from her chair, and Dr. Liu reluctantly let go of her hand.

When she came to Da-Ming's room, he was propped up against his pillows. Once he heard the familiar footsteps, he turned his face toward the doorway. "Mei, is that you? It's you. I know it."

"How are you feeling today?" Her hand was touching his face and then his hair.

"Not so good. I have pain everywhere." Da-Ming ran his searching hand over Mei's face. "Have you been crying, Mei? Don't be like that. You're a soldier's wife, and you need to be strong." He then found her hand and held it tightly. "You see," his tone softened, "for all these years we have been married. . . ."

Mei once again prepared herself for what her husband was about to say. She just knew that these would be his last words.

"I brought you no joy—only worries. It's a shame you married someone like me."

"That's not true." Her voice became hoarse.

"It *is* true. I did whatever I wanted to and never gave too much thought about how you felt. It was very selfish of me. But I did love you, and I always will. You'll always be my wife." She saw tears coming down his cheeks from under the gauze.

"I know." She put her head gently on his chest. "And you will always be my husband."

"I just wish. . . . I just wish I could have given you a family. I did not forget that was what you wanted. I never did."

"I know you didn't." She put her arms over his chest.

"It's too late, and I'm sorry."

"Please Da-Ming. Don't talk like that."

"It wasn't an easy choice. Believe me. It wasn't. I just had this rage when I thought about our country being occupied by the Japanese."

Mei waited for a short moment before she changed the subject. "Doctor Liu suggested that I ask you where. . . . where you'd like to be buried." It took a great effort for her to finish this sentence, as each word felt weighted like a rock.

"I don't want to be buried in Suzhou. I never liked that place." He seemed to have thought about it already. "I want to be with you, Mei." His face kept twitching in pain. "If you are in Shanghai, I want to be buried in Shanghai. Are you staying in Shanghai?"

"I don't know. I don't know what I'm going to do. But I want to be with you too."

"Perhaps Mr. Lee will hire you—I mean to work for him at his company. What's the name of it? Some kind of German company, I vaguely remember."

"Bayer."

"That's it. *Bayer*. They make painkillers, right? But they don't work too well when you've got what I have—a body in pieces." He shook his head. "I'm not as invincible as I once thought I was. Men are absurd. Do you remember when we first came to the city?"

"Yes. I do." She nodded as if her husband could see her.

"You seemed very worried about us. And I told you that I would get a job, and I did."

"Yes, you did."

He smiled. "Do you remember you were reluctant to marry me?"

"Da-Ming, that's in the past."

"And I convinced you that I would take care of you. It's just this terrible war that messed up my plan."

"Don't think too much, Da-Ming." She tried to distract him by touching his face.

"I know I've been talking too much, much more now than in all the talks we've ever had together. Hey, when you don't have much time left, you might as well let it all out." He held her hands in front of his chest. "I should have taken better care of you, Mei." He stroked her hands gently. "I should have."

"You have given your life for our country, and I am very proud of you," she said, wiping her tears from her cheeks.

• • •

August 15th, 1945, was a day Mei would never forget. Under the clear sunny sky, she saw millions of people on the streets celebrating the surrender of Imperial Japan. On that day, everyone donned joyous looks. Not a single vehicle occupied Huaihai Road as miles of people covered the entire street. It took Mei more than two hours to get to the hospital. When she arrived, everyone in the hallway was smiling, and some were singing.

When she walked into Da-Ming's room, he lay there quietly. No longer did she see any signs of quivering in his body. Occasionally, she did see a tremor in his shoulders. When he felt her hands, his mouth relaxed. She leaned over and said into his ear, "The Japanese surrendered today."

His face froze for a moment as if he couldn't believe his ears.

"Yes, Da-Ming, the Japanese surrendered."

With some great effort, he smiled as big as he could. "My job is done and now I can go." He looked peaceful. He put Mei's hand on his left cheek. "My job is done. Thank you, Mei. Thank you." Under the gauze over his eyes, she could see tears. They ran down his cheek and onto his pillow. "I'm very sorry, Mei."

"Sorry for what?" She put her face next to his.

"For . . . all these years we have been . . . together. . . ." He struggled to finish his words. "I never . . . gave you the affection . . . that you deserved."

Her own tears streamed down her face and dropped onto his neck.

"Please forgive . . . me." His breathing soon became short and labored.

She moved closer to him. He suddenly grabbed both of her hands, and she felt his strong fingers squeezing her own. Gradually, the squeeze became weaker and she felt his fingers loosen. She looked at his calm face for a moment, and then wrapped her arms under his back and held his body without moving. She felt the familiar warmth and the soft skin of his chest. Soon she felt his breathing stop and all was silence, except for his familiar laughter, which resonated in her head. Gradually, it became louder and louder.

43

"I am sorry to have missed Mrs. Zhou's husband's funeral." Lily sat closer to Lee, putting her hand on his shoulder. "How did it go?"

"It went smoothly, but it was difficult."

"So, who was there?"

"Well, it was a small gathering—parents from both sides, my mother, some of his friends from the plant, and Manager Wang."

"I should have been there. I should apologize to Mrs. Zhou sometime today for missing her husband's funeral."

"That won't be necessary. I already told her that you weren't feeling well."

"Oh, thank you. Did Mrs. Zhou give a speech?"

"A short one."

"And?"

"It was . . . good but very difficult for her. She really misses her husband."

"I can imagine. She waited for him for all these years. I guess that's the price of war, unfortunately." She pulled up her blanket. "What about you?"

"What do you mean?"

"I mean, how are you doing? This must have an effect on you."

"I suppose I'm all right."

"You *suppose*? De-Chang, I know you like to keep it all to yourself. But once in a while, you need to let it out. Besides, I *am* your fiancée."

"I know. Well, this has not been easy for Mrs. Zhou or me. She has been working in this house for so many years and—"

"And she is part of this family. Is that what you want to say? She *is* part of this family, and we have an obligation to her, just like we have an obligation to Mr. Ma."

He nodded. It was a good point.

"So, what do you think we should do?"

"I'm not sure."

"Why don't you talk to her? She is obviously very comfortable with you. I can see that."

"Maybe we can talk to her together?"

"No, no. I don't think that's a good idea." Lily shook her head in disapproval. "I can tell she isn't comfortable with me because when we both are present, she becomes kind of businesslike. I know I have a tendency to say whatever comes into my mind, and that bothers people sometimes. You probably don't think I know that, but I do." She wrapped her blanket tighter around herself. "You think I didn't know the reason why you and Frau Elke chose Mrs. Zhou to go to Beijing with her instead of me? And I know I've been condescending toward her in the past. It's in my blood. I got that from my father. So it's partly my own fault, and maybe someday I will pay for that."

"We can only be who we are."

"You are always philosophical about things. Actually, I would like her to stay, if you don't object."

"Really?" He was surprised.

"Yes. It's not really about her cooking, though, as much as I like it. I particularly like the way she does my laundry—she gets all the stains out without damaging the fabric, and she presses all my silk blouses and dresses with absolute perfection. She could practically start her own cleaning business!"

"I'm relieved, Lily. Though I never gave too much thought about this laundry business."

"Well, you like the way she does your shirts. Don't you remember?"

He suddenly recalled that sunny Saturday when he had watched her from the kitchen doorway as she pressed his shirts—the day he fell deeply in love with her. "Yep. Mrs. Zhou does everything well," he said, trying to sound casual.

"The truth of the matter is that if she left, all of us would be devastated, and I think you know exactly what I mean." Lily checked her coffee mug. "Could I trouble you again to go downstairs and get me some more coffee?"

44

May 28th, 1946, was another memorable day for Mei. As a result of her hard work and dedication, she received a certificate of achievement from her adult school, and she was overjoyed. Upon entering the kitchen, she handed the large envelope to Mr. Lee without saying a word, but she couldn't hide her happiness.

"I think this must be your certificate of achievement, if I am not mistaken." Mr. Lee proceeded to open the envelope and gently pull out the cream-colored paper, on which words were written in black calligraphy, surrounded by a blue border, and stamped with a raised seal. "Let me see. Let's look at this together, Mei." Mr. Lee signaled her with a swing of his head. "My goodness, this looks impressive. Why don't you read it?"

She leaned over his shoulder and read, "*This is to certify that Zhou*

Mei has completed all the required courses for Level I Classical Chinese, Level III Modern Chinese Literature, and Level II Conversational English and English Composition." She stopped. "I think there is no need to read the rest."

"Congratulations!" Mr. Lee looked animated, his face glowing with genuine joy. "You did it, Mei. You did it!"

"I wouldn't have been able to accomplish all this work without your help, Mr. Lee. You have done so much for me and my husband. I'm sorry to bring him up. It's . . . it's unimaginable."

"The joy is mine, Mei, and I couldn't be happier for you." His smile remained. "Actually, I have some good news too."

"Oh, Mr. Lee, let me guess. Is it about your wedding?"

"I wish, but it's not. Our company is expanding, and we are hiring right now. I wonder," he cleared his throat, "I wonder if you would be interested in working for us."

"Really?" She couldn't believe her ears. "*Me?*"

"Yes, you!" He sounded as certain as the bell tower on the Bund. "You can start as a file clerk, and promotion begins after six months, assuming your work is solid, which I have no doubt it will be. What do you think?"

"I. . . . I don't know what to say, Mr. Lee. I don't think I am qualified."

"Say yes, Mei. We will train you. Come and work for us." His voice was persuasive. "Your salary will be entry-level at first, which is decent, I think. Mrs. Shen can get that information for you."

"When would you like me to start?" She couldn't contain her excitement. But again she thought, *I know nothing about his company.*

"How about Monday so you have a few days to get ready? In fact, there is another person who also starts on Monday. We can train the two of you together."

"What about the housework?"

"Let's try working for the company for five hours a day and see how it goes. Would that be all right with you?"

"That's more than all right, Mr. Lee." She was thrilled. "But I don't think I have the right kind of clothes for this job." *Almost everything I have was given to me by my mother.* She suddenly realized that she had never had a real job outside the household and needed to look professional.

"We can certainly take care of that. I'll ask Lily to take you out to buy some clothes. She knows where to go, believe me. When it comes to shopping, she is the one you want to be with!"

"Thank you very much, Mr. Lee!"

"Good. I'm going to ask her right now." He turned around and started walking toward the kitchen doorway. "Once again," he paused, looking back and smiling, "congratulations!" He gave her a thumbs-up and then went upstairs.

● ● ●

Mr. Lee was right—Miss Wong knew every women's clothing store in the city. It took her several minutes just to go over all the store names. Upon leaving the house on Saturday after lunch, Miss Wong took the opportunity to educate the small-town bumpkin. She named a dozen brands that she liked for herself, which meant nothing to Mei, who nevertheless tried to listen as attentively as she could and nodded as Miss Wong explained the differences between each designer's styles.

"You see, sis, my favorite dresses have always been Dong Fu Lang's. Others include Bonnie Cashin and Maggy Rouf, but some of their clothes tend to be too flashy to wear at work. I highly recommend Sally Craig's suits, which have subdued, subtle tones but are elegant. All her clothes adhere to your body perfectly. With your slim body, sis, you would *love* her clothes."

"Who is Sally Craig?"

"She is actually from Shanghai but she married an American. Good designer."

As they approached a store, Mei saw two young girls in pink suits and white gloves open the large pair of glass doors long before she and Miss Wong got to the entryway.

As soon as the greasy-haired man in a dark suit and square, green-framed eyeglasses saw Miss Wong walking in, he picked up his telephone handset and whispered firmly into it, "Miss Wong is here. Come quickly! Good afternoon, Miss Wong!" He threw his handset in the air, came around the desk in a quick swirl, and gave a deep bow in front of them—well, actually in front of Miss Wong.

Within seconds, four young women in pink suits flew to the front and took the same bow. Mei felt her face getting warm. Miss Wong gave Mei a subtle poke on the arm before she responded, "Oh hello, Mr. G." She removed her sunglasses.

"There is no true sunshine until we have your grand appearance, Miss Wong!" The man was all smiles.

"Actually, I'm not shopping for me today." Miss Wong turned and put her arm through Mei's. "It's for my little sister. I'm just the consultant."

"Oh, my goodness! How come Miss Wong never told us she has a sister?" His long arms gestured in the air like an ape. "How fortunate we are to have Miss Wong's little sister visiting us today!" The man took a few more steps toward them. "Where would you like to sit? The usual place or near the window?"

"Well, since my sister is here, we're going to try the window seats." Miss Wong pointed to a white leather sofa. "Let's sit here, sis. The light is better here, I think."

Mei hesitated, looking at the smooth white leather sofa for a moment before she slowly lowered herself onto it.

"Quick!" The man waved to the pink-suited women. "Bring all the new styles!" Before Mei realized what was going on, piles of boxes began to fly in front of them.

"Wait a minute," Miss Wong said loudly with her hand up. "When did you get these?"

The man pushed his bizarre eyeglasses up. "Only a week ago." He squeezed his small eyes partway shut. "Well, actually five days ago. I promise these are the newest styles on the market, or—"

"Or what? We get these for free?" Miss Wong giggled.

The man gave an awkward smile. "We *love* your sense of humor, Miss Wong."

"Let's have a look." Miss Wong leaned back and crossed her legs.

The young women in pink suits began to open every box.

"No, no, I don't like the buttons on that dress. That style is nice, but I think the color is too-too bright. I love the pattern on that top, but the style is kind of boring." One of the pink-suited women brought in a cup of coffee for Miss Wong. She took a sip and then said to a couple of the saleswomen, "I would like you two to put on these dresses." Then she turned around to face the other two. "And you two, put on these suits." She gave the command with total ease.

In the end, the decision was made for Mei: she would take one dark-gray suit with padded shoulders and a matching skirt with tightly wrapped hips, one light-blue suit with a short-sleeved top and round collar, and one long, dark-brown dress with a closed narrow collar and slightly puffed sleeves.

"We need some shoes too," Miss Wong proclaimed. Before long, shoe boxes piled up higher than the height of the four serving women. "Let me ask you this, sis." Miss Wong leaned over to Mei. "Do you like the pumps, the Cuban heel, or the Continental heel?"

"I am afraid I know nothing and have no clue."

"All right then. Let's put out four pairs of each style so we can see." Miss Wong gave her order, and three of the four women flew in front of Mei, each holding four boxes.

"Why don't you put on that medium brown pair of Continental heels first? They look nice."

Mei obeyed, letting one of the obsequious, pink-suited women put the shiny shoes on for her. When she stood on her feet, she was afraid to walk.

"It takes practice to walk in those, sis. Okay, those are good candidates. Let's try a pair of black pumps. I hate the Cuban heels; they look too cumbersome!"

Mei felt lost, dazed, and confused. "I don't think I have enough money to pay for all these," Mei said quietly to Miss Wong.

Miss Wong heard nothing; she was too busy directing the store staff. After another half an hour, the final decision on the shoes was made: one pair of medium-brown Continental heels, one pair of black pumps, and one pair of light-blue Cuban heels. Even though Miss Wong hated the style, they matched the light-blue suit.

During all this time, the greasy-haired man ran back and forth between the back room and the front with all the boxes, his rolled sleeves up and his matching green tie caught between boxes. Finally, when it looked like he had done all he could to please Miss Wong, he straightened his tie and pulled down his sleeves before walking over to Miss Wong with a large, black-covered book. "We are so pleased that we were able to help with your sister's needs today. Could I just have your gracious signature here?"

Miss Wong grabbed the Mont Blanc pen and signed without looking. Mei felt totally baffled by this. She looked over from a distance, trying not to embarrass Miss Wong, thinking about what all this could mean. Finally, she pulled at Miss Wong's sleeve.

"Don't worry, sis. It's all taken care of," she whispered back to Mei.

"Lovely. We will have everything delivered to your house first thing tomorrow morning." The man made a big bow before he closed the black-covered book.

"My fiancé's house, please."

"That's what I meant—the light-yellow house with the tall *fleur-de-lis* gate."

45

It had been cloudy for two weeks without one drop of rain. It felt like someone was trying to sneeze but could never get it out. Nature had its own agenda. Perhaps this was why Lily had decided not to visit her friends as much. It seemed she purposely locked herself inside the house and spent most of her time reading, mostly newspapers. She had asked Lee to get all the newspapers in the city for her, and he did, although he knew she couldn't possibly finish reading several hundred pages every day.

"You may not believe this." Lily rushed into the drawing-room to find Lee. She was still in her pajamas, a newspaper in her hand. "Gandhi has just been assassinated."

"What? The world has lost a great man." He was in shock. "If he were still alive, he would be very upset to hear this." Lee put his book down and looked at Lily.

"Your father?"

"Yes, he liked him. He thought highly of him. His favorite quote from Gandhi was, 'An error does not become truth because of multiplied propagation, nor does truth become error because nobody sees it.'"

"Your father must have been a man of great integrity." Lily sounded impressed.

"Do you have any good news to share with me?" He wanted to change the topic.

"Well, sort of. The nationalists, or *Guomindang*, have decided to participate in the 1948 Summer Olympics in London."

"Really? That's only a few months away. With all the chaos currently going on in this country, I doubt they'll bring back any medals. Still, I suppose that's good news." He paused, still keeping his eyes on Lily. "I suppose that's all the major news we have for now?"

"Well, there is more, but I don't know what you are interested in hearing about."

"I don't know either."

Lily ran her hand through her hair and then looked into a small mirror on the end table next to where she was sitting. "You sound like something's on your mind."

"No. . . . not really." He couldn't concentrate on his book, and Lily was still waiting for an answer. "I thought perhaps we should talk about us, if you don't mind."

"I knew it. Let me hear it. Here." Lily patted the space next to her on the sofa. "Why don't you come and sit with me?"

He suddenly remembered what had happened at Lily's apartment when she had done the same thing—asking him to sit next to her, but when he had tried to caress her, everything becoming awkward. He didn't want a repeat of that. "Actually, I think I'd like to sit where I am for the moment." He adjusted his body and put the book on the end table.

"Suit yourself then," Lily said carelessly. "So, what is it that you wanted to talk about?"

"Well," he put both of his hands under his chin, trying to overcome his discomfort, "I had a telephone conversation with my mother, and she asked me about our wedding plans."

"I *see*." Lily's eyebrows went up, and then she nodded. "You know, Frau Elke is not the only person who has been concerned about this marriage; my parents, too, have been very concerned. As you are aware, De-Chang, I know as much as you do about what our culture expects of us, and I have no intention of breaking that expectation or tradition." She sounded very serious, her face solemn.

She paused as if gathering something in her mind, something she had been thinking about for a while. "You probably believe that I have never thought about us during all these years we have been engaged. In fact, I have. I've even fantasized about our wedding. I've thought about how beautiful it would be—we would have all our loved ones with us in a beautiful room filled with pink peonies, my favorite flower. All the windows would be decorated with pink and light-green satin ribbons, and all the children would have white doves in their hands." Lily was animated, her eyes filled with rare emotion.

"That's beautiful, Lily." He moved next to her. "What are we waiting for? I've been ready for many years!"

"The fact of the matter is, I have a predicament, and I don't know what to do."

This was the first time he had heard about this. "So, is there anything I can do to resolve this predicament of yours?"

"I wish you could." She sounded disappointed, almost hopeless. "There are a couple of things. . . ." She seemed to purposely stop her sentence to see his reaction.

"I'm all ears," he said, preparing to come up with ideas to solve his fiancée's problem.

"From the day I met Frau Elke, I sensed right away that she didn't like me, and I've been thinking about that for all these years and can't figure out why."

"I'm sorry you feel this way." He kept his eyes on the floor.

"And I know how important it is for you to have her approval of our marriage. She is the only parent you have. Am I wrong?"

"You are not wrong, Lily. We are indeed very close. I wish my father had siblings."

"There is another thing . . ." Lily looked as if she had prepared for this conversation for a while. She removed the newspaper from her lap and looked straight at him. "I think we both know that the communist victory is imminent, and the nationalists will have to surrender or flee to Taiwan or somewhere."

"Yes, but how does this affect us?"

"Because my father is on the nationalists' side, and he does not want me to stay in China after the communists proclaim victory."

Lee felt as if his head had just been hit by a hammer. "I didn't know this. Why didn't I know this? Your father is a nationalist? I thought he was just a . . . businessman."

"Well, he *is* a businessman, but he hates the communists. According to the communists, we both are capitalists. Do you know what that means? It means that when they win, we could lose everything we have. If we don't lose our heads, we will become dirt poor, like the peasants. And I don't want that to happen to us."

"I certainly don't want to lose my head, although I have no trouble getting rid of all the stuff in this house. But the point of the matter is we will always have each other, right?"

"De-Chang, you can't be serious!" Lily raised her voice, seemingly upset. "First of all, the communists wouldn't hesitate to shoot any of us, given our background. And second of all, even if they have mercy on us and let us live, I am not going to share my meal table with some illiterate communist peasants! You can be sure of that."

He was stunned. "I had no idea this has been on your mind, Lily. Why didn't you share these thoughts with me sooner?"

"I couldn't because this is where you were raised, and I didn't want to hurt your feelings. And now you see my predicament."

He had to pause to gather his thoughts, but he never let his eyes move from Lily. "Are you sure about all this?"

"My father doesn't want to lose his daughter. No parent does." Lily kept her eyes on her hands. "And I trust his predictions. Besides, you know how stubborn parents can be. You can't change the old man's thoughts."

"What should we do then?"

"Well, my father had an idea, which he wanted me to share with you." There was a smile on Lily's face. "My father always wanted a son, but he got me instead. I think that must have been a disappointment for him, although he never showed it. But ever since we have been engaged, he's dreamed about the possibility of having you take over his business one day."

"Having *me* take over his business?" He was surprised again.

"Yes. It makes sense to him. You and your father have both run a successful family business, and you are also the head of Bayer of the China Division."

"I see the logic behind this." He nodded, flattered but not excited about the prospect. "I feel very honored that your father has trust in me, though we have never met. However, this also means that I would have to move to Hong Kong, as I don't see how I could run his business in Shanghai."

"You are correct. It would be very difficult."

"I will need some time to think about this, if you don't mind."

"Oh, there is no rush. Take all the time you need. But. . . ." Lily put her hand on his shoulder, looking straight into his eyes, "I will need to go first."

"What do you mean? You need to go *where* first?"

"My father wants me to leave Shanghai as soon as possible because he doesn't trust the communists."

"And what about—"

"You can come later. I am sure you will need time to make all the arrangements, assuming you want to come with me."

"I wish I had known this *planning* was going on between you and your father sooner." He felt he was not prepared for this conversation. "I'll need some time to think about your father's proposal. But I want to clarify this first: I *do* want to be with you, Lily. I do. I only wish our fate, not that I am a big believer of it, was not determined by the political climate of the country—and perhaps that you would even consider staying in Shanghai with me."

"I want to be with you, too, De-Chang, but I think the chance of me staying here after communist victory is very slim. I don't want to disobey my father. A man of his age tends to be obdurate. I am sure you can understand that." She leaned herself against him, and he felt the warmth of her body.

"I don't want to lose you, Lily." He took her hands and held them tight.

"I know."

46

Two days after New Year's Day in 1949, a letter came from Johnny for Lee and Lily. It said that he was engaged to Ah-Fang, the young woman he'd met at the Peace Café that night several years back. The newly engaged couple would be leaving Shanghai for New York, where Johnny had an uncle in the banking business.

Both Lee and Lily wrote congratulatory letters back to the couple. Lee said that even though he would miss his old friend, he thought New York would be the perfect place for him. Johnny had always been fascinated by America, and it would make sense for him to become his uncle's partner. Ah-Fang had met Lily during her junior and senior years at McTyeire. They both liked nightclubs and enjoyed each other's friendship. Like Lily, Ah-Fang came from a family of successful businessmen who controlled much of the silk trade in southern China.

Lily told her friend that she wanted to be the first to be informed about their wedding date.

Three days before the couple's departure, Lee and Lily met them at the Peace Café again. "I need to remember this restaurant because it's my lucky place," Johnny said to everyone at the table, then turned his face to his fiancée, who was blushing.

"Just don't forget about us when you've arrived in New York," Lee reminded his old friend.

Lily joined in. "Hey, Ah-Fang, make sure you find a good nightclub for us in New York so that I can come for a visit!"

"You can be sure of that!" Ah-Fang reassured her friend.

"What do you think is going to happen to China?" Johnny changed the topic.

"I think the communists are going to win. They have the majority support." Lily sounded certain, as always.

"You think so?" Johnny gave her a skeptical look.

"Yes. To tell you the truth, believe it or not, even I sometimes support the communists because they are for all the people and not just a few. At least it seems that way. Mao may get what he wants."

"Then why are you leaving for Hong Kong?" Johnny seemed puzzled.

"Because of my father. He's siding with the nationalists. You know you can't argue with an old man."

"True. I have the same issue with my father, but I'm leaving the country, and he's not stopping me." Johnny looked determined. "So, what about you two?"

"What *about* us?" Lee didn't want to discuss this topic.

"Well, it sounds like Lily may have to take her father's side. What about you, Lee? Are you a supporter of the communists?"

"I'm not sure." That was the truth.

"Not sure?"

"I haven't given too much thought about who is going to win and what's going to happen to China." He was at least honest.

"That's *so* you, De-Chang. Well, Germany has lost. The strange thing is that you still have a job, my friend." Johnny patted Lee on the shoulder. "Life is such an irony!"

"Indeed, Johnny, indeed. That actually baffles me too. I guess I'll stay there until something happens." He had to laugh.

"I like your attitude. I guess in this age of uncertainty, one has to be like that. So, what's going to happen to both of you?" Johnny seemed to have finally cornered Lee and Lily, and Lee looked at Lily with discomfort.

Before he could answer the question, Lily said, "Well, the impending communist victory has made things a bit more complicated for us. As you know, my father would prefer that I move back to Hong Kong, but I think my fiancé would like to stay in Shanghai. So we still need to work out some issues."

Lee shrugged his shoulders and let his silence show his approval of what Lily had said.

"Perhaps we could all meet in Hong Kong sometime soon?" Ah-Fang jumped in, sounding enthusiastic.

Johnny wrapped his arm around Ah-Fang's shoulders. "That's a nice suggestion, my dear, but we will have to wait and see, right?" He looked at both Lee and Lily.

"That's right, Johnny. We will have to see." Lily had an awkward grin on her face, and Lee nodded. "Have a safe journey to New York," she said.

47

Lily's departure came sooner than Lee had wanted. She decided that she would take the passenger ship *The Red Rose* back to Hong Kong. The ride would be long but more comfortable than a train ride. Besides, she would have a good view for a few days. Lee wanted to buy some gifts for Lily before her departure. He bought her three silk scarves, four blouses, and three pairs of shoes. They went back to Yuyuan Garden one more time to have the flower teas again on the second floor of the teashop overlooking the goldfish pond.

Lily appeared nostalgic. "Time goes by so fast," she said, seeming to search for more words.

"I wish you didn't have to go, Lily. It's all right to change your mind."

"If it weren't for my father, I would probably consider staying. He is a very stubborn man." She shook her head regretfully. "As you know,

I am not against the communists. They were the ones that actually kicked out the Japanese. What we don't know is who will be their next enemy. It could be people like us."

"But that's a chance many of us may have to take."

"Not me, De-Chang." Lily seemed to have made her mind up, and no one could change it. "Speaking of *people like us*, many have already left China. I still wish you would change your mind and meet me in Hong Kong. My father said he has a large house in Aberdeen that is not being used. It would be ours if you could come."

"That's very nice. Please give him my thanks."

"He knows enough about you and the Lee family's reputation. He thinks you are the perfect person for me."

"I am already missing you. . . ."

Lily took his hand, and they walked outside and sat on a bench. Lee sat next to her with his arm wrapped around her shoulders. Lily did not resist and said quietly, "This could be our last time together in this lovely place."

● ● ●

On Sunday afternoon, Lee drove her to the Huangpu Port. From a distance, they saw the staff of *The Red Rose* standing outside the ship and greeting the passengers. Since most of Lily's things went on the ship in a large container, she only had a small suitcase with her. The weather was cloudy with a slight drizzle. After parking the car, they walked slowly toward the ship ladder. Lee stared at the big ship, realizing it would take Lily away from him.

When they got closer to the ladder, Lily put her suitcase down and turned to face him. "If you change your mind, I will be waiting."

He nodded silently, holding her hands. He smelled her gentle flowery perfume again, the same scent she'd worn on their first date. All the memories of their time together suddenly rushed into his mind. He remembered how clumsy he'd been at the French café when he'd forgotten to give her the rose. He also remembered their second date at the Beethoven Concert, when he had wanted to hold her hand and couldn't do it.

"Will you write me?" Lily asked.

"Yes, I will. I will miss you." He felt moisture come to his eyes.

Lily looked at her watch and said, "I think it's time."

He let go of her hands reluctantly. When her fingers slid out from his, he reached out a bit as if trying to get them back. To his surprise, Lily leaned over and kissed him on his left cheek. For a fraction of a second, he thought he was going to lose his equilibrium. In all the years they had been together, this was the first and only kiss he had received from her. He fought hard to regain control.

She turned around and walked quickly toward the ladder. He watched her show her ticket to the uniformed staff member before heading to the upper deck. As she, in her red trench coat, reached the top, he saw Lily find a spot among the waving passengers. She put her suitcase down and started searching for him below. Lee began waving at her, and she waved too, but he didn't know if she could actually see him.

Soon, the ladder was removed and the ship slowly moved away from the dock. A loud siren sounded, and blue smoke came up through the top of the ship. He kept waving at the ship until the right side of the deck turned around to face east.

48

"I haven't seen Miss Wong for a while. Is she still in Shanghai?" Mei sounded unusually curious, smoothing out the sleeves of her business suit.

"She actually left for Hong Kong more than a week ago."

"She did? When is she coming back? I've been meaning to thank her for this suit she bought me. I often feel I don't deserve to wear this kind of fancy clothes. But I guess I need to wear whatever my work requires."

Lee kept his hands on the steering wheel. "Unlike her previous trips to Hong Kong, she is not coming back this time."

"She is *not* coming back?"

"That is correct, Mei. Her father wanted her to move back home."

"But why? I thought . . . you two were getting married?"

"I thought so too. Well, it's a bit more complicated than that. It has to do with the current political climate in our country. Her father is a strong supporter of the nationalists."

"I think I get the picture. My husband was in the nationalist army, but he died before the civil war started."

"As much as I regret what happened to your husband, I feel relieved that he did not have to fight the communists, who will most likely take control of this country."

"I think you are right, Mr. Lee. It does look that way. All the news has been about the communists getting more support by the day." She turned her head to look out the window for a moment. "I tried talking to Mr. Ma about your wedding recently, but he was evasive about it. I guess it makes sense now. I'm sorry to learn this news, Mr. Lee."

"Thank you, Mei. I really appreciate you thinking of me. I think neither Lily nor I could predict this would happen—that the beliefs on the opposite political spectrum could push people apart, even though I don't consider myself to have any political inclinations. I do miss Lily, though."

"That's very sad, Mr. Lee. I was hoping that I would be able to do something for your wedding since you have done so much for me and my husband for all these years."

"You are very kind. I did whatever I had to do, and there are no strings attached. You don't owe me anything. It has been a great pleasure for me to see how much you have accomplished."

"Thank you, Mr. Lee. Without your help, I wouldn't have been able to accomplish what I have accomplished, and I am very grateful."

"I am glad I could help. Oh, by the way," he said as he pulled out a yellow envelope, "could I trouble you to give this to Mrs. Shen before you go to your office? And tell her that I need to run a quick errand?"

"Of course, Mr. Lee."

49

Dear Lily,

I hope your trip back to Hong Kong went smoothly. Unlike your previous trips, I feel like this one actually separated us. It was very hard for me to watch you go. When you left, it felt as if part of me left with you. I have spent many days thinking about you, and your face keeps coming up in my dreams.

You have been very patient with me, and I want to thank you for that. I miss our times together and wouldn't hesitate to repeat them over and over again. You have also helped me understand myself better, as I had never taken the time to think about who I am and what I want. Up to this point, I have been doing what was expected, and that part of me will most likely stay the same.

I have given a lot of thought to your father's idea of moving to Hong Kong. However, as much as I want to be with you, I don't think Hong Kong would be the right place for me, for I have no roots there. I wish I could convince you to return to Shanghai.

There has been a lot of fighting between the communists and the nationalists, but mainly outside the city. I am not insensitive about the war, but I think you are much better at understanding politics than I am. After all, I am still a businessman. I hope you are not disappointed with me, and I will do my best to become a politically responsible person. I feel fortunate to be able to go about my life within my small world.

Mrs. Zhou is still living here; she seems to enjoy working for the company. She is an excellent worker, and I wouldn't be surprised to see her get promoted soon.

Please write when you have time.

De-Chang
January 7, 1949

Two weeks later, he received Lily's response:

Dear De-Chang,

It was good to receive your letter. You are a man who always keeps his promises. My trip went well. The boat was comfortable, and the water was calmer than I had expected. I had a corner cabin to myself, and luckily it was probably the quietest spot on the whole ship. The service was impeccable, although the food was mediocre, unlike Mrs. Zhou's.

I, too, miss our times together, and I wouldn't mind repeating them any day. I only wish I had treated you better. I am sorry you had to put up with all my idiosyncrasies; I couldn't help them. Realizing I won't come back to Shanghai for a while, I have begun to miss the city. I miss my times at McTyeire and all my friends there. I hope they come to visit me in Hong Kong someday.

I should be the one to say, "thank you," as you have been so good to me and taken care of me. Unfortunately, by being who I am, I did nothing in return. You are the most generous man I have ever known. I told my father about everything you have done for me, and he was very touched. He really wants to meet you and has been asking me if you have decided whether to come to Hong Kong or not.

I fully understand your predicament and your reasons for not wanting to come to Hong Kong. Shanghai is, after all, your hometown, and that's where you belong. No one can argue with that.

Thanks for the update on the news. I have a feeling that my prediction will be realized soon. I appreciate your honesty about the war and can't imagine what I would do if I were you. I guess criticizing people is easy, but only when I put myself in their shoes do I realize how difficult it must have been for them to confront their dilemmas. Please forgive me if I have been too blunt about things. Since I am the only child in my family, my parents have certainly spoiled me.

It sounds like Mrs. Zhou is doing exceedingly well, and I am not surprised. She is a smart young woman and has a bright future. I just realized that I never asked you if there had been any changes at Bayer *since the downfall of the Nazis. I guess business is business.*

Look forward to seeing your next letter.

Lily
January 21, 1949

50

Ever since Miss Wong left for Hong Kong, Mr. Ma had begun to lock the front gate early. Mei could hear him whistling his music from her room after she finished her cleaning in the kitchen. The odd part of it was that he did not use to whistle when he went to lock the gate. One night, Mei decided to invite him to have dinner in the kitchen, where she asked him about her recent observation.

"Oh, I don't know. Perhaps I am just happy," Mr. Ma said playfully.

"I'm glad you're happy Mr. Ma, but could you share the source of your happiness with me?"

"You see, Mrs. Zhou, everything happens for reason, and that means that our young master can relax now because Miss Wong is gone for good."

"Do you mean—?"

"Yes. When she was here, our young master always seemed tense and nervous, and I don't think that's what he wanted."

"How do you know what Mr. Lee wants, Mr. Ma?"

"My dear young lady—my *friend*—at my age, I can smell things." Mr. Ma squinted his eyes, looking confident. "I have been with the Lee family for a long time. I can tell you this—though promise me you won't disclose it to anyone."

Mei tightened her lips.

"Okay. Since young master and Miss Wong first met, I had a feeling that he wouldn't be able to handle her; they are two very different types of people."

"I feel bad talking about Mr. Lee and Miss Wong."

"You are not. I am. So don't worry. Don't you want our young master to be happy?"

"Yes, but. . . ."

"Let me do the talking, then. You see," Mr. Ma lowered his voice, "our young master is a very honest person. . . ."

"You don't think Miss Wong is?"

"I am not saying that. All I am saying is that I think our young master wants someone gentle and kind—and attractive, of course. But I don't think Miss Wong wants to be someone's wife, not in the physical sense. I think she can only be someone's wife socially and on paper . . . to save face."

"You mean she was doing this only to fulfill her social obligation?"

"Precisely, Mrs. Zhou." Mr. Ma nodded several times.

"I feel bad for Mr. Lee. So, what do you think Mr. Lee should do?"

"Oh, I don't know, Mrs. Zhou. That's the harder part." He sighed and kept his head down. "Perhaps he should find someone like you!"

"Find someone like *me*?"

"Yes!" Mr. Ma seemed to come to a sudden realization. "Someone like you would be perfect for our young master. Don't you think, Mrs. Zhou?"

"You must be joking! I don't think that's such a good idea, Mr. Ma. Someone like me comes from a small town or perhaps even from a farm, has no or very limited education, both parents are poor, and she has no social status. I just don't see that as a good match. In fact, I never noticed anything wrong between Mr. Lee and Miss Wong. They always looked perfect together, at least whenever I saw them."

"My young friend, that's called 'saving face.' Everyone does that." Mr. Ma stood on his feet. "I think it's getting late. Don't you want me to help you with the dishes?"

"That's all right, Mr. Ma. Thank you for chatting with me."

"Oh, by the way, how is everything at Bayer? Do you like working there?"

"I do, Mr. Ma. I'm learning a lot, and everyone is very nice."

51

Even though all the staff was allowed to have an hour's break for lunch, Mei never took it. Since she was only part-time staff, she felt she couldn't justify taking the full break, even though Mr. Lee said it was okay. She also felt she didn't really need a full lunch; a piece of fruit—an apple or a peach—would usually be enough.

Normally, when the rest of the office staff left for lunch break, she would find something to read. One day at the beginning of May, she was asked to join the three women in her office to go to the waterfront for their lunch break. The reason was simple: perfect weather. Sitting on the large boulder and looking at the cloudless blue sky, Mei remembered her first time here, when she had needed to ask Mr. Lee for help with her husband's surgery.

"So, Sis Mei," a high voice interrupted Mei's thoughts. "How come you never take the lunch break with us?" The woman speaking wiped her small red lips and pushed her curly, long hair back.

"I don't know, Ling Ling. I don't usually get hungry during lunchtime. I normally just bring a piece of fruit."

"Maybe she doesn't think we are civilized enough," the middle-aged woman with short, dark hair said, giggling. She was dressed in a red suit, and on her face, she wore thin black glasses

"That's not nice, Laura. Mei, don't mind her. We're just glad you came to join us today. And we should do this more often." Xiu Yun moved closer to Mei while dusting her tight, light-green dress. Mei could smell her strong perfume.

"So, Sis Mei, all of us have been wondering how you got this job. I mean you must be super smart, right?" Ling Ling asked.

"I. . . ."

Before Mei could figure out how to answer the question, Xiu Yun cut in. "Ling Ling, let's not pressure Mei like that. Maybe she doesn't want to share that information with you. You have got to respect her *privacy*."

"Oh, my goodness, Xiu Yun!" Laura shook her head. "Just because you know a couple of foreign words doesn't mean you have the right to use them to scare us."

"Well, let's change the subject," Ling Ling said. "So, Sis Mei, were you once called Mrs. Zhou?"

"I still am. You can call me that if you like." She stared at her peach, no longer wanting to finish it.

"So, where is your husband? Is he still in Suzhou?"

"Oh boy, you sure are nosy, Ling Ling." Even Laura sounded annoyed. "What's that foreign word again?"

"He is dead," Mei answered flatly.

"I am sorry?"

"Mei said her husband is *dead*, Ling Ling!" Xiu Yun sounded agitated. "Are you happy now?" She took the last bite of her steamed bun.

Suddenly, Ling Ling blushed like a peach. "I am so . . . sorry, Sis Mei." She looked at Laura, perhaps hoping for sympathy, but Laura kept her eyes on the river. "May I ask how he died?"

"Oh c'mon, Ling Ling!" Xiu Yun was clearly getting upset.

"It's quite all right, Xiu Yun. I am happy to answer Ling Ling's question." Mei took a deep breath before she turned toward Ling Ling. "He was severely injured in a battle fighting the Japanese and died in my arms."

"How long ago was that, Mei?" Laura turned her head back from the river.

"It was August 1945. He died on the day the Japanese surrendered."

Silence arrived—it felt almost like death itself. Mei had been hoping to have a joyous lunch break and get to know her office colleagues better. It hadn't been joyous at all, but she had gotten to know them a bit.

"I think it's time for us to go back." Xiu Yun stood first and then lowered her face to look at Mei. "Are you all right?"

●　●　●

Upon returning to the office, Mei discovered a red rose on her desk. Next to it, there was a small envelope. She froze for a moment. *Where could these have come from?*

Seeing her standing there like a statue, the three women with her seemed to smell something juicy and closed in at lightning speed.

"What is it? What is it?"

"Oh, my goodness, she got a red rose and a note card. That's great!"

"That's no surprise. If you had a pretty face like Mei's you would get a rose and a note card too!"

"Hey, that's not funny!"

"What's on the note card?"

"Yeah, what's on the note card?"

Mei passed the envelope to Ling Ling, who opened it in a flash. She read aloud:

> *Please meet me at 188 Cherry Road at two o'clock.*
>
> *Your secret admirer*

There was a brief silence followed by a loud scream. A knock on the door was heard, and then a head popped in. "Is everything all right here?"

"Yes. We are fine." Xiu Yun put her index finger on her lips. "Mei, this is great!"

Laura walked back to her desk with a long face, murmuring, "I wish someone would ask me out." The corners of her mouth dropped.

"Hey Laura, you can't blame Mei. It's not her fault she has a pretty face." Ling Ling sounded sarcastic and a little jealous, her face turning a pale yellow. She shuffled the note card back into Mei's hand, creasing the corner of it before she went back to her desk.

It was Mei's turn to read the note card now. She stared at the simple but elegant handwriting, which looked familiar.

"I'm very happy for you, Mei." Watching Ling Ling throw her paper around on her desk, Xiu Yun whispered in Mei's ear, "I hope he is a gentleman."

"Thank you, Xiu Yun, but I'm not ready to go on a date."

The next hour felt like pure torture. She was curious and wanted to find out who had sent the note, even though she felt she wasn't ready for it yet. She couldn't concentrate on her work and needed to stay calm. From time to time, she pretended to look for something and stole a glance at the clock on the wall. She needed to leave the office at one-thirty so that she would have half an hour to find the address. Mrs. Shen would know where it was.

Since the death of her husband, she'd had no desire to find another man. For nearly a year, she'd dreamed about him almost every night. It felt like he was still alive and had never left. At night, she could hear his voice telling her that he was coming home, coming home to have a family with her. During the day, however, she realized that her imagination had made it all up.

The death of her husband had also triggered the memories of her numerous encounters with Captain Aoki. She remembered with crystal clarity all their times together and his persona, especially his deep, confident voice, his polite demeanor, and most of all, his genuine interest in China.

One thought that scared her the most was the fact that both her husband and Captain Aoki had died in her arms; she had seen with her own eyes and felt with her own arms the last breaths of the two dying men. She could still almost hear the last seconds of their palpitating heartbeats as they struggled and fought to stay, until the eternal darkness arrived, like a giant cloud, weakening each pump of blood and eventually stifling the last hope of life.

In the end, she concluded that she was partially responsible for the death of two men. She was convinced that she had not tried hard enough to stop her husband from joining the army. She could have told him that she might be pregnant, but then she hated herself at the thought of dishonesty. She was also convinced that it was her carelessness that had resulted in the death of her only friend, Captain Aoki. It was clear to her that the masked men thought her life was in danger when they saw her surrounded by the three Japanese soldiers. They probably thought they had saved her life by killing the three soldiers. She would have to carry this burden until the last day of her life.

● ● ●

Holding the note card and the rose, she stood in front of an elegant, white-marble-framed entrance with recessed lights behind its front door. A tall man in a tuxedo and white gloves had already opened the door for her. She checked the address one more time, and it was correct. Before she walked in, she reminded herself that she should stay calm and let this "secret admirer" know that she was not ready to have another man in her life.

As soon as she managed to move her heavy feet past the front door, she saw a familiar person sitting behind a window seat and waving at her. It was Mr. Lee. She was embarrassed to have bumped into him on this unwanted blind date. Unfortunately, it was too late to turn around.

"What a nice surprise to see you here, Mei!" He had a big smile on his face.

"Mr. Lee . . . I am . . . so embarrassed." She managed to get a short sentence out, wishing this blind date had taken place in a different location.

He stood from the small table and pulled the chair across from it out for her as if he had been expecting her. "So, what brought you here, Mei?" His eyes were animated.

"I don't even know how to start," she said, shaking her head. "I received a note card today." She proceeded to pull it out and handed it to Mr. Lee, who read over it quickly and then handed it back to her. "I went out to the waterfront with the people in the office during lunch today, and when I came back, I discovered a red rose and this on my desk." She put the rose on the table.

"What a pretty flower!" Mr. Lee took a quick look at the rose. "It suits you perfectly!"

Mei felt warmth on her face. She must be blushing badly, perhaps even sweating. "I didn't expect this awkward coincidence, Mr. Lee," she said, searching for her handkerchief in her purse. It was nowhere to be found.

"Whoever did this must be a courageous man to ask a beautiful woman like you out."

"I. . . ." She couldn't respond and turned her face away toward the window to calm herself. *I wish there was a place where I could hide right now.* Mr. Lee waited, and it felt like his gaze never left her. "Do you know what time it is, Mr. Lee?" She turned her face away from the window.

"Let's see. . . . well, it looks like that 'secret admirer' of yours is not very punctual." He checked his watch. "It's almost ten minutes past two."

She began to feel as if she were sitting on needles. *If he doesn't show up in five minutes, I'll leave. That's what I'll do.* She made up her mind.

"Well, if this person doesn't show up, I suppose I'll just have to take his place today," Mr. Lee said.

She didn't know what to do or say. She began to ponder who the person could be. She quickly ran through all the male staff from all the offices. *Could it be the short, skinny man in the mailroom? He's always very friendly and gives me naughty smiles. Or perhaps it's the quiet, tall bookworm with thin gold glasses in the accounting office? No, that can't be. He has never even looked at me. So, who could this person be?* Suddenly, she felt a soft hand timidly land on hers. She felt her breathing come to a halt. *What is he doing?*

"Mei, *I* am the man." He looked at her with his usual warm smile, except this time, the muscles above the corners of his mouth quivered nervously. "I was the one who wrote that note card."

"Mister . . . Lee?"

"Mei, I'm very sorry for teasing you like this. Please forgive me." His hand was still on hers.

"Mister. . . ." Mei was debating on whether she should try to move her hand from his or not.

"I feel I have been waiting for this moment all my life." His eyes were filled with emotions she had never seen; they seemed to reveal a mixture of joy, love, longing, and nervousness.

This can't be true.

"What about Miss Wong? I thought you two were. . . ."

Mr. Lee shook his head slowly. "I knew you would ask me this question. As I told you before, Lily does not want to live in Shanghai, and I have no plan to move to Hong Kong, ever."

"But after all these years?"

"Yes. Despite all the years we've been together, I think it would be best that we go our separate ways." He paused. "I think I owe you a better explanation. I thought for a very long time that Lily wanted me, and I was very attracted to her. Perhaps it was just an infatuation, not love. But I thought it *was* love. After all, she said she wanted to marry me. I also thought people would do anything for love, and we both failed that test—she didn't want to stay in Shanghai with me, and I don't want to move to Hong Kong."

"I'm sorry to hear this, Mr. Lee. I assumed that you would eventually work it out."

"Thank you, Mei. You are as kind as always. But I have another confession to make." His eyes focused on his hand covering hers.

"A confession?"

"Yes, Mei. For all the years that you have been here, I have felt something deep inside me, something stronger than the force of nature, except I was too ashamed to disclose it because it was immoral." His eyes became moist, and his lips trembled.

"I . . . don't quite follow, Mr. Lee."

"I have been in love with you—a person who had a husband."

Mei froze, feeling that every organ in her body had stopped functioning. She wanted to say something but couldn't form a coherent sentence.

"Would you like some tea, Mei?" Mr. Lee poured tea into the cup in front of her with his free hand. "You look like you've lost your breath."

After a while, she mechanically opened her mouth. "Mr. Lee, I . . . ." The rest of the sentence seemed to have betrayed her.

"Mei, I am not asking you to love me. I know how much you loved your husband, and I'm not trying to replace him. I can't." Mei felt Mr. Lee squeezing her hand. "But I am asking that you would consider letting me love you."

"I . . . am very touched, Mr. Lee, but why me? I am . . . nobody." She was just a small-town woman with no social status.

"That's not for you to decide." A smile returned to Mr. Lee's face. "All I want is to be able to love you, Mei. Nothing else."

"But what if I can't return your love?"

"I think love takes on many forms. You see, suddenly I sound like an expert on love!" He started laughing nervously and loudly, seemingly at himself.

"Actually, Mr. Lee. I, too, have a confession to make."

"You have something to confess?" Mr. Lee's eyes opened wide in disbelief.

"For all these years, I thought. . . ." she couldn't bring herself to finish the sentence.

"You thought what?" Mr. Lee sounded anxious.

"This is going to sound rude, so please don't be angry with me, Mr. Lee." She pulled her hand back gently and wiped her sweaty palm on her skirt. "I thought you . . . didn't have feelings. Yes, I thought you were incapable of feelings. I'm very sorry, Mr. Lee."

"I'm not offended, Mei. Not at all." He had a faint smile on his face. "I do feel, just like everyone else, except I'm not good at expressing *how* I feel."

"I am just . . . . overwhelmed at the moment." Her nervousness returned.

"I understand how you must feel, Mei, and I can wait. I can wait until the last breath of my life departs." Moisture formed again in Mr. Lee's eyes. It was hard for Mei to believe. "And I promise I will always be by your side until the wind takes me away."

"Thank you." That was all the response she could come up with.

"Shall we go for a walk?"

52

After all the years of waiting, Lee was relieved he had finally told Mei how he felt about her. It all seemed acceptable now—he was a single man, and Mei was a single woman.

After returning to the house, he stayed upstairs and did not make any attempt to go to the kitchen for fear of bumping into Mei, who he felt needed some space and time to consider his proposal. He sat in his leather chair, habitually holding a book in his hands, but his mind had trouble focusing on the words on the page. He thought about how Mei had reacted when he'd dropped the bomb on her and how nervous she'd appeared, not to mention his own discomfort and awkwardness. He wished he could do something to make her feel less nervous but realized this was the only time that his help might make things worse. He also realized that if Mei refused him, their future relationship could be very awkward; Mei wouldn't be able to relax around him, and in the end, he might have to find her another place to live. If it came to that point, everything they had built between them for all these years would go down the drain. He could lose her forever.

He flipped through the pages of his book without paying attention to it, preparing for the potential defeat of his romantic endeavor. A "Plan B" must be in place to secure his future relationship with Mei. He still wanted to be able to see her in the event of her refusal. He would apologize to her by explaining that he had lost his mind and that she should not feel burdened or pressured by his actions. He would tell her that she was still an independent person, free to pursue her own dreams.

• • •

After only a few hours of sleep, he woke up earlier than his normal time and walked into the kitchen with a slight headache. As usual, he discovered both his tea and his hard-boiled egg already waiting for him on the kitchen counter.

"Good morning, Mr. Lee."

He detected a slight nervousness in Mei's voice. She was as well put-together as ever—her short dark hair was neatly combed behind her ears, and her white blouse was carefully pressed, its collar spread over the light-gray suit. There was no sign of make-up or jewelry.

"I thought about your proposal last night, Mr. Lee," Mei said. She looked as if she was trying to hide her nervousness.

"Could we sit down for a moment?" Lee moved to the small table with his tea in one hand, egg in the other, and Mei followed.

"I spent almost the entire night thinking about your proposal, and. . . ." her hands moved nervously about her suit, "it was not easy."

"There's no rush, Mei. And no pressure."

"I know, Mr. Lee." She opened her mouth a couple of times with no words coming out, and then she said, "Someone like me, someone from Suzhou, would never in her wildest dreams think about marrying someone rich, someone like you, Mr. Lee. It wouldn't be realistic, and I would be a laughingstock in Suzhou to even pretend it was possible. I don't have that kind of social status. Besides, I have never considered myself 'beautiful,' as you put it. It often surprises me when people say that about me. However, I do have my own desires and dreams, just like everyone else. You have already helped me so much, Mr. Lee, with my schooling. If I have time, I would like to further my education. Also," she paused for a second, "I would like to have a family. I wish I could have a son."

"I would like to do that for you, Mei—I mean, give you a son," he answered as fast as he could.

"You would?"

He couldn't wait any longer. He dashed to the other side of the table and lowered himself to his knees on the floor, taking Mei's hands into his. "Mei, tell me that you want to be Mrs. Lee, and I will always be with you and protect you with all my strength and my soul." He put her hands onto his chest, searching her eyes. "You don't need to love me; your presence is good enough."

Mei's eyes welled up. "That's not fair to you, Mr. Lee. And I can't bear the burden of being responsible for your happiness. We are not equals, and I am not sure if I can return your love." Her lips trembled.

"Just tell me that you would like to be Mrs. Lee! Promise me," he insisted, not hearing Mei.

"I . . . promise."

53

The wedding party was held on Saturday, June 12th. It was Elke's idea. It was also her idea that the party should be small, unlike the annual Chinese New Year's party. She insisted that only the ones who were close to the family should be invited, and both Lee and Mei agreed, except Mei did not want to invite her parents. Because this would be her second marriage, her parents could just stay in Suzhou and share their joy from there. Lee and Mei would send them a small picture frame containing a pair of butterflies as a symbol of their devotion to each other. Lee was disappointed that Mei's parents wouldn't be present, but he had to respect her wish.

Ever since Elke found out about Lee's engagement to Mei, all her aches and pains seemed to go to the other side of the planet. She spent almost a week taking Mei shopping and refused to let her spend a penny. Almost every day Mei walked into the front lobby with bags in both hands and a guilty look on her face, saying, "I couldn't stop her, Mr. Lee. It's too much."

As the self-appointed wedding planner, Elke also took charge of decorating the ballroom, where the party would be. She hung eight red Chinese lanterns, as well as silk ribbons, from the ceiling. On top of the antique furniture and on all the windowsills, she asked Mr. Ma to make flower arrangements. Thanks to Mrs. Shen, the Chang Brother Jazz Band returned as well. She also found a catering service that specialized in Shanghai and other southern Chinese dishes instead of the usual mixture of "east meets west." Mei was very pleased.

And last, Elke insisted that everyone wear red. Elke herself had a custom-made red dress on, and she had a tailor-made red *qi-pao* created for Mei as well. It had pink peonies on it. As the groom (and following specific instructions from Elke), Lee had his signature beige tuxedo on, accentuated with a red bowtie and a matching handkerchief. Johnny and Ah-Fang flew back from New York, but Lily's other friends weren't present. Herr Meyer and his wife showed up in their Chinese New Year attire. Herr Meyer told the bride and groom that he felt lucky to be able to attend their wedding, as he had planned to retire in August.

When the time came for Lee to give a speech to the guests, he put his right hand behind Mei's back, and the two walked in front of the jazz band. Under the bright lights, he turned around to look at Mei, who had a red rose above her left ear. On her ears and around her neck, she wore no jewelry. She looked humble and somewhat uncomfortable.

Her smile appeared polite and modest. Lee gave a slight bow to the guests and everyone went quiet.

"Dear friends, for most of my life, it seemed that everything had been planned out for me. It felt as if there were a path laid out that I must follow, and so I did—I followed it faithfully. But I didn't know that there was more than one path." He stopped to look at Mei, who also looked back at him. "Never in my dreams did I think I would stand before you with Mei by my side. I think you all know what I mean."

The crowd nodded silently.

"For all these years, I had this belief that a good life meant doing well in school and running a successful business. However, I never fully understood how empty my life was. Only until I met Mei did I finally realize what had been missing in my life."

The crowd applauded, and some, Elke included, wiped their eyes.

He checked Mei again. She looked grateful, the same look on her face that he had seen for many years.

"I am thankful to Mei because she made me realize many things, things that I had never thought of or bothered to think about. Having Mei in my life helped me understand what it means to love someone. It has helped me want to explore a journey together, a journey that brings joy, fulfillment, and most of all, love."

The crowd cheered.

"Mei has also made me realize that there is a life outside of my work—the colorful blooms in my beautiful garden, meticulously attended by Mr. Ma, the birds on my kitchen's windowsills, and the many voices of the wind that bring us strength, desire, and hope." He moved closer to Mei and put his hand around her shoulder. "Mei is not just a woman and a wife—she is my dream." He turned his face to her. "Mei, I hope I deserve you."

The crowd cheered again, and Mei smiled at the crowd, wiping her eyes.

54

He sat in the bed with his pajamas buttoned up to right below his neck. He was sweating. The room was filled with pink peonies, and under the warm candlelight, their scent permeated the entire room. For a moment he felt this room was now no longer *his* room, the one that used to be his father and Elke's when he was young, the room that didn't have much in it except books. He pushed his hair back several times to calm himself, but it didn't work. He began nervously smoothing out the comforter, a new one purchased by Elke, but his effort only made it look more wrinkled.

As he became more agitated, the bedroom door opened slowly, and Mei walked in. Dressed in her red, flowery, silk nightgown, she approached the bed quietly and obediently with her head down. She walked to the left side of the bed, and Lee lifted the comforter for her.

He noticed that Mei, too, had buttoned her gown all the way up to her neck.

He saw her preparing herself to get into the bed with noticeable discomfort as if getting into a place where she did not belong. There was a mixture of hesitance, duty, gratitude, and hope in her attitude. Even though it was only a few seconds, it felt as if hours went by.

"I may need some time, Mr. Lee," she finally said, not looking at him.

"I understand. I understand, Mei." He was not sure why he said it twice, and his hands were moving about aimlessly.

"You seem very tense, Mr. Lee. It's my fault that you are not relaxed." There was a quiver in her voice.

"How about we blow out some candles?"

"I . . . guess."

He jumped out of bed quickly. Within seconds, the room was almost pitch-black. Surprisingly, this made him feel a bit more relaxed. He approached the bed slowly and let himself in without making any sound. "Are you all right, Mei?"

"I . . . think I am. I just . . . need some time."

"Yes, Mei. I am not rushing."

It must have been at least four hours of waiting—or four hours of torture, to be precise—until it finally happened, and then, for the first time in his life, he felt a harmony that he had never experienced or imagined. He saw the water meandering joyously in the river, brushing the gentle weeds on the waterbed; the leaves dancing merrily with the wind, waving at the meadow below; and the white clouds rolling sweetly, caressing the sun.

The memory of first meeting Mei suddenly came back to him. He remembered how timid she had been when she'd first walked into his office, and how he was immediately attracted to her. He also remembered standing in the kitchen doorway on that beautiful, warm Saturday morning, watching her ironing his shirts and listening to her sweet, mellifluous voice. Again, he remembered studying her smooth face, her round eyes, and her small lips when he was teaching her how to read at the small kitchen table.

When his euphoria descended, his mind set out on a new journey. He began to have some understanding of what it was like to take ownership of her body in the literal sense. For a moment, he felt as if Mei had become a part of his body, an extension of who he was or what he had wanted to be. Did he also possess her soul? He wasn't sure.

55

In one night, Mei thought she had become another person, a person Da-Ming wouldn't have liked. She had betrayed him. In fact, she had betrayed him twice. She'd first betrayed him when she befriended Captain Aoki, the Japanese soldier, while he was away fighting the Japanese. And now, she'd made herself the newlywed Mrs. Lee. She imagined Da-Ming coming back from his eternal destination to curse at her, accusing her of conceiving the plan to marry someone rich while he was still alive. She also imagined Da-Ming finding out about her friendship with Captain Aoki and going to the authorities about her crime. Although Mr. Lee was next to her, she did not feel him, not in the flesh and blood, nor anything beyond. His body felt clean but vacant of odor, pulse, and breath. She kept her eyes closed and told herself that the person next to her was still Da-Ming.

She felt a combination of gentleness and uncertainty from Mr. Lee, as if he doubted his own natural abilities. When she woke from her half-sleep, she felt a chill from the core of her heart. In almost total darkness, she saw Mr. Lee lying right next to her. His breathing produced no sound, as if he were not alive; his eyes were closed tightly, as if they were impenetrable; the corners of his mouth moved subtly from time to time, but his lips never opened. When she felt his lips on hers, she experienced uncertainty instead of passion, as if the soul of the kisser was still wandering in the ocean of unforeseen dreams.

• • •

Within days, she discovered more about Mr. Lee. He never let her near him when he was brushing his teeth because he thought it was embarrassing to have toothpaste around his mouth. On his shoe rack, all his shoes were lined up in perfect alignment with the shoelaces tied. All books had bookmarks in them, and he never creased the corners of his books as page-markers. He always kept a small comb in the right pocket of his jacket, and his home office door was always locked when he was not inside.

Although his kindness was still the same after their wedding, Mr. Lee seemed less talkative—not that he had been a big talker to begin with. She often saw him sitting in a chair doing nothing, his eyes staring into the distance as if he were searching for something. He smiled at her more often, though sometimes it seemed forced, and he would come from behind to caress her and kiss her neck. This surprised her because Da-Ming had never done that. She wasn't sure if she liked it because it reminded her of her intimate times with Da-Ming.

"Oh, I'm sorry, Mei. Did I make you feel uncomfortable?" Mr. Lee asked.

"It's . . . fine. I'm just not used to it, that's all." She regretted her short answer.

"I realize that it must be difficult for you to get used to me, even though we have both lived in this house together for so many years." He seemed to know what she was thinking. "Perhaps you could address me by my first name now?"

"I will try, but I'm used to calling you Mr. Lee."

56

He felt a soft touch on his arm. It was Mei's hand. "Sorry to wake you up. Dinner is ready." She pulled a chair next to him. "You look exhausted."

"Oh, Mei. I . . . haven't been sleeping well lately." He grabbed her hand. "And I had a long day at work."

"You forgot to shave this morning before you left for work." Mei had a smile on her face. "This is very uncharacteristic of you. You never touched your tea, either." He felt her hand on his face.

He kissed her hand gently and pressed it closer against his skin. "Ah, I can't seem to get myself together these days."

"I see you have some dark circles around your eyes." He heard her sigh. "I haven't been a good wife, as far as I can see, and—"

"Please don't say that, Mei. I just don't know what has gotten into me these days."

Mei moved her chair in front of him. "I think I know the reason, and I'm sorry . . . sorry for the fact that I have not been—"

"That's not what I meant, Mei. I—" He felt Mei's finger on his lips.

"Let me finish." She took a deep breath and kept her head low. "You have probably been thinking about our marriage a lot. I must confess that part of the reason I married you was out of gratitude because you did so much for me and my deceased husband. Although I did sense on some occasions that you were paying attention to me beyond what was normal for business, the thought of you being interested in me romantically never occurred to me simply because we both come from very different backgrounds. Besides, you were engaged to Miss Wong."

"I know you really loved Da-Ming, and I also know that I can't replace him. I am not trying to. Do you think you could love me, perhaps just a little?" He looked into Mei's eyes.

"I think I *do* love you, just not the same way I loved Da-Ming." She sounded as if she had prepared what she wanted to say beforehand. "I also want to apologize because for all these years, I thought you were incapable of feelings because you always seemed very calm and sedate. . . ."

He covered his eyes with his hand. "I do feel, Mei. I do. I'm just not good at expressing how I feel. It's like everything I say is inadequate, so by keeping myself calm, at least I don't lose myself. But as you can tell, I am not doing a very good job."

"I'm so sorry, Mr. Lee. I promise I will try to. . . ."

"I hope I deserve you." His voice quaked.

"Oh, Mr. Lee, I have a surprise for you!" Mei ran to her room and came back with something in her hand. "I made this for you. Try it on!"

He couldn't believe his eyes.

"Here, let me put it on for you." Mei put the new cardigan on him and dragged him in front of the mirror. "It looks like it fits you! Well, the sleeves seem a bit long." She folded the parts that covered his hands. "There. Much better!"

He was overcome with emotion, and tears started running down his cheeks.

"Isn't navy blue your favorite color, Mr. Lee?"

He nodded, and he kept nodding because no words could come out.

57

Four years of civil war between the communists and the nationalists officially ended on October 1, 1949, when Mao Ze-Dong, on top of the Gate of Heavenly Peace and facing three hundred thousand people, declared the birth of the People's Republic of China. Mei remembered his speech clearly: *The Chinese people have stood up. The era of Chinese people being bullied by foreign powers is over.* The celebration lasted for almost a week. On the new National Day, both Lee and Mei joined the crowd on Huaihai Road with the new Chinese flags in their hands. They kept waving the flags and singing patriotic songs. Mei learned the new songs very quickly; soon she was singing along with the crowd. Mr. Lee seemed less capable of singing. Mei saw him moving his lips but couldn't hear any sound as the singing volume from the crowd overpowered his voice. She could barely hear herself.

Mei's dream of having a son came true in September 1950, when He-Ping was born. She had to stop working so that she could stay home with the baby. The boy grew fast and loved everything. Mr. Lee managed to find some little ducks from a farmer's market and kept them in the backyard. Every day, Mei brought her son out to play with the ducks, which made the baby very happy. His constant giggling worked like the magic of massage, relaxing every bone and nerve in her body.

Soon, it became apparent that the little ducks were convinced that He-Ping must be their parent, and they started following him around. With the assistance of Mei, the boy began tumbling throughout the garden fearlessly, often treading onto the flowers. This inevitably made Mr. Ma very upset. He stood far away with a frown on his face, watching the young boy relentlessly destroy his masterpieces.

When Herr Meyer went back to Germany, Bayer replaced him with a woman representative from Hamburg named Frau Leni. She was a tall, middle-aged woman who wore her blonde hair in an elegant Chignon updo. As Bayer increased its production at the beginning of 1950, Frau Leni started asking Mr. Lee to stay longer at work. As the result, he had to change his dinnertime from six to seven. One night after dinner, he asked Mei, "Do you think we should hire a housekeeper so that it would be easier on you?"

"I think I can manage, Mr. Lee," she said, wiping He-Ping's mouth. "Besides, it will save us some money since we are still adjusting to this new salary system implemented by the new people's government."

"True. I just don't want to exhaust you, that's all. I wish Mr. Ma cooked." He came around and put his arms around her shoulders.

"Actually, you are the one who appears exhausted these days. Just look at those dark circles around your eyes! Is the new boss giving you too much work?"

"Gee, I can't even recall the last time I looked in the mirror." He rubbed his eyes and loosened his shirt collar. "I think I'm doing all right. Frau Leni is a nice woman but is on the pushy side sometimes."

"That doesn't surprise me. Having worked there myself, I know what it's like when the deadline comes near. Everything has to be perfect, just like you!" She walked to the other side of the kitchen and came back with an envelope in her hand. "By the way, this came for you today."

Lee noticed familiar handwriting below the postal stamp with the head of the Queen on it. He felt awkward but did not say anything.

"So, has Miss Wong been writing to you?" Mei asked directly.

"Yes, she has."

"And have you been corresponding with her?" She pushed a bit further.

"No, not since I proposed to you. I keep all her letters in my desk drawer and have never even opened them. There is nothing for you to worry about." He put his arm on her shoulder.

"I'm not worried, just curious. After all, you two were together for almost ten years. You must miss her sometimes. Do you?"

"Occasionally I do. I wonder how she is doing. She is a decent person, although we were not meant to be husband and wife."

"For some reason, I feel responsible for your breakup, even though I never intended for it to happen."

"You did nothing wrong, Mei. I was the one who fell in love with a married woman, shameful to say."

"Do you think you should tell Miss Wong that we are married? Otherwise. . . ."

"I probably should. I probably should."

"I know it will be a hard letter to write, but to keep her guessing is perhaps even worse." The baby started to cry and Mei moved to take him upstairs. "Oh, by the way," she said, stopping, "there's another piece of mail for us. I think it's from the city government." She pointed to a large yellow envelope before she left.

Alone in the kitchen, Lee opened the letter. It read:

Dear Mr. and Mrs. Lee:

> *In searching for an ideal location for our new Youth Activity Center and after considering all possible locations, the Xuhui District Committee has decided that your residence is the perfect choice for this educational and recreational endeavor.*
>
> *You should expect a visit from Secretary Wu sometime within the next two weeks, and your cooperation is greatly appreciated.*

Sincerely,
Xuhui District Housing Authority

58

Secretary Wu was a veteran of both the Second Sino-Japanese War and the Civil War. Since the beginning of 1950, he'd been assigned by the Communist Party to oversee the Xuhui District, where the old French Concession was located. A short, stocky man in his fifties, with a round face and a red complexion, he was courteous and direct. He seemed like a no-nonsense type of person, which had made him very popular in the area. Whenever he walked by people's homes, everyone waved at him. He would ask them how they were doing and if there was anything he could do to help. Mei had met him a few times through local meetings, but Mr. Lee hadn't because he was always at work.

On Sunday, at the agreed-upon time, Secretary Wu showed up after lunch, when Mei had just put her son to bed for a nap. Secretary Wu wore a clean, well-fitting, four-pocket, light-gray Mao jacket with a matching hat. In his upper-left pocket, a black ink pen rested neatly inside. This seemed to be the typical official look for local district leaders. Mei was almost finished cleaning the dishes in the kitchen, and Mr. Lee was upstairs, but he came down as soon as he heard the guest come in. They all sat in the kitchen. As soon as Secretary Wu sat down, Mei brought him tea.

"Thank you for letting me see the house, Mr. and Mrs. Lee," he said, the teacup in his hand. "I have never been to a home this beautiful; it looks like a palace! It must be a lot of work."

Mei looked at Mr. Lee, who gave an awkward smile.

"Well, you both know why I'm here today. So let's get to business. We are looking for a large house with many rooms and a garden outside for the new Youth Activity Center for the Xuhui District, and your house seems to be a perfect choice. I think the children would be very happy to come here."

"We certainly hope this place is good enough for what the district is looking for." Mr. Lee sounded diplomatic.

"The space is certainly large enough, but we may need to do some renovations to fit the equipment in." He took a sip of his hot tea. "For your family, we have found a three-bedroom apartment, and it's not far from here. It's nothing compared to this house, but you do realize that living in a space like this is against our communist principles."

"We do. Only capitalists would live in a place like this," Mr. Lee said matter-of-factly. "That's how it was said in *People's Daily*," he whispered in Mei's ear.

"So, what does it look like?" Mei asked.

"Well, it's on the top floor of a four-story building. The space is quite large by the common-people standard. But the best feature is that all the bedrooms and the living room face south. You'll have plenty of sun throughout the day. If you like, I'd be very happy to show it to you. This is manager-level housing because of Mr. Lee's position at the pharmaceutical company." He gave Mr. Lee a piece of paper that showed the address of the apartment, and Mei came around and looked over her husband's shoulder.

"We want to comply with whatever is expected of us," Mr. Lee said.

"So, Secretary Wu, what exactly does this *manager-level* mean?" Mei grabbed the piece of paper from her husband's hand.

Smiling, Secretary Wu put his teacup on the countertop and put his hands together. "It just means that it is more than one hundred square meters, and it has three bedrooms, plus a kitchen and a bathroom. Most people can't have this, regardless of how big their families are. I know a family that has seven people, and they live in a space less than sixty square meters. It's quite common."

"We are very lucky and grateful. Thank you, Secretary Wu." Mr. Lee looked at Secretary Wu with a smile.

"Secretary Wu," Mei raised her voice and felt Mr. Lee pull at the corner of her blouse discretely. "There are a lot of big houses in this area. I'm just curious why *we* have to vacate our home. I'm sure you recall that my husband has just donated a large amount of money to the district and—"

"The apartment sounds very nice, Secretary Wu," Mr. Lee cut in, and Mei caught the look in his eyes. It displayed a mixture of blame and fear.

"Mr. Lee is a very wise man." Secretary Wu nodded, which seemed to imply authority. "He shows a good understanding of our Communist Party policy."

"So, when can we see the apartment, Secretary Wu?" Mei realized the gravity of this conversation and softened her voice reluctantly.

"How about tomorrow right after dinner, say around seven?"

59

In the weeks that followed, Lee began making arrangements for the move. He invited the director of the Shanghai Museum to come over to see his antique collection and was told that the museum would be happy to take most of what he had, which included antique furniture, porcelain, and the artworks on paper. Lee told the director that it would make sense for him to donate his entire collection so that everyone could come to the museum to enjoy it.

Two nights before their move, he wanted to sit in his backyard after dinner. The sky looked calm and pink, with a few clouds laced with golden outlines from the receding sun. Sitting in his cane chair, he admired the beautiful sky and felt the gentle breeze. He knew this peace and quiet would come to an end soon. Within a short moment, he felt a hand on his shoulder, and a soft voice said, "I hope you don't mind me joining you."

"Not at all, Mei." He sat straight, putting his hand on Mei's.

"How are you feeling, Mr. Lee?" Mei sat down.

"I think I'm all right."

"You are *always* all right. That's something about you I never seem to understand." He sensed the edginess in Mei's voice.

"It's the truth, Mei."

"You must feel something. They're taking away your house, your home, the place you grew up in. And you must have memories of your father, Frau Elke, your school, and everything!"

"I see what you are getting at, Mei." He turned around and took Mei's hands. "There's something about me you don't know. All I want is *you*, Mei. You!"

"But you have me now." Mei seemed calm.

"I know, and I'm grateful. As you can probably tell, everything in this house I inherited; the only thing that is mine is my clothes. What I feel attached to is something you don't see, and that's my memories. I miss my father very much. He was very kind to me." He stroked Mei's hair. "He would be so happy to know that I married you."

"But I don't think I have been giving you the kind of love you deserve, Mr. Lee. You deserve to have a better wife instead of—"

"Please don't say that, Mei." He put his hand over Mei's mouth. "Whatever you have given me is more than I could have ever dreamed of, and I have never been better since I met you. You are the very reason that I look forward to waking up each morning so that I can see you.

And to have you by my side makes me a better person and a stronger person. You are the air and water of my life."

Mei did not respond. He felt her head on his arm, and soon her tears soaked through his sleeve. He should say no more. The silence was all they needed.

● ● ●

The next morning, after Mei finished cleaning the kitchen, Lee asked Mr. Ma to come in so that he could tell him what he had planned for the elderly man.

"Mr. Ma, both Mei and I wanted to share a piece of important news with you, and we want to apologize for not informing you about this sooner. But once you hear what we have to say, we hope you will understand our reluctance." He gave Mei a quick glance. Her face was sad. He said, "You may recall seeing Secretary Wu visiting here recently, and you must have wondered what brought him here."

"Yes, yes, young master. I have been wondering about that, and I can't say he doesn't make me nervous, although he seems like a very nice man."

"Secretary Wu has informed us that this house will be the new Youth Activity Center and the district has found us—meaning Mei, myself, and our son—an apartment." He looked at Mei again, whose eyes were locked onto Mr. Ma, her head shaking.

Mr. Ma did not react immediately. He gave a long sigh and slowly reopened his mouth. "I just knew this would be coming. I read the newspapers every day, and I guess we all have to conform to the new system."

"Precisely, Mr. Ma. But you have given this family your loyal service for many years, so we feel responsible for your life and your well-being."

"We have found a small apartment for you, and we think you're going to like it." Mei put on a forced smile.

"Mrs. Lee and young master, you are my only family, and I wouldn't know what to do without you. I would be lost." Mr. Ma began to choke up. He kept his head low and took out a handkerchief to cover his eyes. "I just knew this was coming."

Lee gave Mei a gentle poke on the arm, and she got up.

"Mr. Ma." She lowered herself. "We are not abandoning you. As you can imagine, our new apartment is too small for all four of us. But the good news is that our apartments are only a few blocks from each other, so we can see each other often. And we will make sure that your rooms are comfortable and that you have enough to eat."

"Thank you, Mrs. Lee, and thank you, young master. I don't know what's wrong with me; perhaps it's old age. As I have gotten older, I have become more sentimental. Please forgive me."

"We know how you feel, and there is nothing to forgive, Mr. Ma. Mei is right; we will be seeing each other a lot. And we will always take care of you as you have taken care of us."

60

Ever since they moved to their new apartment, Mei had been attending the district family meetings required by the city government and organized by Secretary Wu. The purpose of these meetings was for the community to learn about recent party policies and keep everyone in sync with the government so that no one would fall behind. At each meeting, Secretary Wu would introduce the latest party policy and procedures on how to implement them. He began each meeting by reading from handwritten papers and then reiterated what he had read to make sure that everyone had a clear understanding. Mei listened attentively and made notes every time so that she could explain everything to Mr. Lee later.

One night, when they sat at the dinner table, Mr. Lee asked Mei to explain something that she had told him the night before. "I was a bit unclear about our government's effort on achieving equality in our society."

She looked into space, making sure that what she remembered was accurate. "Well, from what I understand, equality needs to be achieved on several levels. On the educational level, within our government there are many of our leaders who were either less educated or uneducated. The government is making an effort to increase the literacy level among its leaders."

"What about within our society?"

She had to check the notes in her notebook. "The reason that we have inequality in our society is that there is a discrepancy among the proletarians, which are the working class, such as factory workers, peasants, soldiers, and others who are not in the non-proletarian category. The non-proletarians include intellectuals and people with a lot of money. While the intellectuals are usually considered bourgeois or bourgeoisie because they possess capital, whatever that means, the rich ones are regarded as capitalists because they are greedy and lazy."

"I see. Are the bourgeois and bourgeoisie considered the enemies of the people?"

"Not from what I understand, *but* anyone who is not a proletarian must work hard to bring himself to the level of the proletarians." She was pleased to be able to convey this clearly.

"So from what you have just said, I guess I'm not a proletarian." He sounded disappointed.

She moved closer to him. "Not yet, but we can work on it. We have already moved out from that big house and donated most of the things in the house to the museum."

"Does that count?"

"Yes, it does. Secretary Wu said so. He even praised me in front of the group today."

"What did he say?"

"This is how he said it to the group: 'This is Mrs. Lee. Even though she married a capitalist or a rich man, she comes from a humble working-class background, and because of that, she should be able to influence her capitalist husband to become one of us!'"

"And how did the group react?"

"Everyone applauded."

"Are there any other people in the group that resemble our background?"

"Not really. I think our background is rather unique. I overheard one woman telling another that I married a filthy capitalist pig."

"What did you say to that woman?"

"I pretended I heard nothing."

"Well, I guess I have some work to do." He sounded as if he were preparing himself for something.

Mei went inside to check He-Ping for a moment and then came back when she saw Mr. Lee reading the newspaper. "You seem . . . different lately, Mr. Lee."

"How do you mean, Mei?" He put the paper down.

"Well, ever since the establishment of the People's Republic, you have been very attentive to what's going on in our country, not that I think you never cared about it before."

"That's a good observation, Mei. Perhaps you are right; it's just I didn't realize it."

"So. . . ."

"I've been reading quite a bit about Chairman Mao lately, and there's a lot about him I didn't know before. He is an amazing person. It must have not been easy to fight both Japanese and the nationalists, both of which were much better equipped and trained than the communists. But Chairman Mao did it. The communists have won. And now I can say—*all* of us can say—that centuries of fighting in China have ended. Don't you find that remarkable?"

"*Only the Communist Party can save China*. That's what Chairman Mao said."

"And because of that, I want to follow the steps of our new government, the people's government."

Mei was impressed. "Well put, Mr. Lee." She paused. "Gee, I'm starting to sound like you!"

They both laughed.

61

Winter 1950 was colder than usual. On most days, clouds occupied the sky and refused to leave. It also seemed unusual that the wind insisted on coming every other day. When inside, Mei put on several layers of clothes to make herself feel warm. He-Ping, on the other hand, did not seem to mind the cold rooms. He only had a couple of layers on him, but his hands were always warm. He spent almost the entire day doodling; he had a fascination with paper and colored pencils, although Mei couldn't easily tell what kind of masterpieces he was creating. On the rare days when a little sun came through the windows, Mei moved there and watched her son, realizing he had quite an imagination.

He could have been Da-Ming's son if Da-Ming had not been killed. She wished she could remove her former husband from her mind.

One day, after putting He-Ping to bed for his post-lunch nap, she went downstairs to collect the mail as usual. As she came back up the stairs, an article on the front page of the *People's Daily* caught her eye. It was from the central government regarding new policies for enemy collaborators during the war.

The New Campaign against the Counterrevolutionaries

> We have knowledge that many people in this country either served in the nationalist army or collaborated with the enemies. It's now the time for those people to come forward and tell us what they did. For those who voluntarily come forward and confess what they did during the war with the nationalists or the Japanese, our government's policy is always lenient. They will receive a lighter sentence or no sentence at all.
>
> However, for those who purposely hide their crimes or shameful secret pasts, the punishment could be severe. Should anyone have any questions regarding this matter, they should contact their local party secretaries.
>
> Trust the Party and trust the people.

She put the newspaper on the table, feeling a chill going through her spine. Old memories of her husband came back. He was the one who joined the nationalist army. Even though he died before the civil war started, the nationalists were still regarded as the enemy of the state, and having a nationalist husband was not a good thing. It could earn her a black dot on her record, according to the new system. She also thought about her friendship with Captain Aoki, with whom she had spent time on many occasions.

We were just friends, she said to herself. She imagined herself explaining her past to Secretary Wu. *Would he believe that I am innocent, or would he have me arrested?*

She was usually talkative during dinnertime. This evening, however, she was reticent and couldn't stop thinking about what she'd read earlier.

"You seem preoccupied with something, Mei. Is everything all right?" Mr. Lee had a worried look on his face.

"There was an article I read in today's newspaper." She pushed the newspaper in front of Mr. Lee, who put down his rice bowl.

He read it silently and quickly. "I can see why you seem worried. Are you thinking about telling the government about your deceased husband?"

She nodded.

"I see. From what I understand, you should be all right because your husband was the one who decided to join the nationalist army, not you. Besides, Secretary Wu seems like a nice person."

"That may not get taken into consideration, Mr. Lee. I'm not worried about myself." She was thinking about her secret friendship with Captain Aoki. "I'm just worried about He-Ping. If I do receive some kind of sentence, someone needs to be at home to take care of him."

"Are you seriously considering turning yourself in?"

"I think I have to. *Trust the party and trust the people.* That's what the *People's Daily* said."

"Will they have a way to find out if you don't tell them?"

"I really don't know. They must have their ways. They must."

That night, Mei couldn't sleep. She turned back and forth on her pillow until she felt Mr. Lee's hand. "Mei, I don't want to lose you." His voice was soft and sad.

She turned to him. "I know, Mr. Lee. I'm just worried about He-Ping, that's all."

"But I'm worried about *you*!"

"The better side of my situation is that I am a proletarian. I own nothing. For that reason, I may receive a lighter sentence, I hope."

"That certainly is an important factor, which I hope the government will take into consideration. But, Mei. . . ."

"Yeah?"

"I have a feeling that our destiny has already been decided for us. I just have this ominous feeling. . . ." He put his arms around Mei.

"Let's try to sleep."

62

After some serious debate, she decided to turn herself in to the district authority. Specifically, she wanted to tell everything to Secretary Wu. She would tell him that Da-Ming decided to join the nationalist army on his own, and it was Captain Aoki who pursued her—and she had no choice but to follow his orders for fear of being killed. All of it was true. Once she put things in perspective, she felt better and calmer. All she needed to do was come up with a plan for the care of He-Ping during her absence.

In the morning, after Mr. Lee left for work and after she and He-Ping had breakfast, she took her son to see Mr. Ma, who was just getting ready to go out for his daily morning walk. He removed his hat as soon as Mei sat down with He-Ping.

"I was just thinking about you and your family, Mei." Mr. Ma put his hat on the table.

"We were thinking about you too, Mr. Ma. How have you been?"

"My back has begun bothering me lately; other than that, I guess I'm all right. The funny thing is, when I was working in the gardens every day, I was fine. But now, since I no longer have to work, my health has started to go bad. Isn't that strange?"

"People say one needs to stay active. That must have some truth in it."

"I have a feeling that you have something important to see me about. Am I wrong?"

"You are not wrong, Mr. Ma. After all these years, you can still always tell if there is something wrong." She opened the *People's Daily* that she'd brought with her, and Mr. Ma put on his reading glasses.

"Is this about your former husband?"

"Yes. I would like to go see Secretary Wu soon."

"And would you like me to watch He-Ping while you are gone?"

"That would be nice. Only briefly, Mr. Ma, if you don't mind."

"Not at all. But does young master know about this?"

"He has some idea but doesn't know how I am going to do this."

"When would you like for me to watch He-Ping?"

"I was thinking tomorrow after I put He-Ping down to nap. Would that work for you?"

"That would be fine." Mr. Ma looked pensive, nodding his head.

"Don't worry, Mr. Ma. I will prepare something for He-Ping when he wakes up. And if I don't make it back by the evening, Mr. Lee should return between six-thirty and seven."

"You can trust me on this, Mei. I hope all goes well with Secretary Wu." Mei felt his hand on hers. "I know I said he seems like a nice person, but something about him scares me a bit, and I don't know why."

"It's all right, Mr. Ma. I used to be scared, too, about a lot of things. But now I feel I am stronger. I'm just worried about my son."

"Don't worry, Mei. Your son will be in good hands."

"Mr. Ma. I can't thank you enough." She held Mr. Ma's hand. "He-Ping is very easy to take care of. He never cries, and he entertains himself. He likes to draw all day. I'll make sure to prepare a lot of food before I go." She stood. "Would tomorrow around four o'clock work for you?"

"See you tomorrow at four, Mei."

63

She did not want to disclose her plan to Mr. Lee, not because she was planning to surprise him but because she was afraid that he would try to stop her. It would be easier if she wrote him a letter explaining everything. Lying right next to him that night, she looked at his peaceful face; his eyes were gently closed, and his lips were even and serene. She moved closer to him and put her head on his pillow. Within minutes, she felt the slight movement of Mr. Lee's head leaning toward hers, but he did not wake.

After thinking all night about what she wanted to say to Mr. Lee, she finally was able to begin her letter after lunch the next day.

Mr. Lee,

I still hope that one day I will be able to address you by your first name. It has been an unforgettable journey with you all these years. Every day, I tell myself how lucky I am to have known you and to have you as my husband. You are a very kind man. I only wish I deserved your love. Since the very first day I met you, my life changed forever. Without you, I would never be able to write this letter. You have made me who I am today, and I am forever grateful to you.

After some very serious debate, I thought it would be wise for me to go see Secretary Wu regarding my deceased husband. As we both believe, given the fact that I played no role in his decision to join the nationalists, I should be able to receive a lighter sentence. What does this mean? I am guessing between a couple of weeks of confinement and community service. These are the kinds of things I have been hearing about. However, I don't know Secretary Wu well enough to make any predictions or to know what will happen to me.

Once I turn myself in, as you can imagine, my life will be in the hands of the government. But I will try to give you a call tomorrow from Secretary Wu's office and let you know their verdict.

He-Ping has a bit of a cough this morning, so I have cooked some bosc pear syrup, which should soothe his throat. Make sure he takes it three times a day. Please tell him that his mother is away on some personal business and that she loves him very much.

I have asked Mr. Ma to come help. If he can't stay long due to my absence, perhaps we could ask Mrs. Shen to find someone for us. I am very sorry for this imposition. I have always had good intentions and

tried my best to be a responsible person. If there is anything that I have done wrong, I can only ask for your forgiveness.
    Please remember me.

Yours forever,
Mei
December 12, 1950

She carefully put the letter in an envelope and sealed it before placing it on the dining table in the hallway for Mr. Ma to give to Mr. Lee. She took a small bag from her closet and put a few personal items in it. A few minutes before four o'clock, she thought she should put on a new jacket, a light-gray cotton jacket given to her by Mr. Lee. She'd been saving it for a special occasion.

When the clock above the dining table struck four, she heard a gentle knock on the door. She let Mr. Ma in quietly, as she did not want to wake up He-Ping. "Thank you for helping me, Mr. Ma."

"Are you sure you want to do this?" Mr. Ma looked as if he wanted to persuade her to change her mind.

"I am all set. I just want to see He-Ping one last time, just in case."

She walked into her son's room, where she saw the young boy sleeping soundlessly, face-up, just like his father. She leaned over and kissed his forehead before she tiptoed out of the room.

"Let me show you something, Mr. Ma." She walked into the kitchen, and Mr. Ma followed. "I have made a lot of food that will last at least a couple of days. And please help yourself whenever you are hungry." She came out from the kitchen and grabbed a sheet of paper from the dining table. "Here is a list I have made for you."

"You have my assurance, Mei. Don't worry." There was a tremble in Mr. Ma's voice. He held the paper in both hands.

"And please give this letter to Mr. Lee when he comes home." She picked up the envelope and put it into Mr. Ma's hand.

"And what should I say to our young master?"

"Everything I needed to say to Mr. Lee is all in this letter." She put her light scarf on and grabbed her small bag. "He-Ping normally sleeps until five, and he can get some snacks when he wakes up. He knows where they are and will be thrilled to see you. If he asks about me, just tell him that I have gone out for some errands."

She felt Mr. Ma's hand on hers. "I hope all goes well for you, Mei, and I look forward to seeing you back." Mr. Ma had a worried look on his face.

"Thank you, Mr. Ma. I am indebted to you." She opened the door, stepped out, and closed it quickly behind her.

As she walked out of the building, she felt the chilly wind on her face. She tightened her scarf and looked up at her windows one last time before she stepped into the wind. Even though she did not know what was awaiting her, she felt she was prepared this time for the unknown destiny ahead.

64

With Mei's letter in hand, he ran as fast as he could. When he arrived at the District Secretary's Office, he saw Mei sitting on the wooden bench alone in the outer room, where he was embraced by cold, damp air. On top of that, there was a strong odor of tobacco.

Mei appeared calm, her eyes fixed on the opposite wall, where there was a large photo of Chairman Mao. Below that were two large slogans written in bold calligraphy:

Without the Communist Party, There Will Be No New China.

Help Us Clean Up Our Society.

"What are you doing here?" Mei looked surprised when she turned her head to face Lee. "You look out of breath and sweaty." He felt her hand on his forehead.

"I was going to ask you the same thing, Mei." He sat next to her. "I was just surprised to see this letter that you left me. Perhaps you could. . . ."

Mei looked down. "You shouldn't have come here, Mr. Lee. I can handle this by myself."

"I don't follow you, Mei. What's going on?"

He saw her tightening her lips as if trying to prevent what was about to come out of her mouth. "Do you remember that Japanese captain who came to our house one night?"

"Yes. That was several years ago. I . . . don't suppose you have anything to do with him?" He put Mei's letter and the newspaper on the bench. "Wait a minute, did something happen between the two of you, and is that the reason you came to this office?" Suddenly, Mei's letter made sense. He felt a sudden surge of blood rush to his head.

She put her index finger next to her mouth. "Shhh. . . . *nothing* happened. Nothing, Mr. Lee. We were just friends."

She sounded innocent and he believed her. "There is no need to say anything anymore. Let's go home." He put his hand under Mei's arm.

She glanced down at the newspaper under the letter he was carrying. "Wait." She removed the letter partially covering the newspaper and read the headline:

THE DAY OF RECKONING FOR ALL TRAITORS OF OUR MOTHERLAND HAS ARRIVED.

Mei's face suddenly looked as white as the wallpaper. Before they could say anything to each other, two tall men in Mao uniforms appeared in front of them. "Secretary Wu is ready to see you, Mrs. Lee."

Mei stood with a formidable force. "I just need to see my son one last time." Lee felt Mei's firm grip on his arm. She turned to look at the uniformed men. "I just need to see my son, very quickly." She walked swiftly toward the door.

"Wait!" both Lee and the two uniformed men said simultaneously behind her.

By the time Lee rushed outside, Mei was already running. He needed to catch her. "Wait, Mei!" He ran after her, his face catching her flying scarf. Mei was faster, and he saw her make a sudden left turn onto another street. "Watch for the traffic!" he shouted from behind. But it was too late.

He heard a loud squeal and a dull punching sound as if someone had punched a sandbag. By the time he made the turn and reached the next street, he saw Mei lying in the middle of the road in front of a large truck. He dashed over to her. "I'm here, Mei. I'm here." He gently grabbed her shoulders. Only then did he see the blood coming from her head.

The old truck driver emerged from his truck slowly, mouth wide open.

"I panicked, Mr. Lee. I just . . . want to see my son one last time." Her lips were shaking, but her face looked calm.

"Shhh. . . . please don't talk." He put his cheek onto hers.

"Let's go . . . home. I just want . . . to see . . . my son. Can you help me stand?"

"I'll try, but let's take it slow." He felt Mei's hands on his shoulders and saw her legs aimlessly struggling. He put his arms under her to pull her up.

"I can't." Mei sounded faint. "I feel cold. Could you hold me?"

Her face looked pale, and he saw blood slowly coming from the corner of her mouth. "I'm . . . so . . . sorry, Mr. Lee, but I did not betray. . . ."

"Shhh. . . . I know."

Mei's breaths were getting shorter. "I just . . . wish you'd get the love . . . you deserve, Mr. Lee. You are . . . a . . . good man."

"Please say no more, Mei. I have my love in my arms." His vision became blurry from his tears.

"Could . . . you promise me. . . ."

He nodded as hard as he could. "Yes, Mei. I promise. Anything."

". . . to take good care . . . of our . . . son?"

He nodded again and buried his face in her chest.

"Thank you, Mr. Lee." A forced smile appeared at the corner of her mouth. She struggled to keep her eyes open, but soon he felt the tight grip of her hands on his arms loosen, and he watched her eyes shut. He held her close to his chest until she became lifeless.

65

Two weeks after Mei's funeral, Elke wanted to meet. "How are you holding up these days, my dear?" she asked quietly, staring at his black armband.

"I haven't been sleeping much lately."

He felt Elke's warm hand on his. "I miss her too. I have fond memories of her as my travel companion. She was an amazing young woman." Elke wiped away tears. After a minute or two, she regained her composure. "I have wondered for quite some time about the true reason she turned herself in to the authorities, although I *do* recall that her then-husband served in the nationalist army."

"That was one of the reasons."

"Was there something else?"

"I think she might have befriended a Japanese captain, Captain Aoki, who came to our house one night several years ago."

"I *see*." Elke looked surprised. "But I assume that she didn't do anything wrong."

"She didn't, but the incident haunted her for all these years, and she couldn't let it go. And I don't believe she told anyone about this other than me, so in the end, she was in a way punished by her own conscience."

"So what do you think really took place between Mei and that Japanese captain?

"Nothing. My guess is that he probably pursued her when he saw her on the street. And she couldn't resist for fear of being taken away. Besides, Captain Aoki seemed like a nice young man. The only problem was that he was an officer of the occupying army. Their 'relationship' was most likely platonic. From what I know about Mei, she had a clear sense of boundaries."

"Then why didn't she tell you about it sooner so that you would have a chance to talk to her and ease her anxiety?"

"Mei probably struggled with confiding this to me for a long time, but in the end, she wanted to keep it to herself to protect our family."

"That makes sense." Elke nodded and took a sip of her coffee. "For some reason, the way Mei died puzzled me. As I thought more about it, I wondered if, since you did not catch her until after she'd already been struck by the truck, you think there might have been a possibility that she ran toward the truck on purpose?"

"You think she wanted to kill herself?"

"I don't know. I just have this eerie feeling. . . ."

"I hadn't thought about that possibility. I would have a difficult time accepting this idea, the idea that she wanted to leave us—her family. This is too hard to process. . . ."

He felt Elke's hand on his arm. "I have been meaning to ask you about the years that you two spent together," Elke said, changing the subject.

"What do you mean, Mom?"

"Well, I noticed that you sometimes seemed . . . subdued. I know that you really loved her. I'm just not sure what happened. It's a puzzle to me."

"Nothing *happened*." He paused to gather his thoughts. "It seems that marriage can exist in the absence of love, at least in this culture, and I don't know what a good marriage constitutes. Mei was good at household tasks, but I think she married me out of gratitude."

"I think I see your point here, my son. I have thought about this for quite some time, mostly from my observations and my limited understanding of Chinese culture. It seems that couples don't usually open up about how they feel about each other, at least not as much as we do in the West. The concept of love is perhaps too platonic; instead, the foundation of it seems like more of a mutual consent rather than an open expression."

"It does seem that way." He looked outside the window, then turned his head back to her. "I had this feeling from the very beginning that Mei was unable to reciprocate my feelings toward her, but she couldn't bring herself to tell me. Still, I was content that she allowed me to love her. When she was around, I felt more complete."

Elke took out her handkerchief and put it in his hand. "I sensed that, and she probably didn't want to hurt your feelings. So in the end, it seems that 'saving face' is more important than anything else in this culture."

He nodded. He didn't feel the need to add anything more.

"I hope you don't mind me changing the subject." She paused for a moment. "Another reason I am here today is that I wanted to let you know that I have decided to go back to München for a while because my parents are getting quite old—they are in their nineties—and they are not well. People of their age don't manage very well on their own, as you can imagine. But before I leave, I wanted to see if you would like to come with me."

He took a deep breath. "Mom, you are very kind to think of taking me to Germany, but I think I should stay in Shanghai, at least for a while, to collect myself."

Elke nodded. "I can understand that. After all, you have gone through a lot lately. But if you change your mind, you know where to find me, right?"

He gave Elke's hand a gentle squeeze. "So, when are you leaving?"

"In two weeks."

"Can I come to see you off?"

"Please don't, *mein Schatz*. Please don't. I am not very good at saying goodbyes. I get emotional—an old lady like me gets emotional!" She laughed. "And besides, it's not a goodbye—it's *Auf Wiedersehen*, or see you again!"

A young waiter in a white tuxedo came to the table. "Your taxi is here, Frau Elke."

As they walked outside, he felt Elke's hand on his arm. "Do be careful, *mein Schatz*."

"I will write you, Mom." He opened the passenger side door and lifted the corner of her coat before closing it.

When she rolled down the window and waved to him, he saw tears in her eyes.

He kept his hand in the air long after the taxi disappeared into the evening traffic.

Acknowledgments

I would like to express my deep gratitude to the following people, whose help has contributed to the publication of this manuscript:

First and foremost, I owe a huge thanks to my publisher, Sheri Williams, and deputy publisher, Ashley Carlson, for giving me the opportunity to publish this manuscript. The suggestions that Ashley provided have made this manuscript stronger, and I very much appreciate our discussions.

My editor at TouchPoint Press, Kimberly Carlisle-Coghlan, has done amazing work in polishing this manuscript as well as everything else that needed to be checked and edited. She is so good at what she does.

Becky Marietta, associate editor at TouchPoint Press, worked tirelessly, even on the weekends, to double-check and edit this manuscript. I really appreciate her hard work and thoroughness.

I feel so fortunate to have Erin Brown's help on my manuscript. Her professional guidance and suggestions were invaluable. I am grateful for our discussions.

Laurie Rosin has done a wonderful job in helping me with my query and synopsis, which every author dreads.

As a first-time author, I was fortunate to have Cate Fedele as my first audience. She has provided useful feedback on the building of the characters in this manuscript.

I am grateful to my readers, Nonie & David Gilbert, for their support and interest in this manuscript.

And last but not least, I would like to thank everyone at

TouchPoint Press for their hard work and help in every step of the publishing process.

• • •

Thank you so much for reading *Unpredictable Winds*. If you've enjoyed the book, we would be grateful if you would post a review on the bookseller's website. Just a few words is all it takes! ♥

CPSIA information can be obtained
at www.ICGtesting.com
Printed in the USA
LVHW090214100722
723127LV00011B/478